family of liars

e. lockhart

DELACORTE PRESS

Text copyright © 2022 by Lockhart Ink
Map and family tree art on pages vii–ix copyright © 2022 by Maxime Plasse
B&N Bonus Material copyright © 2022 by Lockhart Ink
Jacket art used under license from Getty Images and Shutterstock.com

Visit us on the Web! GetUnderlined.com

Educators and librarians, for a variety of teaching tools, visit us at RHTeachersLibrarians.com

Library of Congress Cataloging-in-Publication Data is available upon request.
ISBN 978-0-593-48585-9 (hc) — ISBN 978-0-593-48586-6 (lib. bdg.) —
ISBN 978-0-593-48587-3 (ebook) — ISBN 978-0-593-56853-8 (int'l ed.) —
ISBN 978-0-593-56880-4 (B&N edition)

The text of this book is set in 11-point Joanna MT.
Interior design by Ken Crossland

Printed in the United States of America
10 9 8 7 6 5 4 3 2 1
2022 Barnes & Noble Edition

For Hazel

The Sinclair Family Tree

Dean Sinclair

Pevensie
and Philadelphia

Harris Sinclair & Tipper Taft Sinclair

Clairmont
and Boston

Yardley
Sinclair

Thomas Sinclair
(Tomkin)

Penelope
Mirren Taft
Sinclair
(Penny)

Rosemary
Leigh Taft
Sinclair

Caroline
Lennox Taft
Sinclair (Carrie)

Elizabeth
Jane Taft
Sinclair
(Bess)

Cadence

Dogs in 1987:
Wharton
Albert
McCartney
Reepicheep

Johnny

Will

Mirren

Bonnie

Liberty

Taft

contents

Dear Readers,

This book contains spoilers for the novel
We Were Liars.
    I love you, and I wrote this for you—
with ambition and black coffee.

xo
E

PART ONE
A Story for Johnny

1.

MY SON JOHNNY is dead.

Jonathan Sinclair Dennis, that was his name. He died at age fifteen.

There was a fire and I love him and I wronged him and I miss him. He will never grow taller, never find a partner, never train for another race, never go to Italy like he wanted, never ride the kind of roller coaster that flips you upside down. Never, never, never. Never anything.

Still, he visits my kitchen on Beechwood Island quite often.

I see him late at night when I can't sleep and come down for a glass of whiskey. He looks just like he always did at fifteen. His blond hair sticks up, tufty. He has a sunburn across his nose. His nails are bitten down and he's usually in board shorts and a hoodie. Sometimes he wears his blue-checked windbreaker, since the house runs cold.

I let him drink whiskey because he's dead anyway. How's it going to hurt him? But often he wants hot cocoa instead. The ghost of Johnny likes to sit on the counter, banging his bare feet against the lower cabinets. He takes out the old Scrabble tiles and idly makes phrases on the countertop while we talk. *Never eat anything bigger than your ass. Don't take no for an answer. Be a little kinder than you have to be.* Stuff like that.

He often asks me for stories about our family. "Tell about

when you were teenagers," he says tonight. "You and Aunt Penny and Aunt Bess."

I don't like talking about that time. "What do you want to know?"

"Whatever. Stuff you got up to. Hijinks. Here on the island."

"It was the same as now. We took the boats out. We swam. Tennis and ice cream and suppers cooked on the grill."

"Did you all get along back then?" He means me and my sisters, Penny and Bess.

"To a point."

"Did you ever get in trouble?"

"No," I say. Then, "Yes."

"What for?"

I shake my head.

"Tell me," he pushes. "What's the worst thing you did? Come on, spill it."

"No!" I laugh.

"Yes! Pretty please? The absolute worst thing you ever did, back then. Tell your poor dead son all the gory details."

"Johnny."

"Oh, it can't be that bad," he says. "You have no idea the things I've seen on television. Way worse than anything you could have done in the 1980s."

Johnny haunts me, I think, because he can't rest without answers. He keeps asking about our family, the Sinclair family, because he's trying to understand this island, the people on it, and why we act the way we do. Our history.

He wants to know why he died.

I owe him this story.

"Fine," I say. "I'll tell you."

4

MY FULL NAME is Caroline Lennox Taft Sinclair, but people call me Carrie. I was born in 1970. This is the story of my seventeenth summer.

That was the year the boys all came to stay on Beechwood Island. And the year I first saw a ghost.

I have never told this particular story to anyone, but I think it is the one that Johnny needs to hear.

Did you ever get in trouble? he asks. *Tell me. What's the worst thing you did? Come on, spill it . . . The absolute worst thing you ever did, back then.*

Telling this story will be painful. In fact, I do not know if I can tell it truthfully, though I'll try.

I have been a liar all my life, you see.

It's not uncommon in our family.

PART TWO
Four Sisters

2.

MY CHILDHOOD IS a blur of wintry Boston mornings, my sisters and I bundled in boots and itchy wool hats. School days in uniforms with thick navy cardigans and pleated skirts. Afternoons in our tall brick town house, doing homework in front of the fireplace. If I close my eyes, I can taste sweet vanilla pound cake and feel my own sticky fingers. Life was fairy tales before bed, flannel pajamas, golden retrievers.

There were four of us girls. In the summers, we went to Beechwood Island. I remember swimming in the fierce ocean waves with Penny and Bess while our mother and baby Rosemary sat on the shore. We caught jellyfish and crabs and kept them in a blue bucket. Wind and sunlight, small quarrels, mermaid games and rock collections.

Tipper, our mother, threw wonderful parties. She did it because she was lonely. On Beechwood, anyway. We did have guests, and for some years my father's brother Dean and his children were there with us, but my mother thrived at charity suppers and long lunches with dear friends. She loved people and was good at loving them. Without many around on the island, she made her own fun, having parties even when we hadn't anybody visiting.

When the four of us were little, my parents would take us to Edgartown each Fourth of July. Edgartown is a seafaring village on the island of Martha's Vineyard, all white picket fences. We'd get deep-fried clams with tartar sauce in paper containers and then buy lemonade from a stand in front of the Old Whaling Church. We'd set up lawn chairs, then eat as we waited for the parade. Local businesses had decorated floats. Vintage car collectors proudly tooted their horns. The island fire stations paraded their oldest engines. A veterans' band played Sousa marches and my mother would always sing: "Be kind to your fine-feathered friends / For a duck could be somebody's mother."

We never stayed for the fireworks. Instead, we motored back to Beechwood and ran up from the family boat dock to the real party.

Clairmont house's porch would be decked out in fairy lights and the large picnic table on the lawn dressed in blue and white. We'd eat corn on the cob, hamburgers, watermelon. There would be a cake like an American flag, with blueberries and raspberries on top. My mother would have decorated it herself. Same cake, every year.

After supper she'd give us all sparklers. We'd parade along the wooden walkways of the island—the ones that led from house to house—and sing at the top of our lungs. "America the Beautiful," "This Land Is Your Land," "Be Kind to Your Fine-Feathered Friends."

In the dark, we'd head to the Big Beach. The grounds-keeper, Demetrios in those days, would set off fireworks. The family sat on cotton blankets, the adults holding glasses of clinking ice.

Anyway. It's hard to believe I was ever quite so blindly

patriotic, and that my highly educated parents were. Still, the memories stick.

IT NEVER OCCURRED to me that anything was wrong with how I fit into our family until one afternoon when I was fourteen. It was August, 1984.

We had been on the island since June, living in Clairmont. The house was named for the school that Harris, our father, had attended when he was a boy. Uncle Dean and my cousins lived in Pevensie, named for the family in the Narnia books. A nanny stayed the summer in Goose Cottage. The staff building was for the housekeeper, the groundskeeper, and other occasional staff, but only the housekeeper slept there regularly. The others had homes on the mainland.

I had been swimming all morning with my sisters and my cousin Yardley. We had eaten tuna sandwiches and celery from the cooler at my mother's feet. Sleepy from lunch and exercise, I set my head down and put one hand on Rosemary. She was napping next to me on the blanket, her eight-year-old arms covered in mosquito bites, her legs sandy. Rosemary was blond, like the rest of us, with tangled waves. Her cheeks were soft and peach-colored, her limbs skinny and unformed. Freckles; a tendency to squint; a goofy laugh. Our Rosemary. She was strawberry jam, scabby knees, and a small hand in mine.

I dozed for a bit while my parents talked. They were sitting in lawn chairs beneath a white umbrella, some distance away. I woke when Rosemary rolled onto her side, and I lay there with my eyes closed, feeling her breathe under my arm.

"It's not worth it," my mother was saying. "It just isn't."

"She shouldn't have it hard when we can fix it," my father answered.

"Beauty is something—but it's not everything. You act like it's everything."

"We're not talking about beauty. We're talking about helping a person who looks weak. She looks foolish."

"Why be so harsh? There's no need to say that."

"I'm practical."

"You care what people think. We shouldn't care."

"It's a common surgery. The doctor is very experienced."

There was the sound of my mother lighting a cigarette. They all smoked, back then. "You're not thinking about the time in the hospital," Tipper argued. "A liquid diet, the swelling, all that. The pain she's going to suffer."

Who were they talking about?

What surgery? A liquid diet?

"She doesn't chew normally," said Harris. "That's just a fact. There's 'no way out but through.'"

"Don't quote me Robert Frost right now."

"We have to think about the endgame. Not worry how she gets there. And it wouldn't hurt for her to look—"

He paused for a second and Tipper jumped in. "You think about pain like it's a workout or something. Like it's just effort. A struggle."

"If you put in effort, you gain something from it."

An inhale on the cigarette. Its ashy smell mixed with the salt of the air. "Not all pain is worth it," said Tipper. "Some pain is just pain." There was a pause. "Should we put sun lotion on Rosemary? She's getting pink."

"Don't wake her."

Another pause. Then: "Carrie is beautiful as she is," said Tipper. "And they have to cut through the bone, Harris. Cut through the bone."

I froze.

They were talking about me.

Before coming to the island, I had been to the orthodontist and then to an oral surgeon. I hadn't minded. I had barely paid attention. Half the kids at school had braces.

"She shouldn't have a strike against her," said Harris. "Her face this way, it's a strike against her. She deserves to look like a Sinclair: strong on the outside because she's strong on the inside. And if we have to do that for her, we have to do that for her."

I realized they were going to break my jaw.

3.

WHEN WE FINALLY discussed it, I told my parents no. I said I could chew just fine (though the oral surgeon disagreed). I said I was happy with myself. They should leave me alone.

Harris pushed back. Hard. He talked to me about the authority of surgeons and why they knew best.

Tipper told me I was lovely, beautiful, exquisite. She told me she adored me. She was a kind person, narrow-minded and creative, generous and fun-loving. She always told her daughters they were beautiful. But she still thought I should consider the surgery. Why didn't we let the question sit? Decide later? There was no rush.

I said no again, but inside, I had begun to feel wrong. My face was wrong. My jaw was weak. I looked foolish. Based on a fluke of biological destiny, other people would make assumptions about my character. I noticed them making those assumptions, now, pretty regularly. There was that slight condescension in their voices. Did I get the joke?

I began to chew slowly, making sure my mouth was shut tight. I felt uncertain of my own teeth, whether they ground up food like other people's did. The way they fit together began to feel strange.

I already knew boys didn't think I was pretty. Even though I was popular—went to parties and was even elected freshman delegate to the student council—I was always one of the last to be invited to dances. Boys asked girls in those days.

At the dances, my dates never held my hand. They didn't kiss me, or press against me in the dark of the dance floor. They didn't wonder if they could see me again and go to the movies, the way they did with my friends.

I watched my sister Penny, whose square jawline was nothing to her, shove food into her mouth while talking. She would laugh with her jaw wide open, stick her tongue out and let people see every shining white molar.

I watched Bess, whose mouth was fuller and sweeter, and whose jaw was a forceful, feminine curve, complain about her six months of braces and the retainer that followed. She snapped the blue plastic retainer cover open with a groan when Tipper reminded her to replace it after meals.

And Rosemary. Her square face mirrored Penny's, only freckled and goofy.

All my sisters, their bones were beautiful.

4.

THE SUMMER I was sixteen, we spent our days on Beechwood, as always. Kayaks, corn on the cob, sailboats, and snorkeling (though we didn't see much besides the occasional crab). We had the usual Fourth of July celebration with sparklers and songs. Our annual Bonfire Night, our Lemon Hunt, our Midsummer Ice Cream party.

Only that year—Rosemary drowned.

She was ten years old. The youngest of us four.

It happened at the end of August. Rosemary was swimming at the beach by Goose Cottage. We call it the Tiny Beach. She wore a green bathing suit with little denim pockets on it. Ridiculous pockets. You couldn't put anything in them. It was her favorite.

I wasn't there. No one in the family was. She was with the au pair we had that year, a twenty-year-old woman from Poland. Agata.

Rosemary always wanted to swim later than anyone else. Long after we all went to rinse our feet at the hose by the Clairmont mudroom door, Rosemary would swim, if she was allowed. It wasn't uncommon for her to be with Agata on one beach or the other.

But that day, the sky turned cloudy.

That day, Agata went inside to get sweaters for them both.

That day, Rosemary, a good swimmer always, must have been knocked down by a wave and caught in the undertow.

When Agata came back outside, Rosemary was far out, and struggling. She was beyond the wicked black rocks that line the cove.

Agata wasn't a lifeguard.

She didn't know CPR.

She wasn't even a fast enough swimmer to reach Rosemary in time.

5.

AFTERWARD, WE WENT back to boarding school, Penny and I. And Bess began it.

We left our parents, only two weeks after Rosemary died, to be educated on the beautiful campus of North Forest Academy. When our mother dropped us off, she hugged us tight and kissed our cheeks. She told us she loved us. And was gone.

It was up to me to take care of Bess. I was a junior that year. She was a freshman. I helped decorate her dorm room, introduced her to people, brought her chocolate bars from the commissary. I left her silly, happy notes in her mail cubby.

With Penny, there was less to do. She already had friends, and there was a new boyfriend by the second week. But I showed up anyway. I stopped by her room, found her in the cafeteria, sat on her bed and listened to her talk about her new romance.

I was there for my sisters, but we dealt with our feelings about Rosemary alone. Here in the Sinclair family, we keep a stiff upper lip. We make the best of things. We look to the future. These are Harris's mottoes, and they are Tipper's, as well.

We girls have never been taught to grieve, to rage, or even to share our thoughts. Instead, we have become excellent at silence; at small, kind gestures; at sailing; at sandwich-making. We talk eagerly about literature and make every guest feel welcome. We never speak about medical issues. We show our love not with honesty or affection, but with loyalty.

Be a credit to the family. That's one of many mottoes our father often repeated at the supper table. What he meant was Represent us well. Do well not for yourself, but because the reputation of the Sinclair family demands respect. The way people see you—it is the way they see all of us.

He said it so often, it became a joke among us. At North Forest, we used to say it to each other. I'd walk by Penny, pushed up against some guy, kissing in the hall. I'd say, without interrupting them, "Be a credit to the family."

Bess would catch me sneaking a box of shortbread into the dormitory—same thing.

Penny'd see Bess with tomato sauce on her shirt—same thing.

Making a pot of tea. "Be a credit to the family."

Or going to take a poop. "Be a credit to the family."

It made us laugh, but Harris was serious. He meant it, he believed it, and even though we laughed about it, we believed it, too.

And so we did not flag when Rosemary died. We kept up our grades. We worked at school and worked at sports. We worked at our looks and worked at our clothes, always making sure the work never showed.

Rosemary's would-have-been eleventh birthday, October fifth, was Fall Carnival day at school. The quad was filled with booths and silly games. People got their faces painted. There was a cotton candy machine. Spin art. A pretend pumpkin patch. Some student bands.

I stood with my back against my dorm building and drank a cup of hot apple cider. My friends from softball were together at a booth where you could throw beanbags at one of the math teachers. My roommate and her boyfriend were huddled over a lyric sheet, going over their band's performance. A guy I liked was clearly avoiding me.

Other October fifths, back when I was home, my mother made a cake, chocolate with vanilla frosting. She served it after supper, decorated however Rosemary wanted. One year, it was covered with small plastic lions and cheetahs. Another year, frosting violets. Another year, a picture of Snoopy. There'd be a party, too, on the weekend. It would be filled with Rosemary's little friends wearing party dresses and Mary Jane shoes, dressed up for a birthday the way no one ever does anymore.

Now Rosemary was dead and it seemed like both of my sisters had forgotten her entirely.

I stood against the brick dorm at the edge of the carnival, holding my cider. Tears ran down my face.

I tried to tell myself she wouldn't know whether we remembered her birthday.

She couldn't want a cake. It didn't matter. She was gone.

But it did matter.

I could see Bess, standing in a cluster of first-year girls and boys. They were all drawing faces on orange balloons. She was smiling like a beauty pageant queen.

And there was Penny, her pale hair under a knitted cap, dragging her boyfriend by the hand as she ran over to see her best friend, Erin Riegert. Penny took a handful of Erin's blue cotton candy and squashed it into her mouth.

Then she looked over at me. And paused. She walked to where I stood. "Come on," she said. "Don't think about it."

But I wanted to think about it.

"Come watch the dude make the cotton candy," Penny said. "It's pretty sweet, the way he does it."

"She would have been eleven," I said. "She would have had a chocolate cake with decorations on it. But I don't know what."

"Carrie. You can't go down this hole. It's like, a depressing hole and it's not going to do you any good. Come do something fun and you'll start to feel better."

"She told me she had this idea for a Simple Minds cake," I said. Simple Minds was a band. "But I think Tipper would have steered her away. It's too hard. And kind of, I don't know, cheap-looking."

Bess came to stand with us. "You okay?" she asked me.

"Not really."

"I'm advocating cotton candy," said Penny. "She needs to do something normal."

Bess looked around at her new friends, and at the older kids she didn't know yet. "The timing is bad right now," she said, like I had asked her for something. Like I'd asked her to come over. "I have people waiting for me," she added.

My sisters loved Rosemary. I knew they loved her. And they must have mourned her. But I didn't know how to talk to them about it. When I tried, like now, they changed the subject.

They hadn't come to see how I was feeling.

They had come to tell me to stop feeling that way.

I LEFT THE carnival.

I climbed to the top of my dorm building and went out on the catwalk that led around its roof.

I took a felt-tip marker from my bookbag and wrote on the weathered wooden railing:

> ROSEMARY LEIGH TAFT SINCLAIR
> She loved
> Snoopy and chocolate cake,
> potato chips and big cats,
> and the band Simple Minds.
> She loved
> her green bathing suit and swimming in the wicked ocean.
> She loved
> her sisters
> even though they were not worthy of her.
> She would have been eleven years old today.
> And I loved her.
> Happy birthday to Rosemary, now and forever.

WHEN WE WENT home for Thanksgiving, Tipper put on a bright face. She helped us unpack our suitcases. She baked beautiful pies and had relatives in for the traditional meal. Harris was jocular and intense, wanting to play chess and discuss books and movies.

The closest either of our parents came to mentioning Rosemary was to say that the house seemed nice and noisy now that we were home. It had been a quiet fall.

I know my parents did what they thought best—for us, and for them. It hurt to be reminded of our loss, so why remind anyone?

6.

DURING WINTER BREAK of that same year, Harris brought up the jaw surgery again, this time with new urgency. He insisted it was medically necessary. Postponing the decision, as we had done since I was fourteen, was dawdling. We should take care of things when they neeeded taking care of.

I tried saying no, but he reminded me that *don't take no for an answer* is one of his life philosophies.

I was forced to comply.

Now that I am grown, I think *don't take no for an answer* is a lesson we teach boys who would be better off learning that *no means no*. I also see that my father wanted me to look like him even more than he wanted me to be pretty. But back then, some part of me felt relieved. Harris was in charge, and I had always been told that he knew best.

I left school in February for what was supposed to be two

weeks. The doctors cut open my jawbone and put a wedge inside it. They built the bone up and moved it forward and reattached that part of my skeleton. Then they wired my teeth shut so everything could heal in position.

They gave me codeine, a narcotic pain medicine. Instructions were to take it every four hours at first, then as needed. The pills gave me a strange sensation—not numb, but aware of the pain as if it were happening to someone else.

My jaw. The loss of Rosemary.

Neither one could hurt me, if I took that medicine every four hours.

The liquid diet was not so bad. Tipper brought me frozen yogurt. We no longer had a nanny, but our housekeeper, Luda, was exceptionally kind. She was from Belarus, thin as a pole, with bleached hair and eye makeup my mother found vulgar. Luda made me soft, almost-liquid custards, chocolate and butterscotch. "To get your protein in," she'd say. "So nourishing."

The family dogs took to sleeping in my room during the day. McCartney and Albert, both golden retrievers, and Wharton, an Irish setter. Wharton was noble-looking and stupid. I loved her best.

The infection came on suddenly one night. I could feel it arrive, underneath the haze of my medicated sleep. An insistent throbbing, a thrumming red ball of pain in my right jaw.

I woke up and took another codeine.

I made myself a bag of ice. Pressed it to my face.

It was five days before I asked my parents to bring me to the doctor. Harris believed that complaining isn't the behavior of a strong-minded person. "It adds nothing to the company you keep," he often said. " 'Never complain, never explain.' Benjamin Disraeli said that. Prime minister of England."

When I mentioned the pain, to Luda and Tipper, I was lighthearted. "Oh, this one side is just giving me a little trouble," I said. "Maybe we should have it checked out." I didn't tell Harris at all.

By the time the doctor saw me, the infection was severe.

Harris told me I was a fool to have ignored an obvious problem. "Take care of things when they need taking care of," he reminded me. "Don't wait. Those are words to live by."

The infection rampaged through my system for eight more weeks. Antibiotics, different antibiotics, a second doctor, a third, a second surgery, painkillers and more painkillers. Ice. Towels. Butterscotch pudding.

Then it was over. My jaw was healed. The wires removed. Regular braces installed. The swelling was down.

My face in the mirror was foreign to me. I was paler than I'd ever been. Thinner than was natural. But mostly, it was my chin. It was now set forward, giving me a strong line along the jaw to my ears. My teeth hit one another at unfamiliar spots, too sensitive for nuts or cucumber, too weak to chew a pork chop, but lined up.

I would turn my profile to the mirror and touch my face, wondering what future this bit of artificial bone had bought me. Would some beautiful boy want to touch me? Would he listen to me? Want to understand me? I hungered to be seen as unique and worthy. I wanted it in that desperate way that someone who has never been kissed wants it—

vague but passionate,

muddled with fantasies of kisses I've seen in movies,

23

mixed up with stories from my mother about dances and corsages and my father's multiple proposals.

I longed for love,

and I had a pretty urgent interest in sex,

but I also wanted to be seen

and heard

and recognized,

truly, by another person.

That's where I stood, when I first met Pfeff. I think he saw that in me.

I WAS BACK at school in May and finished out the semester as best I could. I returned to softball, where I had always been a strong hitter and a credit to the family. We won our league championship that season. I stepped back into my group of friends. I worked hard in pre-calc and chemistry, doing extra hours in the library to get up to speed.

But I was not well. I found myself thinking obsessively about stories I read in the newspapers—stories of men dying from AIDS, this new health crisis. And flooding in Brownsville, Texas; families whose homes were drowned. Photographs in the paper: a man in a bed, his weight down to nothing. Protestors on the cobblestone streets of New York City. A family in a rubber raft, with two dogs. A woman waist-deep in water, standing in her kitchen.

I'd think of these images—

people dying, a city drowning—

instead of thinking about Rosemary, dying, drowning.

They let me hurt without looking at my own life. If I didn't think about them, I'd have never stopped thinking about her.

Codeine helped dull these obsessive thoughts. I'd been prescribed it by several different doctors, so there was a seemingly endless supply of little brown bottles in my drawer. The school nurse gave me more, with permission of my parents, when I said my teeth were aching.

At night, I took the pills to sleep. And sometimes, night came early.

Like, before supper.

Like, before lunch.

PART THREE
The Black Pearls

7.

OUR ISLAND IS quite a ways off the coast of Massachusetts. The water is a deep, dark blue. Sometimes there are great white sharks off the shore. Beach roses flourish here. The island is covered with them. And though the shoreline is rocky, we have two sweet inlets edged with patches of white sand.

At first, this land belonged to Indigenous people. It was taken away from them by settlers from Europe. Nobody knows when, but it must have happened.

In 1926, my great-grandfather bought the island and built a single home on the south shore. His son inherited it—and when he died in 1972, my father and his brother Dean inherited it. And they had plans.

The Sinclair brothers demolished the home their grandfather had built. They leveled the land, where needed. They carted in sand for the island's beaches. They consulted with architects and built three houses—one for each brother, plus a guesthouse. The homes were traditional Cape Cod style: steep roofs, wood shingles, shutters on the windows, big porches.

Some of the money for these projects came from my mother's trust fund. Tipper's family money came (in part, going back some generations) from a sugar plantation near Charleston, South Carolina. That plantation used enslaved people for labor. It is ugly money.

Other money came from my father's family. The Sinclairs

were owners of a long-standing Boston publishing house. And more came from my father. Early in his career, Harris bought a small company that puts out a number of literary and news magazines.

That's ugly money, too. Just in different ways. The history there includes exploited workers, broken contracts, and child labor overseas—along with journalistic integrity and belief in the freedom of the press.

When the Sinclair brothers were done with their improvements, there were two docks, a boathouse, and a staff building. The island was crisscrossed with wooden walkways and planted with lilacs and lavender.

I have spent every summer here since I was five.

IT IS JUNE now, 1987. The summer the boys arrive. The summer of Pfeff.

We drive from Boston to the Cape. Gerrard, the Beechwood groundskeeper, meets us in the town of Woods Hole. He has brought the big motorboat. Gerrard is about sixty years old, short and smiley. He says very little, except to my mother. She has eager questions about rhododendrons and lilacs, various repairs that are needed, the installation of a new dryer. In a few days, Luda will take a rental car down with more stuff from the Boston house.

With the boat loaded up, we motor two hours to the island with Gerrard at the wheel. Penny, Bess, and I sit together, our hair whipping around us.

It is the same ride as every year, only without Rosemary in her orange life vest.

Without her.

30

CLAIRMONT HOUSE LOOKS the same as ever—three stories and a turret up top. The wooden shingles are gray from salt air. A wide porch stretches around two sides. There is a hammock on one end of the porch and a collection of cozy armchairs on the other. On the lawn is an extra-large, custom-made picnic table. We eat supper there most nights. At the foot of the lawn stands a maple tree. From a low branch hangs our tire swing on a single thick rope.

Coming up from the dock, Penny throws her suitcases on the lawn and runs to the swing. She hurls herself into it and spins wildly. "Carrie, get over here. You need to say hello to the swing!" she calls.

Okay, then. I'm feeling melancholy, thinking of Rosemary—but I go over anyhow. I run and climb on, standing with my feet on either side of Penny's legs. The rush of air in my ears, the dizziness—for a moment, I forget everything but this.

"It's summer now!" cries Penny.

When Bess gets up from the dock, she leaves her bags and comes to join us. We are too big, and it's hard to fit, but we get gloriously dizzy together, the way we did when we were children.

Inside Clairmont, the carpets are worn but the woodwork is oiled. The kitchen's round table boasts the stains and scrapes that are inevitable with a big family. The living room features a number of oil paintings and a bar cart glistening with bottles, but the den is more comfortable. It bursts with books and blankets, plaid flannel dog beds and stacks of newspapers. There's a study for my father, filled with framed *New Yorker* cartoons and fat leather furniture; and a crafting studio for my mother, all quilting fabrics and jars of buttons, calligraphy pens and boxes of pretty stationery.

MY PARENTS' ROOM is on the third floor, away from the noise of us girls. When I go in, about a half hour after our arrival, Tipper is unpacking, sliding shirts into a drawer. Her beige linen dress is creased from traveling.

Wharton (our Irish setter) stretches across the bottom of the bed. I lie down beside her. "Make room, you dumb queen of a dog."

"Oh, don't say that," scolds Tipper. "She'll feel bad."

"Stupid is part of her charm." I stroke Wharton's soft ears. "She's eating Harris's sock."

My mother comes over and takes the sock from Wharton's mouth. "That's not a food," she tells the dog.

Wharton looks up soulfully, then begins to lick the bedspread.

Tipper putters from the dresser to the dressing table, in and out of the closet, and back and forth to her suitcases. When I was sick, we were often just the two of us, but since school ended, I have only seen my mother with my sisters around.

She changes her dress and combs her hair at her dressing table. "Come here." She pulls out a wide, shallow jewelry drawer lined with black felt. "I keep things here year-round," she says, touching her fingers to the pieces. "That way it's like getting presents every time I open this drawer. I forget what I have, and then it's like, oh, hello! Aren't you pretty?"

A game like that is typical of Tipper. She looks for ways to squeeze any last drop of pleasure from a situation, to create joy and surprise whenever she can. "This was my granny's ring," she says, holding up a square-cut diamond. She goes on, pointing out pieces, ancient jade and newer sapphires. She sets the treasures gingerly on the table so I may try them on. Each one is a piece of our feminine family history, stretching back through her lineage and Harris's.

One is her engagement ring, an emerald surrounded by diamonds. My parents met at Harvard Radcliffe, where Harris proposed to Tipper four times before she said yes. "I wore her down," he always tells us. "She accepted me just to shut me up."

My mother laughs when he tells that story. "The fourth time you figured out to buy a ring," she reminds him.

Now, she pulls out a double-strand of dark, glowing pearls, deep gray with galaxies spinning inside them. "Your father bought these for our second anniversary, when I was pregnant with you." She lets me hold them. They are slippery, and heavier than I expected. She takes them back and clasps them around her neck, where they glisten against the blue of her fresh dress. "It was a very meaningful gift," she says. "Things weren't easy then."

"Why not?"

"I can hardly remember." She reaches out to touch my cheek. "But I'd like you to have them someday."

"Okay."

"The black pearls," she says, fingering them at her throat, "are Carrie's."

Beneath the drawer liner, I catch a glimpse of a photograph, edged in white, with faded orange color. I can only see the bottom right corner. "What's the picture?" I ask, reaching for it.

She stops my hand. "It's nothing."

"Is it Rosemary?"

A look crosses her face. Grief. "No."

I put my hands behind my back. "I wanted to see it if it was Rosemary."

My mother looks at me, and for a moment I think she's going to cry—breaking down in tears over her lost baby. Or maybe, instead, she will tell me it's okay to miss Rosemary. To be thinking about her all the time, the way I do.

But she steels herself. "Know what?" she says. "I think you should wear them tonight."

She takes off the black pearls and fastens them around my neck.

8.

LET ME TELL you more about Penny and Bess. People often comment that we are like princesses in a (Western) fairy tale. Three tall blondes with willowy figures. Copies of our mother. We are appealing to people, that way. They like our serious eyes and our merry laughs. We might be waiting to be rescued, people think. We are white cotton and sandy feet, old money and lilacs, each one.

But we are easy to tell apart.

Bess (Elizabeth Jane Taft Sinclair) is fourteen, always running to catch up with me and Penny. She is the hard worker, the people pleaser, the martyr. She cooks with our mother in the kitchen, churning ice cream and baking pies. She sorts her lip gloss by shade, lining up the tubes on a pretty tray on her dresser. She stacks her shirts and sweaters in color-coded piles.

Bess has acne on her forehead. She can't leave it alone—smearing creams on it, tonics, alcohol, concealer. She wants to take care of that acne, conquer it. She is like our father that way. She has absorbed his work ethic and his pride in that ethic, but also his indignation when effort isn't clearly rewarded. Bess is a Liberty print, a jar of sharpened pencils, a weekly organizer filled out in neat handwriting. She isn't always pleasant—not at all. But she is always good.

Penny (Penelope Mirren Taft Sinclair) has a remarkable ability to make people like her, selfish though she is. They want to touch her. She is the beauty of the family, the one you'd pick out of a photograph. When Granny M was alive, she used to remark on it—the magnetism of Penny's physical presence. "What a belle," she'd often say, pulling Penny aside and giving her butterscotch candy.

She labeled me "a good girl" and Bess a "little helper."

If my hair is the color of butter and Bess's early spring sunshine, Penny's is cream. She is sixteen and a sleek greyhound of a person. She plays hard when she wants to. She works hard almost never. She loves beautiful things and despises the people she despises with an inflexible hatred.

Penny likes order, but in a different way than Bess does. She wants things to happen easily, without conflict. "Just be normal," she says to me. Meaning, don't be angry, don't rock the boat, just go along. Signs of unrest and turmoil bother Penny. She turns cold and quiet, and that cold and quiet protects her from her feelings. What I mean is, she prefers a smooth surface.

Me, I am an athlete and a narcotics addict.

A leader and a mourner.

On the outside, I am gray-eyed and butter blond, with a strong line to my jaw now, and a mouth full of braces. Pale skin, pink cheeks. A little taller than my sisters, taller than a lot of boys my age. I have the confident walk and good shoulders of an excellent softball player. I stand up in front of crowds with a smile. I fix my sisters' problems. Those are the qualities anyone can see.

But my insides are made of seawater, warped wood, and rusty nails.

9.

THE MORNING AFTER our arrival, I am up at six. I pull on a sweater over my nightgown, since mornings on Beechwood are chilly. On my way downstairs for coffee, I pause at the door to Rosemary's old room.

Inside, it is bare. The bunk beds are made up neatly with old quilts from my mother's collection. Used to be, Rosemary kept about thirty stuffed animals on the upper bunk with her, mostly lions. But they are not here anymore. Not even her favorite lion, a floppy white one named Shampoo.

Rosemary's books are absent, too: old picture books and chapter books, collections of fairy tales. Gone are her Barbies, her spiral drawing thing, her Magic 8 Ball. The room's built-in shelves display a few pretty objects I don't remember—a green-and-white vase, a few books on botanical subjects. When I open the closet, it is empty except for some neatly folded blankets.

Tipper must have worked hard to put every reminder of Rosemary out of sight, not wishing to cause pain to anyone who might wander in here without thinking.

I climb to the top bunk, where my sister used to sleep.

I should have played more "lion family" with her.

I should have done her hair in French braids, though Bess did that.

I should have made cookies with her more, though I did sometimes.

She was the baby who wanted to go up and down the porch steps a thousand times, right leg always stepping up, left leg following. The four-year-old in tutus, running along the walkways with a magic wand. The seven-year-old in a snorkel mask and flippers, stomping in frustration that no one wanted to take her down to the beach. The ten-year-old with a battered stack of Diana Wynne Jones novels; asking for seconds of strawberry rhubarb pie; baking cookies studded with butterscotch chips; demanding I read her fairy tales, even though she was too old to be read to.

"Mother cleared this out when?" Penny stands in the door. Her shiny, pale hair is chaotic from sleep. She wears her green North Forest gym shorts, an old chamois shirt, and beloved slippers that have lamb faces on the toes.

"Don't know. Maybe Luda did it last fall."

"I need coffee," says Penny. But she climbs into Rosemary's bunk with me.

I know she doesn't want to talk about our sister. About our feelings. She never does. She'll lash out if you push her, so I stay silent.

Penny puts her feet in the air, still in the lamb slippers. They touch the ceiling.

I put my feet in the air, too, in blue scrunchy socks.

We wiggle our toes on the ceiling together.

"Would you want to go hunt in the attic?" I ask, getting an idea. "Just to look for maybe some of the old books? And maybe games? We might want them." I don't mention Rosemary's other things, her clothes and stuffed lions and so on.

"I wouldn't say no to a game of Clue."

"Also those Diana Wynne Jones books," I say.

"Those are sweet," says Penny. "I could do a reread of some of those babies, for sure."

WE PAD UPSTAIRS to my parents' floor. At the end of the hall is a doorway to a narrow wooden staircase. That goes up to our attic space—the turret. It is a hexagonal room with two windows and a finished wooden floor, but it tends to be stuffy and hot, so Tipper uses it for storage.

The room smells of wood and dust. There are a couple of carpets, in rolls. Trunks and cardboard containers are carefully labeled in our mother's handwriting. As I expected, there's a cluster of new-looking boxes against one wall, neatly taped.

38

Penny and I spend the next half hour looking through the contents. I say hello to Shampoo and the other stuffed lions, to Rosemary's shorts and T-shirts. Oh, I miss her. But I want to keep Penny with me, so I close those boxes quickly. Instead, I focus on games. We find Clue, Scrabble, and the Magic 8 Ball. Do we want the Spirograph art thing? No.

Penny shakes the 8 Ball while I rummage some more. "Will I fall in love?" she asks it.

Better not to tell you now, it says.

"Will I at least make out with someone? This summer? Anyone?"

Reply hazy. Try again.

"Ugh. Will there be kissing?" she asks, exasperated.

Signs point to yes.

"That's more like it," Penny says.

Boys have lined up for her attention ever since she started at North Forest, but Penny claims that she was never in love with any of them. "Some were extremely cute," she told me once. "But they were too stupid to love."

It seems unfair that this magnetism and beauty should be so heavily gifted to Penny, as if by some fairies at her birth, and that she should value it so little. She has kissed too many people to keep count, is asked early to every dance, is never alone unless she wants to be. She is valued for the good fortune of her cheekbones, the blue of her eyes, the extra length of her neck. And she has never known any other way of being in the world.

"Will Carrie fall in love?" she asks the 8 Ball.

As I see it, yes.

"Ooh, Carrie, you're falling in love."

"It didn't say when," I remind Penny. "I might be falling in love when I am thirty."

"Will Carrie fall in love *this summer?*" Penny asks the 8 Ball.

It is certain.

"There's no one to fall in love with," I tell the ball. "There's not anyone for Penny to kiss, either."

She sighs. "That's true."

We do not know the boys are coming then. We don't know how they will spin us around, rile us; change our conceptions of ourselves and upend our lives like drunken gods playing with the fates of mortals.

But we are both in the mood to be upended.

Penny goes on asking the ball ridiculous questions. "Will I ever memorize the periodic table?" "Will I marry Simon Le Bon?" He is the lead singer of a band she likes. "Is Bess the biggest pill on earth or are there bigger pills in existence?" "Will Wharton overcome her fear of seagulls?"

We take Clue, Scrabble, and a backgammon set for ourselves, plus some worn Wynne Jones novels. Last, we open a box of Rosemary's fairy-tale books. Many of them are old, having belonged to my father when he was young, and to his mother before that. They are grand, their pictures deep with mystery. Curlicue letters begin their chapters. These are the books I used to read to Rosemary before she went to bed.

"Mother used to read those to me and Bess," says Penny, touching the fairy book on the top of the stack. "But I don't remember Rosemary having them."

"She did."

"I hope they didn't scare her. Some of them are pretty bloody."

"She was never scared of stories."

I take the books to my room. Then Penny and I go downstairs, where Tipper has made fresh carrot muffins studded with raisins, coconut, and walnuts. We drink mugs of milky coffee and eat hot muffins on the porch, where the air is warming in the sun.

I beat Penny at Scrabble.

10.

"CARRIE," BESS CALLS from the sand as I walk onto the Big Beach. "We need you."

My sisters say this all the time. They say it because I am the eldest. In this case, they need me to set up the umbrella, a large white contraption with a persnickety mechanism—but it began with "We need you" to tie our shoes. That became "We need you" to play mermaids with us, became "We need you" to cut out paper dolls, became "We need you" to tell the nanny we didn't mean to paint the dining table.

More recently, it evolved into "We need you" to show us how to shave our legs, to help Bess write a paper, to get Penny reinstated on the tennis team when she's missed so many practices. To help Penny pack when she's left it till the last minute, to convince Tipper to let Bess have a low-cut dress she wants, to redirect the gossip that swarms around school now that Penny's dumped Lachlan two weeks before the end of term. "We need you" means my sisters love me, they rely on me, they admire me.

After I set up the umbrella, the three of us spend the middle of the day stretched out beneath it. Our parents come for shorter periods, and Gerrard takes a dip during his break, but my sisters and I have set up camp. Two printed cotton blankets are laid end to end. The umbrella gives us shade. We have strawberries, blackberries, ham-and-Brie sandwiches on baguettes, and thin buttery cookies. A cooler of drinks. We have a pile of magazines and a boom box we only play when our mother isn't around. She hates music on the beach.

We listen to cassettes: Terence Trent D'Arby, Pet Shop Boys, R.E.M., Duran Duran. We lie on our backs and dance by waving our legs and arms in the air.

When we swim, we do it together. We don't speak about it, but none of us ever swims alone.

"Tipper has a secret photograph hidden in her jewelry drawer," I tell my sisters as we flop onto the blankets, dripping and breathing hard. I didn't intend to blurt what's on my mind, but it pops out.

Bess's eyes widen. "What of?"

"I didn't see it," I say. "Only the corner. She shoved it underneath so I wouldn't see."

"It's probably Rosemary," says Penny.

"She would let me see Rosemary. I asked if it was Rosemary."

"Maybe not. If she thought it would make you sad."

"Maybe it's Uncle Chris," says Bess. My mother's brother, Christopher Taft, ran away to South America with a woman quite a bit older than he. That is all I know about him. None of us kids have ever met him, and as far as I know, Tipper never hears from him. Her parents "washed their hands of Chris"— that's what our late Granny M used to say.

"Oh, yeah, Christopher," says Penny. "Should we go peek at it?"

"Ooh, yes," says Bess.

"We can't go prying in her stuff." I am suddenly worried they'll run upstairs and dig out the photograph, leaving a trail of sand and making a mess of our mother's jewelry drawer.

"She shouldn't be keeping things from us," says Bess, pouting. "We deserve to see all her pictures."

"Come on," Penny says to me. "You wouldn't have told us if you weren't curious."

"We could sneak in when she's busy in the garden," adds Bess. "You could be the lookout while Penny and I steal the photo."

"No," I say sharply. I don't want them upsetting our parents. "What if it's her and Harris naked?"

"Oh, blech. No." Penny sticks out her tongue.

"Gag me," says Bess. "But it's probably not."

"You could never unsee it," I tell them.

"Okay, fine, whatever," says Penny. "You brought it up."

11.

TONIGHT, TIPPER CUTS early summer flowers from the kitchen garden. She lays the picnic table with a runner down the center. She wears a clean white apron and grills salmon. There are round slices of lemon in our glasses. After we eat, since Luda isn't here yet, my sisters and I help with the dishes.

Later, Penny steals a bottle of wine from the cellar. I get a corkscrew and we leave to go to sit on the porch of Pevensie, Uncle Dean's house.

Pevensie is not as big as Clairmont. It looks out across the newly built tennis courts and the wooden walkways that go from place to place. In the distance, you can see the family dock. The small motorboat (Guzzler) is tied up there, and so is the sailboat. The big motorboat is usually at the back dock, which the staff members use.

We pour the wine into paper cups and talk, mostly about school, even though we're finally free of it. Penny's friend Erin Riegert arrives tomorrow for an indefinite stay. The two of them were inseparable at North Forest.

"I hope she doesn't hate me when she gets here," says Penny thoughtfully.

"Why would Erin hate you?" I ask.

"She would never," says Bess.

"She lives in an apartment. With only her mom. She's like, on scholarship, I think."

"You don't know if she's on scholarship?"

"She *is* on scholarship. Okay? She is."

"I wish I could have had a friend up," says Bess.

"You could have someone," says Penny.

"Mother told me no. She said there'd be too many people and it was your year."

That sounds like Tipper. She has never tried to parcel things equally among her children, but instead decides that it's someone's turn, or someone is the queen today.

"You can come with us out in the kayaks," Penny says to Bess, "and down to the beach, and all that. We can all make ice cream in the machine. But if me and Erin are playing tennis, or we want to be alone in my room, or if we're going to Edgartown, you have to leave us and go do your own thing."

"You're mean," says Bess, pouring more wine into her cup.

"No," says Penny. That is her usual way—to categorically deny having hurt anyone's feelings. "I just said a ton of things you can do with us. The rest of the time you can hang out with Carrie."

"Carrie will have Yardley," complains Bess. And that is true. Our cousin Yardley is a year older than I am, and when she is around, we fall in together.

It is late, so we head back to Clairmont, but when we come upon the house, our parents are sitting on the porch. A record sings out through the screen door that leads to the dining room. Classical music, a string quartet.

"Oh damn. The wine," I say. The bottle is empty, in my hand. Bess holds the paper cups.

"If they see it, they'll lock us down all summer," says Penny.

"I know," adds Bess, who knows nothing. "Can we throw it over the edge?" She means the edge of the wooden walkway we are standing on. Below it are grass and low bushes of beach roses.

"No," says Penny. "Someone will find it and know it was us."

"We can scootch it under the walkway," says Bess.

"Shhh," I tell them. "I have an idea."

I lead them back toward the northeast side of the island. "Where are we going?" asks Bess.

"You'll see." It is fun to have her wide-eyed and following. The feeling slides around me like a warm sweater. It was I who made that mean girl from the soccer team leave Bess alone in the locker room. It was I who thought to tell our parents that Penny was visiting Erin when she wanted to go off with Lachlan. It was I who got Penny reinstated on the tennis team. I am like our father this way. He always has a way forward. He's a fixer.

We head to Goose Cottage. It's a small house compared to the others, with four sweet bedrooms under slanted ceilings, and only a galley kitchen. No one is staying there at present.

I open the door—our doors are always unlocked on the island—and put the wine bottle in the recycling bin there. I take the paper cups from Bess, rinse the wine off them, and put them in the trash. "Problem solved."

We stand in the empty living room, touching familiar objects and reacquainting ourselves with the space. The windows look out over the sea. The television set is dusty.

"Hey hey hey hey." A sound carries on the wind. It is almost like a voice, very soft. It sings the words. Just a whisper.

"What was that?" asks Penny.

"Hey hey hey hey." It comes again.

"It sounds like a cat," says Bess.

"There can't be a cat on the island," I say. "How would it even get here?"

"It could be Gerrard's," says Bess.

"He doesn't live here," I say. "He goes home most nights."

"It's not a cat," says Penny. "It—it sounds like Rosemary."

"Hey hey hey hey." The sound is musical, like the opening of a Simple Minds song that was popular a couple summers ago.

"She loved that song," says Bess. "Oh my god. She was always singing it."

Penny starts singing. "La, la la la la. La la la la." A bit from the bridge.

"Don't be creepy," I say sharply to Penny. "You'll scare Bess."

"I'm already scared," says Bess. "Doesn't it sound like Rosemary?"

A chill scuttles through me.

But I don't believe in ghosts. And we are a little drunk. There is no reason to work ourselves up.

"Woooooooo!" says Penny. "In the guesthouse, no one can hear you scream."

"Penny!" cries Bess.

"Penny, stop," I say. "It's probably a seagull looking for its mate. Or a seal or something. We need to rinse our mouths out. There will be toothpaste in the upstairs bathroom."

My sisters follow me upstairs. We flip on the bright bathroom light and the exhaust fan whirs, drowning out the sounds of the sea and whatever else.

The toothpaste is stiff and yucky from sitting in the medicine cabinet all year. We squeeze it onto our index fingers and rub our teeth and tongues, cleaning the wine off our breath.

Bess is giddy, now that she's done being scared, and the wine has gone to her head. "We're so bad," she says. "And we're all high schoolers now. I'm gonna be hanging out with you. Erin'll be here. So much fun, right? This is going to be the best summer."

I am suddenly angry. "Stop." I grab Bess's shoulders, hard. "Don't say that."

"What?"

"The best summer."

"I just—"

"It is *not* the best summer."

"I just meant, we're going to— It's going to be fun, that's all. Staying up late, sneaking in the guesthouse."

"Rosemary is gone," I say, close to her face. "How can you say *best summer*? She is *gone*."

"I'm sorry. I just—"

"You can't just erase her like that. And be so happy. What kind of person are you?"

"I didn't mean it," whispers Bess. "I was just talking."

"Let her look forward to the goddamned summer," says Penny, affecting disengagement and putting on lip gloss in the bathroom mirror. "Let her have a little happiness. Good Lord, Carrie."

"Yeah," says Bess, switching moods now that Penny is defending her. "Let me look forward."

"You're always so dramatic," says Penny. "It's really okay for her just to be happy. Happy is better than being, what, a grieving puddle or whatever. Am I right?" This to Bess.

Bess nods. "You shouldn't tell me how to feel, Carrie," she says. "You always tell me how I should feel."

"Fine." I cave immediately. These are the sisters I have left. "I get your point."

As we step onto the Goose Cottage porch, I listen for the sound, the "hey hey hey hey." I can't help it.

But it is gone.

We head to the Clairmont kitchen, where we raid the freezer. We find a quart of chocolate and a quart of mint chocolate chip.

We sit around the kitchen table together, dipping our spoons straight into the cartons.

12.

I TAKE A codeine to help me sleep. The sea lapping at the shore seems loud and unfamiliar as I lie in my bed.

When I finally drift off, I dream that Rosemary is crawling on her hands and knees up the long steps that lead from the Tiny Beach. Her hair is wet and she wears her green bathing suit, the one with the pockets. The one she drowned in.

I fear her at first, in the dream. She is a ghost climbing out of the sea, returning to the spot where no one loved her quite enough to keep her safe.

Though we did love her.

We always loved her.

I will always love her.

"I love you, Rosemary," I tell her.

And in my dream, when Rosemary reaches the top of the stairway, she is smiling. Glad to see me. "Hey hey hey hey," she sings.

She lies down on the walkway, her wet suit making marks on the dry wood. She stretches her arms over her head. "La, la la la la. La la la la."

When I wake, the sun is streaming through the cracks in my curtains. I am up early again, despite the pills.

And Rosemary is kneeling on my carpet, wearing a floral summer nightgown and Penny's lamb slippers.

13.

SHE HAS THE Scrabble board in front of her—the one Penny and I left on the porch yesterday morning. She hums to herself as she makes words with the letter tiles. *Pancake*, crisscrossing with *kangaroo*, crisscrossing with *shampoo*, crisscrossing with *pumpkin*.

I stare.

She looks exactly like her old Rosemary self. She has a summer tan and freckles on her nose. Her dirty-blond hair is streaked with lighter threads. She has a large bag of potato chips next to her and is eating them absently.

I know she is dead.

I do not believe in ghosts.

But I do not think I am hallucinating, either.

"Good morning," says Rosemary without looking up.

"Morning, buttercup." I gaze at her in wonder. "How did you get here?"

"I missed you," says Rosemary. "So I came back for a bit." She smiles at me and picks up the bag of potato chips. "I'm having chips for breakfast."

Chips for breakfast—that's something she and I did once. It's nearly impossible to get junk food in this house first thing in the morning, because our mother and Luda are always up so early, frying bacon and squeezing orange juice. They play NPR on the kitchen radio and bustle about, almost like friends. Well, it is only Luda who takes the trash to the bins by the staff building; only Luda who wipes the grease off the stove. And it is only Tipper who decides the menus. But they do seem to enjoy the kitchen together.

Anyway, one morning when she was seven, Rosemary woke at five a.m. and for some reason came to get me. We tiptoed downstairs together and made ourselves tea with lots of milk and sugar. We got two kinds of potato chips from the pantry: ridged ones with ranch flavor and regular ones with just salt. We took our chips and our mugs of tea down to the family dock. We watched the sun finish its rise. Rosemary wanted us to sing the song she called "Billie Jean Is Not My Lover," so we did. She liked that song. She had no idea what it was about.

After that, she often asked me if we could have potato chips for breakfast. Sometimes I said "Wake me early and we'll do it"—but she never came in early enough. Tipper and

Luda were always in the kitchen. Other times I said "Ugh, no, buttercup. I want to sleep in. Have an egg and be a credit to the family. 'Kay?"

Now I'm sorry for every time I ever said no to her. But isn't that how people always feel when someone dies? It's a cliché. You wish. You're sorry.

"You were a good sister," says Rosemary, as if she knows my thoughts. "I wouldn't come back for Penny or Bess. Not even for Mother and Daddy."

I sit up and rub my eyes. "You love Mother and Daddy."

"Okay, I came back for Mother, too," she says. "'Cause she's the mom. I went up there last night and saw her."

"You did? How was it?"

"Hm."

"What 'hm'?"

She fiddles with a piece of her hair. "She turned away."

"What?"

"She— I thought she'd want to see me. But she didn't."

Rosemary crawls across the Scrabble board, messing up all the words she just constructed. "You coming on the lap?" I ask.

"Yep."

She is too big, but she gets on my lap anyway. I put my arms around her. Her tangly Rosemary hair smells of conditioner and seawater. She feels solid, not ghostly at all. She's breathing.

We cuddle for a bit. "Mother saw me and just left," says Rosemary eventually. "She turned right around with like, a shocked look on her face, and went out of her bedroom and down the hall. So I followed her because I thought she'd hug me or maybe cry or maybe be happy, but when she got to the top of the stairs, before she went downstairs, she turned back around. She said, 'Please don't follow me. Don't visit me and don't follow me. I have to keep it together now. For the rest of the family.'"

"Oh, buttercup."

"She was scared of me."

"She loves you. She just— She does love you," I say.

"I guess." Rosemary climbs off my lap, picks up her bag of potato chips, and goes to sit on the foot of the bed. "Will you read me a story?"

"Seriously?" I say. "You come back from the dead and after a quick reunion cuddle, you want a story?"

"Yup."

It feels so much like none of the past year ever happened that I touch my jaw to be sure about the surgery.

"You look different—you look great—it's kinda weird—but I'll get used to it," says Rosemary, running the sentences together and rolling her eyes.

"Thanks."

"Did it hurt?" she asks. "'Cause dying hurt a lot, but only for a second, and then it was fine. Mostly it was being scared of dying that was awful. And I was thinking, when I saw your face before you woke up, your different face, that you probably had a lot more hurt than I did, right?"

"Yeah, it hurt." I am so glad she didn't suffer.

"Like, what they did to your face hurts way more than *death*."

I laugh.

"Okay, now read." Rosemary grabs a fairy book and hands it to me. "You know the one I want."

14.

THE STORY SHE wants is "Cinderella." It was always her favorite, though Tipper and I often tried to get her to pick something else. You know, because it's a marriage plot—the kind of story where the best reward for a good girl is a handsome prince. Even Tipper thought it was antiquated. But Rosemary loved it.

"Why 'Cinderella'?" I asked her once.

"Pretty clothes and parties, and I also like the pumpkin part," she answered. "The pumpkin is the best."

So I read aloud "Cinderella," marveling that I get to do this, trying to stretch out this strange, cozy moment.

When the story is over, Rosemary stands up. "Bye for now, Carrie. I'm tired."

She skips out the door of my room like it's an ordinary day.

I sit there with the book in my hand.

The Scrabble tiles are strewn across the rug. The potato chip bag is empty.

OUR FAMILY HAS always loved fairy tales. There is something ugly and true in them. They hurt, they are strange, but we cannot stop reading them, over and over.

I want to tell you Rosemary's favorite now. My own version of it.

I want to tell it because the story feels to me like a way to tell the story of my family and that summer when I was seventeen. I can't yet figure out how to explain what happened, any other way.

Cinderella

THERE ARE THREE sisters, living in a house together.

Two of them have pretty faces, but their hearts are twisted.

The third sister, their stepsister—Cinderella—is not only pretty but pious and good.

She has it tough, though. She scrubs their floors on hands and knees. Her hands and face are covered in ashes. Her nails are black with soot.

One day, the prince announces a festival, with balls and parties going on for days. There will be music and delectable things to eat.

Of course, everyone wants to go.

Cinderella wants to go, as well, but more important, she wants her sisters to accept her. Could she go to the festival with them? Please?

The answer is no. The sisters, vain and consumed with their own internal lives,

blind to the suffering of others,

drunk on the hot liquor of the desire for parental approval,

desperate for love and validation—

they see Cinderella as competition.

The stepmother replies that Cinderella may not go to the festival because she does not have a dress. Everyone leaves without her.

So Cinderella goes to the grave of her late mother. Above the grave, there is a bird in a hazel tree. The bird throws down a golden gown for Cinderella to wear.

We all know how the story goes from there. After dancing with the prince, Cinderella runs away. She runs from the prince because she is ashamed of being the unloved, ash-covered sister.

She drops a slipper.

The prince picks it up. He searches for her.

When he comes to their home looking for the woman whose foot will fit the slipper, the stepsisters try for his affection. They maim their own feet, trying to please their mother (who wants them to marry well) and hoping to find love.

One cuts off her big toe.

The other slices off the back of her heel.

They slide their butchered feet into the slipper, but the blood seeps out each time. The prince can tell they do not really fit the shoe.

When the prince asks if the third daughter might try on the shoe, her own father replies that she is only a "deformed little Cinderella."

But she does try it on, and her foot slides into the blood-caked slipper easily. She is not deformed at all.

The prince recognizes her and takes her off to be married.

THIS IS MY story.

That is, I am Cinderella.

I am the good sister,

the outsider,

the one who mourns.

Like me, Cinderella is made over from deformity to beauty and social elevation.

Her new appearance is my new appearance.

But I am also a stepsister.
I am vain and consumed with my own internal life,
drunk on the hot liquor of the desire for parental approval,
desperate for love and validation,
self-mutilated,
seeing my sisters as competition.
Bloody.

PART FOUR

The Boys

15.

A COUPLE DAYS after Rosemary first appears, my uncle Dean arrives with his kids, Yardley and Tomkin (full name: Thomas). Dean brings Penny's friend Erin Riegert with him as well. Gerrard drives them all over in the big boat, which has a cabin below.

Dean is a good time. He lives in Philadelphia. He's a lawyer, though he doesn't seem to work that much.

When he divorced his wife eight years ago, he let her have the kids during the year. He gets them for the summers and brings them to the island. He's the fun dad, making up for lost time. When he's here, Luda does his laundry, unloads his dishwasher, and rinses the soap scum out of his bathtubs, but Dean has always been the grown-up who did the most things with us kids. He happily takes us sailing or to Edgartown for ice cream, when Tipper is busy with domestic matters and Harris on the phone with his office. Dean seems to be fully on holiday when he's here. He horses around with Tomkin in the water. He lives large, drinks beer, slaps backs.

He and my father own Beechwood together, but today, Harris greets Uncle Dean like a guest. The boat arrives at noon. We all go down to the dock.

"Where ya been?" Harris calls jovially as Dean disembarks. "We had to start the summer without you."

"Business got messy," says Dean. "Is there lunch? I could eat a Cadillac."

"Sandwiches and potato chips," says my mother. "Should be ready at Clairmont in an hour."

"That sliced beef I like with the horseradish?"

"On sourdough. And tuna salad. Your own fridge is full if you can't wait." Pevensie has been aired, cleaned, and restocked.

"Tomkin has to pee," says Dean. "Bess, will you take him up to pee?"

"I can pee by myself," says Tomkin. He is narrow and freckly, with brown hair and a nose that turns up. His eleven-year-old legs are covered with scrapes and bug bites. Here on the island, he spends his time staring into tide pools and climbing rocks. Last year, he and Rosemary built a collection of fairy houses around a stump at the back of Pevensie. Some were made of stones, and others were held up by twigs and roofed with leaves, fitting homes for Rosemary's smallest dolls but mostly left empty for actual fairies. They were furnished with shells and bits of moss, plucked rose hips and beach roses. Tomkin is good that way. He'll go along with girls. This year he hardly seems taller than before.

Bess goes with him, carrying his suitcases.

Penny is already gone from the dock. She captured Erin and the two of them ran toward the house squealing, lugging Erin's bags. Erin could sleep in Rosemary's old room, of course, but Penny wants her. There are twin beds in Penny's room anyhow.

My mother nudges me. "Yardley."

I am hanging back. I have not seen any of these people since Christmas, before my operation. I did talk to Yardley on the phone a couple times. She sent a card when I first had the proce-dure. I know her mother must have made her write it, but it was

62

well done. Yardley's fat, bouncy handwriting filled the whole inside of the card, both sides, and spilled over to the back.

> That %&$* sucks about the liquid diet. I only just now thought about how attached I am to chewing. I'm like, obsessed with chewing, actually. Gum! Licorice! Only the red kind. Other chewy stuff like caramel! Or crunchy things like nuts!
>
> Okay, I don't give a poop about nuts. But I do chew a lot of gum.
>
> Sorry. I don't mean to make you jealous about all the chewing I do. This card is meant to cheer you up!
>
> Oh, here is something fun. New boyfriend! I got rid of Reed that I was talking about at Christmas because he was NOT supportive about my college application angst. He kept wanting to come over and make out when I was literally *applying to Harvard* and the form was due the next day.
>
> So I said, no more Reed.
>
> New boyfriend = George.
>
> George wants to make out all the time, too, but my college applications are in now, so it doesn't matter. He's a canoe racer, which I didn't know was even a sport, but apparently it is.
>
> Okay, out of room now, write back soon.
>
> > Love,
> > Yardley

She didn't get into Harvard. She is going to Connecticut College and wants to be pre-med.

Dean is disappointed. He and Harris are Harvard men. But in general, Yardley is a "credit to the family." She's narrow of face and body, efficiently built, with strong, sturdy legs. Her face is freckled, with a snub nose like Tomkin and very thick brown hair, so that she radiates health and American sportiness. Her voice is firm and arresting; her jaw a sharp line from chin to ear.

Yardley has seriousness of purpose and knows how to work hard, but she can be extremely silly. She's not creative— she herself says that—so she's sweetly in awe of my mother's summer parties and extravagances, and even of my occasional sketches and woven friendship bracelets.

"Carrie!" shouts Yardley, climbing off the boat with a tote bag full of Pop-Tarts and tennis ball canisters. "Get over here, cutie. Oh my god, you look amazing."

I hug her. "Welcome to another summer."

"This one's going to be different."

"Not that much."

"Oh yes it is. Come meet the boys."

I squint at her. "What boys?"

"I brought you a present."

"What?"

"Just kidding. But also not." Yardley drags me onto the boat and down into the cabin, where two teenage boys are hovering over a third, who has clearly just puked into a green bucket. "Terrible sailors but cute as hell," she says.

"I'm a good sailor," says one. He's broad-shouldered with light skin, thick black hair, and high cheekbones. His nose looks like it's been broken several times. He wears a Live Aid music festival T-shirt and baggy seersucker shorts.

"It was very choppy," says the boy who vomited. He is less conventionally handsome, beaky and tall, with close-cropped red hair. He has the look of New York City around him. He's wearing a leather jacket, despite the heat.

The third boy comes over and leans in to Yardley's ear. "That vomit was the most heinous moment of my life," he fake-whispers. He is generally beige—tan skin, tan hair that flops over his forehead, a medium build. He compensates for his beigeness by wearing red plaid shorts and a pink polo shirt with the collar popped.

This must be George. The canoe racer. Unless Yardley has someone else now. She is ordinary to look at—pretty but not gorgeous, nothing special about her clothes—but she has always had boyfriends. I don't know what makes guys like her so much. Maybe it's her confidence. Yardley doesn't think—or at least, doesn't seem to think—about all that stuff that keeps me unsettled. She is certain of her place in the world, oblivious, happy, better able to just love and be loved. Anyway, I adore her.

"This is my cousin Carrie," she announces. "She's seventeen, she can outswing any of you with a baseball bat, she knows where all the bodies are buried on this island, and you're all very happy to meet her. 'Kay?"

Beige George shakes hands.

The broad-shouldered boy with the broken nose bows comically.

The redheaded boy in the leather jacket looks up from the bucket. "Sorry I'm so disgusting."

"Thank you for the present, Yardley," I say. Cheeky, but I mean it.

"You're welcome." Yardley marches over to the bucket of vomit and picks it up. "Major," she says to him. "Are you finished ralphing?"

"I am."

"Promise?"

He squints. "We're going on dry land now, right?"

"Yes, we are."

"Then I promise."

Yardley climbs out of the cabin and goes to the back of the boat, where she dumps the contents of the bucket and rinses it in the sea. We all follow her, the boys lugging backpacks. Their duffel bags have been taken out by the staff.

"Do you want a mint, Major?" Yardley says. "I bet you want a mint before you meet my aunt and uncle."

Major nods.

She gives him a mint from a paper tube in the back pocket of her shorts. "Okay, you weenies, get off the boat and meet everyone. Make big eyes at my auntie Tipper, 'kay? And shake hands with my uncle Harris."

And so in a bustle, my parents meet George Bryce-Amory, the beige yet pink-and-plaid canoe-racing boyfriend of Yardley. George is all toothy smile, strong forearms, hearty proclamations ("Nice little place you got here") interspersed with self-mocking asides. "Oh, I'm a terrible cook," he tells my mother when she offers to stock the Goose kitchen for him and his friends. "It's really shocking and even scary. I make, like, burned coffee and, let me think, kind-of-raw oatmeal and that's it."

She promptly invites him to come up to Clairmont for breakfast any morning, and says he can help himself to leftover pie. "The coffee's always on by six a.m.," she says. "And by eight there will be eggs and muffins." She promises to buy him cereal for the cottage and extracts favorite brands from each of the boys. George likes Lucky Charms. "It's revolting, I know. I should be eating oat bran, but I love it so much," he says.

Jeremy Majorino, known as Major, is the ralpher with no sea legs, the red hair and leather jacket. He is the product (we learn) of an artsy private school in Brooklyn, friends with George from years of summer camp. "When George decides he's friends with you, you don't have a choice," Major says, shaking Harris's hand awkwardly. "Loyalest guy I know."

While all this is happening, the boy with the broad shoulders and the broken nose is loafing behind his friends, his hands in his pockets as he stares out at the sea. His worn T-shirt blows in the wind. All three of our dogs come up to him and he bends over to stroke their soft heads. I hear him saying in a low voice: "Oh, hello, good-looker. Oh, yes, you too. And you. Ack, you slimed my hand. You slimed it with your dog nose! I'm wiping it off on your fur, you slimy dog. You deserve it. Yes you do. Are we friends anyway? I think we are friends."

He feels me looking at him and stands up. Smiles. His eyebrows are thick over dark brown eyes. His nearly black hair hasn't been cut in ages.

His name is Lawrence Pfefferman, he says to my parents. "Call me Lor, for short. Or Pfeff," he says.

"Watch out," Yardley whispers in my ear.

"Why?" I ask.

"Just watch out, is all," she says. "Pfeff is a lot."

It is pronounced "Feff." To my parents, George explains that he and Pfeff are friends from school in Philadelphia.

"You a boating man, Lor?" says my dad, tossing his head mockingly at Major.

"Yes, sir."

"All right, then. We'll take the sailboat out this evening, for the sunset. Everyone but that guy." Another dig at Major, because he threw up. "You in, George? A little sailing?"

George looks hesitant to leave Major alone on their first night here, but he doesn't have to say anything because Tipper interjects.

"Harris, we have the Lemon Hunt tonight."

"Oh, but the weather is—"

"No," says Tipper firmly. "I have been working for days on the Lemon Hunt. This evening is not the time."

She takes her parties very seriously. My father grins. "To-morrow, then," he tells George and Pfeff. "We'll get a good sunset. Let me show you boys to Goose Cottage."

He grabs someone's backpack and heads down the walkway to the guesthouse. Yardley and the boys go along.

Pfeff is the last to follow, and as he goes, he reaches out to touch the beach roses. He leaps up to tap the branch of a tree that arches over the walk.

16.

MY MOTHER TURNS to Uncle Dean. "Hello."

"You're beautiful as ever, Tipper. Good to see you." He smiles.

"What were you thinking?" Her manner is perky, like she's a wife on an old black-and-white sitcom. She tilts her head to one side.

"What? They're nice boys," says Dean, lighting a cigarette. He is a big man, quite a bit taller than my father, and running slightly to pudge. "Yardley's been going out with George five months. I've taken the guy out to dinner. We hit the golf course a couple times."

"You didn't ask me," my mother says. "You didn't even tell me they were coming."

Dean looks out at the sea and shakes his head. "I don't have to tell you, Tipper. And I certainly don't have to ask you."

He's right, technically. He co-owns the island. But since Harris is the elder brother, and since Dean is divorced, and probably for a million other reasons, Dean sits number two. My mother is the hostess, and Dean lets her handle the staff who do his housework and the stocking of his refrigerator. His pantry is full of favorite cookies and bottles of expensive beer, thanks to her.

Tipper smiles. "What if I'd had people in Goose Cottage already?"

He shrugs. "It has four bedrooms. The guys could double up, or someone could sleep on the foldout."

"Not every guest would appreciate sharing with three teenage boys."

He gives her a look. "Do you have someone in Goose, Tipper? And if you did, would you have asked me first? Or even let me know?"

She looks away.

"Yardley's eighteen," says Dean. "She wants to be with her guy before she goes off to college and probably never sees him again. So he's here for a bit, and he brought some buddies. It's nothing."

"Three unexpected boys," says Tipper. "You think I have enough chicken for those appetites? For tonight?"

Dean turns conciliatory. "They'll eat hot dogs. They won't care."

"I care. I don't want to feed them hot dogs."

"They're Yardley's friends," I put in. "She said they're from good families and all that."

Tipper turns to me. "You have no idea what it is to run this property with unexpected guests."

"You can't send them home," I tell her. "It would be rude if you don't let them stay at least a week."

She frowns. I know she hates to be rude.

"They'll brighten up the place," I add. I don't have to mention Rosemary, but she knows that's what I mean. Rosemary not being here, that's what needs brightening. "It could be fun," I continue. "You know, for me and Penny. We can take them out in the kayaks, and like Harris said, on the sailboat. We could do a tennis tournament or something." I'm selling her on wholesome group activities.

My mother folds her arms.

"Please, Tipper?" I say, putting my head on her shoulder. "Best person, nicest mother in the world. Let me have some good distraction. I neeeeeeed it."

She sighs, but I can tell I've won her over. "I really have a very full plate," she snaps at Dean. "I'd be grateful if you wanted to man the grill. Tonight. And often. As soon as you're settled."

Dean grins. "Always glad to man the grill."

When Dean is gone, my mother turns to me. "Make sure they have a good time, okay?"

"The boys?"

"Of course the boys. If they're staying, I'm going to be a good hostess. You take them down to the beach, show them the kayaks. And make sure they understand how the VCR works, the washer, that stuff, so they're comfortable. I can't believe Dean's nerve." She shakes her head. "Three boys and no warning. I haven't even got the beds made up in the cottage. You'll do that for me?"

Major, George, and Pfeff. I can feel them from here, like a pulsing or a heart beating, over in the guesthouse. Testosterone, entitlement, cold beer, and laughter.

I tell her yes.

17.

WHEN I GET to Goose, it is all kinds of chaos. In the yard that opens off the wooden walkway, George and Major are playing Ping-Pong, having dragged an old table from the garden shed, where it has languished for years. They have their shirts off. George is muscled and evenly tan to match his beige hair; Major pale and lithe. Their boxer shorts peek out of their waistbands. George's are Black Watch plaid, clashing wildly with his red plaid shorts. Major's are a simple blue.

"Ho!" George grabs the ball to stop the game. "Carrie, is it?"

"Yeah."

The duffel bags are piled on the porch. Clothing bursts out of them. Tennis rackets, bags of taco chips. A typewriter is open and a piece of paper stuck into it.

Pfeff sits on the porch with his back against the house, a Coke in one hand, the blue kitchen phone in the other. Its curly cord stretches through the window. "I'm sorry. . . . I'm sorry. . . . I said, I'm sorry," he's repeating. "I know, but I'm calling you now. . . . Yes, George's girlfriend, Yardley. She invited us." He looks up at George and Major. "When did Yardley invite us?"

"Me, a while ago," says George. "You two hosebags on Tuesday night."

"Tuesday night," says Pfeff into the phone. "No, I don't have her dad's number. He's like, in a different house than we are. We're in a guesthouse. . . . Massachusetts, I think." He looks up again. "We're in Massachusetts, correct?"

"Correct," I tell him.

"Yuh-huh," says Pfeff into the phone. "She said—Major, how long are we staying?"

Major shrugs. "Forever, maybe. This place is amazing."

"Maybe forever," says Pfeff.

"His mother," George explains to me. He tosses the Ping-Pong ball in the air and catches it again.

"I know I'm a terrible son," says Pfeff. "And I know you deserve a delightful son, so it stinks that you got me, but I also know you love me anyway. . . . Of course I love you. So can we be friends? . . . Also, I'm a legal adult. That means I don't have to come home. Okay."

"I'm here to show you how to work the washing machine and whatever else," I say.

"Yardley showed us all that," says Major.

"We're fully up to speed," says George.

And maybe it's the two shirtless boys, because I can't stop looking at them. Or maybe it's the way they've already disrupted everything about how Goose Cottage usually feels. Or maybe it's just because it's baking hot out—but I surprise myself. "Let's go swimming, then," I say. "You haven't really been to Beechwood until you've been in the water."

"Hell yeah," says George. And Pfeff hangs up with his mother.

Beach towels are in a cupboard by the door. The boys find their swimsuits, Pfeff riffling through his duffel, tossing shirts and jeans across the porch in his search, then changing in the mudroom, yelling, "Don't come in and look at my weenie."

Major yells back that it's not the kind of weenie anyone would be interested in, and Pfeff says "What on earth does that mean?"—still from the mudroom. "It's a perfectly normal weenie. A good weenie, even. Oh god, now Carrie's going to think terrible things about me. Major, you've never even seen it. Carrie, he's never seen it. Seriously."

George tells him to shut up and Major says he *doth protest too much*. The two of them change quickly upstairs in the bedrooms. George phones Yardley, who is over at Pevensie, and together we troop down the long wooden staircase to the Tiny Beach.

TWO O'CLOCK IS the perfect time to swim on Beechwood. The sun has heated the water all day. The cove is protected from the wind. The shore is rocky. The sand on the Big Beach is nicer, but there is a private feeling to the Tiny Beach that's magical.

All three boys run whooping into the water, diving under the gentle waves as soon as they hit knee-deep. I stand for a moment and watch them. The muscles in their backs ripple. Their shoulders are sleek with water. They flip their hair out of their eyes and splash each other. George swims a serious-looking crawl toward the sharp rocks that edge the cove, then stops to tread water and look around. Major floats on his back, looking up. Pfeff shouts and swims out to join George.

"You coming?" Major asks me. "We won't bite."

I strip down to my swimsuit and go in. The codeine I took earlier blocks all thoughts of what happened to Rosemary in this very same water. Instead, I hear the echo of the waves,

feel the warm drumbeat of the sun and the cucumber cool of the seawater against my skin.

I am awake. I am expanding.

The nerves in my fingertips cry to touch someone,

the pulse in my veins jumps.

They are here on our island, these boys. Transforming it. Possibly desecrating it.

They may last a week.

They may stay forever.

18.

BEFORE SUPPER, I put on one of several white cotton dresses I own. I feel too old for yellow, and for the Lemon Hunt, we all must wear yellow or white. I comb my hair and dust blush on my cheeks.

The black pearls sit on my dresser, still there from several nights ago, and it occurs to me that I wasn't meant to keep them. Tipper will be cross that I didn't return them sooner. She can be sharp about things like that, small breeches of etiquette that she thinks mean you don't appreciate something. "Manners are kindness," she always says. She feels they show you value other people; that you consider their time, their possessions, their creative effort.

I know she is downstairs, apron on, working with Luda in the kitchen, so I write a short note.

> Dearest best mother, loaner of pearls,
>
> Thank you for the chance to wear these, and for saying they will someday be mine.
>
> > With love,
> > Carrie

MY PARENTS' DOOR is open. The room is empty except for Wharton. She lies sleeping on a cotton blanket at the foot of the bed and doesn't stir when I come in.

Harris's clothes are tossed over an armchair. His bedside table is cluttered with a couple pairs of eyeglasses, books (*The Fatal Shore*, *Lonesome Dove*, a book about the CIA), nasal spray, tissues, and an orange plastic jar of prescription sleeping pills. Halcion, they're called.

Tipper's table has only a pretty glass container of scented hand cream and a small dish where I know she puts her earrings.

I stare for a moment at Harris's side of the bed.

He uses nasal spray.

He needs pills to sleep.

He forgets to throw away his tissues.

The Harris Sinclair I know is always alert, always decisive. His tennis serve is brutal, his opinions likewise. But his nightstand seems vulnerable. It speaks of discomfort and fatigue.

Looking around to be sure I am alone, I open the bottle of Halcion. I shake a small handful into the pocket of my dress, leaving a good amount in the bottle. I recap it.

Then I go to Tipper's vanity. I place the black pearls inside the jewelry drawer, tucking my note underneath them like a surprise.

She will like that.

I am about to shut the drawer when I feel the pull of the photo. Though I told myself otherwise, part of me has intended to look at it all along. And I did not want my sisters with me.

I lift the black velvet liner and slide the picture out from underneath. It has been crumpled, then flattened out again. Folds crisscross the image.

It looks like it was taken in the late sixties or early seventies. On one side is my mother. She looks as she did in college and when she was first married: her hair in a headband, with a tease behind it. She's sitting on a bench, outdoors. Her dress has a Peter Pan collar. Behind her, I'm guessing it's Harvard Radcliffe. Old brick and large trees, a snatch of lawn. She's laughing, and her eyes are directed at a man—who isn't there.

His face has been scratched out, as if with a box cutter.

I can tell that he's white, and average weight. It could be my uncle Chris, whom I've never met. Or it could be someone else. The man wears a plain white T-shirt and blue jeans that sit high on his waist, the way jeans used to. His feet aren't in the picture, and he's pointing at the camera, as if to give instructions to the photographer, who snapped the picture at just the wrong moment.

Did my mother scratch this photo, then crumple it—then change her mind?

I tuck the picture back beneath the black velvet of the jewelry drawer, making sure it's exactly as it was.

19.

THE LEMON HUNT is an evening tradition. Sometimes it is done at the start of a summer, sometimes near the end, and some years skipped. Tipper has a dress for it, a lemon-yellow cotton sundress with pintucks. She wears it with a white cotton cardigan. I can remember her in that dress when I was three.

Penny and I wore pinafores printed with lemons, bought specially for that night.

When I get downstairs, fairy lights outline the porch, and torches glow along the edges of the lawn. Bess is spinning our younger cousin Tomkin on the tire swing that hangs from the big tree in the front yard. Tomkin wears a white button-down and white Bermuda shorts, already fairly dirty. Bess is barefoot, wearing a bright yellow dress with puffed sleeves and a sweetheart neckline.

Uncle Dean mans the grill, as promised, dressed in white Bermudas and a terrible checked yellow shirt that I think he wears to play golf. He is in his element, managing a huge number of chicken breasts marinated with lemon.

The epic picnic table is covered in my mother's lemon-printed tablecloths. On a separate table, the beginnings of the buffet are laid out. There are stacks of green napkins, bouquets of white and yellow flowers, trays and bowls of "nibbles"—meaning things to eat during cocktail hour. Bowls of salty olives mixed with lemon rind, salmon mousse and sesame crackers, cashew nuts and yellow cherry tomatoes.

My cousin Yardley's sporty figure is wrapped tight in a yellow floral dress with her bright blue bra straps showing. Her hair is pulled off her face with a headband. She helps Luda (all in white with a white apron) lay out the final details of the drinks table. There are three different kinds of lemonade—regular, strawberry, and lemon-lime—with club soda, tonic, and alcoholic options for mixing. Beethoven's Ninth Symphony plays on the stereo. It is one of my mother's favorites.

Penny and Erin walk up from the Big Beach, carrying their shoes. Erin is wearing Penny's clothes—a yellow T-shirt and a pair of white carpenter overalls. Penny wears her white sundress. Erin is short and sturdily built, with wavy red-brown hair that she's pulled back in a high ponytail. Her face is like an angel's—heart-shaped with pretty red lips and dark eyebrows—and at school she favors black turtlenecks and long, narrow skirts with Doc Martens. Next to languid Penny, Erin always seems bristling with energy.

I walk down to them as Penny flops on the grass, heedless of her dress, to brush the sand off her feet. "I hardly saw you on the dock," I say to Erin.

"My head was spinning from all the manhood in the boat," she says. "I didn't know Yardley was bringing an entourage."

"Neither did I."

"That Pfeff is pretty fine," says Penny from her seat.

"Major will look better when he's not ralphing," says Erin. "I told you, he's the cool one."

"I don't know how you can think about a guy who chundered his guts out right in front of you," says Penny. "Mother's good with them all being here?" she asks me. Feet clean, she puts on her espadrilles.

"She's pissed. But they charmed her. And I put some pressure on her to let them stay."

"Where will they all sleep?" asks Erin.

"There's room in Goose," says Penny. "They're in Goose, right?"

"Um-hm."

"Oh my god, this place," says Erin. "I was saying to Penny: I had no idea what to expect."

I don't want her to feel strange here. "It's just a—"

"It's just a *whole island*," interrupts Erin. "With an extra house for when you have guests. Who has an extra house? You weirdos."

"You can get stuff out of the kitchen whenever you're hungry," I tell her. "I mean, like, if you see a whole pie or something, don't eat that, but apples or potato chips or cookies or whatever. Drinks and coffee. Definitely help yourself. And supper's usually at seven unless it's a special night, like tonight. And um, let's see, what else? Use all the shampoo and conditioner and that stuff. Sunblock. And did you meet Luda?" I point her out. "You can ask her if you need anything."

Erin grins. "Thank you. Penny didn't tell me any of that."

"Oh please," says Penny. "I would have gotten around to it."

"She didn't tell you to bring white clothes, either. Did she?" I ask.

"No." Erin looks at the group on the lawn. "I'm underdressed."

"It's okay," I tell her. "The entourage will be underdressed as well."

THE BOYS ARRIVE late, making an entrance as they run together down the walkway and up the sloping lawn to pay tribute to my mother. George is all in white. The color is unflattering to his beige face and hair, but he looks extremely put-together: polo shirt with a jacket and trousers, like a tennis player from the 1920s. The other two are in white T-shirts and pale tan chinos, Major with black Converse (a bit of New York edge) and Pfeff wearing flip-flops (devil-may-care).

Tipper is smiling and laughing, making sure everyone has

drinks. She is glad to have guests, I realize, whatever she said to Uncle Dean. The family has always hunted lemons, so many summers past. We take for granted Tipper's lemon pound cake, her foamy lemon mousse in jelly jars. These boys and Erin are a fresh audience.

We eat on the lawn instead of at the picnic table. White and yellow cotton blankets, old and mismatched, some of them patchwork quilts, are laid out for people to sit on as supper is served.

George cozies up to Yardley on the porch hammock. Penny, Erin, and I sit with Pfeff and Major, while Bess and Tomkin get out croquet mallets and hoops. Those two have little interest in chicken and salad and sourdough bread. They are saving themselves for dessert.

We watch them play. Our croquet set is old and used to belong to Harris's mother. We don't use it often. It's more of an affectation than an actual game. Bess and Tomkin perform beautifully, batting the colored balls, running and laughing, being picturesque.

Major talks about a movie, Ferris Bueller's Day Off, that no one else has seen. He's explaining the story, beat by beat, but Pfeff interrupts him. "Don't tell them the plot."

"Why not?"

"People don't want to hear the plot of a goddamned movie, Major. It ruins the fun."

"I want to hear it," I tell him. "We're movie starved. Boarding school and now here—I never see anything."

"We have a couple VCRs," explains Penny. "But there's nothing to watch." She flops back on the picnic blanket. The boys' eyes all go to her legs as her skirt slides up above her knees.

"I think we own twelve movies between all three houses," I say.

"It's eleven," corrects Penny from her lying-down position. "And the most random movies you could ever own."

"Kids' movies, mostly," I add. "From when we were little."

"We have *Bedknobs and Broomsticks*," says Penny. "I have seen that thing like a million times."

"And some classics our dad thought would be good for us," I add.

"They're not even real classics," says Penny. "It's just things that old men like, like *Ben-Hur*." She shakes her head. "God, that's a stupid movie."

All the while we're talking, my eyes are on Pfeff. It isn't that he's so handsome. His lips are thin. The space between his nose and the top of his mouth is probably a bit too short for actual beauty. But he is voracious—eating hungrily and enthusiastically, declaring his adoration of the chicken, the sourdough. Getting up for seconds. "I'm going to move in and live with your mom instead of mine," he tells me. "I'm done with my mother entirely. Adopting your family. That's it, you have to take me. I'm going to eat like this every day until I go to college."

"Don't be vile," says Penny. *Vile* is her favorite word this season. She says it when *vile* is not what she means at all.

He keeps looking at me but answers her. "The way to my heart is through my stomach, I'm just saying."

"It'll be all cafeteria food at Amherst," says Major. "You better eat up now." Major and Pfeff are both going to Amherst, a college in western Massachusetts.

"I'm on it," says Pfeff.

TIPPER HAS ASKED me to proclaim the rules of the Lemon Hunt. For all her hostessy impulses, she never likes to stand up in front of a crowd, and I have done this announcement for the past couple years. I don't mind public speaking. I know I have a strong voice, and it contradicts what people think when they look at my jaw. Or what they used to think.

When she gives me the signal, before dessert, I stand on the Clairmont steps and ring a bell.

"The nearly annual Sinclair Family Lemon Hunt will commence momentarily," I proclaim as everyone gathers at the foot of the steps. "With tremendous thanks to my mother, the miraculous Tipper Sinclair, you will find that there are one hundred lemons and a single lime hidden across Beechwood Island. There are none that will endanger you to retrieve. None on rooftops or in brambles. And none indoors, though they may not be visible to the naked eye. Each of you, adults and children, is to take a basket."

I gesture at a collection of baskets Luda has brought out. They are wicker, some dark and some light. They're all different shapes, but each is tied with a pale yellow ribbon.

"Collect lemons," I continue. "Wander near, wander far. Please do not go swimming on your own." I see Tipper wince, but I feel I have to say it. The idea of Tomkin or Bess or anyone, really, swimming alone on those beaches chills me. "You needn't bother around the staff building, but anywhere else is potential asylum for a citrus fruit." Though I say this every year, there is a ripple of laughter. "At the end of the hunt, you will hear this bell again. At that time, lemons will be counted—by Tipper"—here, I curtsy toward my mother—"and two prizes will be awarded. One for maximum lemons, the other for the lime."

"Off you go!" calls Tipper, waving to the group. "Good luck!"

The baskets are collected. Flashlights are turned on.

The music inside the house gets louder as people leave the lawn.

One hundred lemons (and the single lime) await.

20.

THE BOYS HEAD out together. Penny grabs Erin and they head for the boathouse. Uncle Dean grabs Tomkin and the two of them run off. Bess, a serious hunter, disappears around the back of Clairmont, skirting the house.

I start off with Yardley. We agree to walk toward the tennis courts and the wooded area around them. We pass Tomkin, who is hunting in some bushes off the walkway. "I told Dad to leave me alone," he tells Yardley proudly. "I don't need his help to find lemons. I'm eleven years old!"

"Yes, you are, butthead," says Yardley. She takes the lime from her pocket and throws it at him. "Here you go, though."

Tomkin catches it. "For real?"

"Shut up," says Yardley, and we walk on.

"Where did you find the lime?" I ask. "And when? We just left Clairmont."

"It was in the grass, blending in, right at the foot of the steps," she says. "No one in this family can see what's right in front of them."

We walk in silence for a bit.

"I found a photograph of my mother," I blurt, finally saying what has been on the tip of my tongue all evening, with no one to say it to. "When she was first married, I guess, with this guy I don't know."

"Mm?"

"His faced was scraped off. Like down to white paper. I couldn't tell who it was."

Yardley stops walking. "That sounds like a horror movie."

"No, it was like someone hated the man in the picture, hated him enough to want to scrape his face off."

"Still a horror movie."

"But why would Tipper keep the photo?"

Yardley starts walking again. "Where'd you find it?"

"Her jewelry drawer."

"Oh god," she said. "Like she's keeping it, like it's precious? With the face scraped off?"

"Uh-huh."

"But it's an old picture?"

"From before I was born. I think."

"Hm." We walk in silence for a moment. "Honestly, Carrie, I'd say leave it alone. Ever since my parents got divorced, there's no end of stuff I just totally ignore. Legal documents, evidence that my dad has girlfriends, or hookers, even. Angry phone messages from my mother, stuff about money and schedules and—you know what? I just fast-forward. Don't need to know it, happier without it. Let those stupid grown-ups deal with their emotional garbage and their illegal this and that, shady guys coming over or whatever. You start digging in adults' lives and things get ugly so fast, you don't want to eat your breakfast anymore. I figure it's my job to like, get an education, then become a doctor and help people. Be nice to my friends. Not get pregnant, not drive drunk. I'm gonna just like, be in love with George and enjoy the summer."

I try to push the image of that photograph down, burying it in the thick cool dirt of my mind, dirt that is heavy with things I do not think about but carry with me nonetheless. "You two are in love?"

"I think so," she says. "Not totally sure."

"I think I would know if I loved somebody," I say. "All the people I love, there's no question." My sisters. Even when they're petty or annoying, I love them and it's just a fact. I held Bess when she was a baby. Penny and I have been together as long as I can remember.

"I thought I would know, too," says Yardley. "But with a new person? I've only been going out with George five months. I feel like I love him, but I could totally fall out of love if he started acting like a dick."

"He seems very, very into you."

"Yeah. But it could be the private island. You have to consider that, right?" says Yardley. "When you come with fun extras, you never know if a person loves you for yourself."

"Cynical."

"Yeah, well, I don't think like that all the time," says Yardley. "It's just now. In the dark. When he didn't pick me for his Lemon Hunt partner."

We arrive at the tennis courts. Yardley flicks the lights on. We squint as we do a quick run across the clay. Two lemons, both mine. Then we plunge the courts into darkness again. Then we depart the walkway and head through the woodsy area behind the courts, up to the perimeter path.

A lemon for Yardley.

At Pevensie we circle, looking in the grass, the slats of the fence, the trellis for the climbing vines, under the steps and under the pillows of the porch swing.

A lemon for me.

When I come down from the Pevensie porch, Yardley is not to be seen.

I circle the house again, and when I come back to the front, she and George are kissing. She is pressing him against the house with her hand up his shirt.

I stand there for a moment. George's hand is cupped under her bottom like he's done this a thousand times. Yardley is transformed from the funny, practical girl I know into an experienced woman, someone with the courage to push her boyfriend against the house and run her hand up his stomach to his chest, like she knows what makes him feel good.

She turns. "Carrie, go on without me," she says. "I'm going to hunt for lemons with George. 'Kay?"

"Hunt for lemons, that's a good thing to call it," says George, low and laughing.

"This is my house," says Yardley. "You wanna see my room?"

I turn and run into the dark walkways of the island.

21.

I AM HEADING along the perimeter path that curves around the island, going toward the Big Beach, when I run into Pfeff.

"Ahoy," I call as he comes into sight.

"Oh, ack. You scared me."

"How's your hunt?"

He shows me a basket with two lemons. "Terrible. I lost George and then I lost Major and— I don't know. There are like no lemons anywhere. It's possible I need glasses. I should get myself tested. Do you want to give me hints?"

"I didn't hide them." In the moonlight, his skin is glowing. I'm suddenly aware of the straps on my dress, the feeling of my hair down my back, the braces on my teeth, the balm on my lips.

"You didn't?" he says. "You gave that speech and seemed so impressive and official, I thought you would know all the secret places."

"Nope."

We are standing at a spot where the path traverses a rocky ledge. Over the edge, far below, waves hit dark rocks. Pfeff leans against the railing and peers down. "This is a dangerous spot."

I lean over the rail beside him. His bare arm is inches from mine. "When we were little," I tell him, "we were forbidden to go on this path alone. In case we'd get the idea to climb the barrier."

He leans out a little farther. "It makes you feel alive, though. Am I right?"

I lean out and feel a spike of adrenaline stab me.

"Should I climb up?" asks Pfeff. "Just to see how it feels to be in mortal danger?"

"Don't be a fool."

"Oh." He sounds chastened. "Okay."

"I'm all about water safety," I say. "The cool kids all care about water safety."

"Ha." He grins. "You're clever. You know that?"

"Sometimes."

Pfeff looks at me. His thin white T-shirt is loose at the neck and shows his collarbone. His eyes flash.

He leans down, slowly, and when I realize he is going to kiss me, I cannot move, I'm so surprised. He brushes his lips ever so softly across mine. It feels like a feather against my mouth, so light. When he pulls away, I can still feel the spot where we touched.

I have never been kissed before. It's like

diving into cold water, like

eating a raspberry, like

listening to a flute, and it's like

none of those things.

"I adore clever people," Pfeff says, his voice low. "And with the moonlight, and all the danger, and the lemons, and everyone in white, I feel like I'm in a movie or something. Don't you?"

"Not really," I say. "This is my regular life."

"You're like a girl from a movie," whispers Pfeff. "I had to kiss you. Because look at where we are. Right?" He gestures at the sea, the sky, the moon. "It would be a shame to waste it." He tilts his head and cracks a smile. "I hope that wasn't gross or anything."

"No," I say. "It wasn't gross."

"Oh, good."

I reach my hand up around his neck and kiss him back then, standing on tiptoe. His neck is warm beneath my fingers, and suddenly, my mouth is no longer

defective,

scarred,

infected,

inadequate,

as it has seemed ever since I first learned I needed jaw surgery. Instead, my mouth is all

connection and

sensation.

Pfeff leans into me and parts his lips, sliding his hand up my waist to my chest. I am floating and dizzy with this new feeling. He moans, softly, and kisses me a little harder, his breath hot.

And then it is over. He pulls back and smiles. "I should go," he whispers.

"Okay." I am stunned and disoriented. I don't know what people do after suddenly kissing in the moonlight. I don't want him to go.

"Did you forget there's a lemon hunt going on?" Pfeff asks.

"Almost, yes." I laugh.

I want him to kiss me again, or give me a chance so that

I can kiss him again, but his mood seems to have changed. "I better get busy with my lemon hunting," he says. "I like to win things, if you haven't guessed."

"You'll need a lot more than two lemons if you want to win."

He picks up his basket. "I'm going to hunt the hell out of some lemons, then," he says. "Good luck, beautiful Carrie." And with that, Pfeff is gone, running down the walkway and into the night.

22.

I SPEND MUCH of the next hour down on the family dock. I find several lemons on the boats, but my mind is not on the hunt.

I keep replaying what happened. Was that first kiss just a moment of impulse on Pfeff's part? A boy and a girl in the moonlight, the surf crashing below them?

Or does he like me, because he thinks I am *clever* and *impressive*? He used those words.

What else did he say? "You're like a girl from a movie." "Good luck, beautiful Carrie."

But he talked like the kisses were sort of a joke, merely something fun to do so as not to waste the beauty of the evening and the drama of the landscape. And he left in search of lemons.

There was that look in his eyes before he kissed me. The feel of his mouth on mine, the whiff of seawater in his hair.

I am sitting on the edge of the dock when I hear the bell ring. Tipper wants us all to return at the sound of it. The Lemon Hunt is over.

AS EVERYONE CLUSTERS on the Clairmont lawn, Harris announces that it's time for prizes. Tipper stands by his side like a game show assistant.

Tomkin wins for the lime, of course. The gift is a cube kite: three cubes attached to one another, a bright red bit of geometry to fling into the sky. Then people begin counting up their lemons.

Pfeff arrives last for the reckoning, lemons bulging comically in his front and back pockets and held in his hands. "I lost my basket," he announces, kneeling dramatically at my mother's feet. "I suspect it was stolen by one of these weenies." He gestures at Major and George. "Sorry, one of these buttholes."

Tipper laughs.

"Anyway, it was stolen with two lemons in it, I might add, but nonetheless, I persevered, and now, my lady, I present you with"—he begins taking the lemons from his pockets, laying them all on the grass—"twenty lemons."

He wins, beating Bess and Erin, who were tied with fifteen each.

My mother presents Pfeff with a one-hundred-dollar gift certificate to the Edgartown bookshop.

Dessert is lemon mousse topped with fluffy blobs of whipped cream, and rich lemon pound cake soaked in lemon syrup.

I hope Pfeff will come over to me.

I want to go to him.

I can sense him everywhere he goes—talking with my father, horsing around with George and Major, pouring himself lemonade. People bring their dessert plates to the picnic blankets. Bess puts Madonna on the stereo. "Where's the Party," "True Blue," "La Isla Bonita."

I want to talk to Penny, to tell her about the kissing with Pfeff, but she and Erin have claimed the tire swing and don't seem easy to interrupt. Yardley is helping her brother put together his kite. So I am alone with my new experience, the secret of what happened on the walkway in the moonlight.

Pfeff, Major, and George settle themselves on a blanket, plates full of cake. I choose a blanket near them, stretching myself out and staring at the stars.

"You *have* to play tennis," Pfeff is saying to Major. "Because George will just beat me constantly, and that's no fun. I need someone at my level."

"I'm not that vigorous," says Major. "I didn't come to this island to exert myself."

"Tennis is not exertion. It's a game," argues Pfeff.

"I exert myself when I play tennis," George tells Pfeff. "That's why I'm so much better than you."

"Look at all this peer pressure," says Major. "Play Yardley or one of her cousins, Pfeff. I'm sure they all play."

"Yah, but I have dreams of manly comradeship and competition and stuff," says Pfeff.

"Oh god, save me," says Major.

"Well, I just remembered I didn't bring my racquet," says Pfeff.

"They'll have spares," says George.

"Also, no socks," says Pfeff. "I'm realizing. And I think no underwear."

"Uck," says George.

"I packed in a rush."

"But you've been at my house for nearly a week," says George.

"That's where my socks and underwear are. In that bottom shelf thingy in your guest room."

"You left all your underthings for my mom to find?"

"Not on purpose!" Pfeff laughs. "Oh god. I need to get underwear somehow."

"You can wash it," says Major. "There's a machine in the cottage."

"But what if I forget one night?" says Pfeff. "What if I forget and then I have only used underwear to wear? Tipper will know."

"She will," says Major.

"She'll smell me," says Pfeff, still laughing. "Or even if she doesn't smell me, she'll have like a second sense that I'm a filthy creep who doesn't belong on her island."

I see my chance and take it. "I can bring you to Edgartown," I call over. "Solve all your problems."

"Oh no." Pfeff clutches George comically. "Carrie was eavesdropping."

"You were talking loudly about your underwear in my immediate vicinity," I say.

"Is Edgartown where the bookstore is?" asks Pfeff. "Where I have my gift card I got for being a lemon god?"

"Mm-hm. There are lots of shops."

"Yeah, okay. Can we go tomorrow?"

I sit up. "Sure."

"What time is good?"

"Eleven," I tell him. "Meet me on the dock."

Pfeff stands. "I'll be there." He picks up a croquet mallet from the lawn. "Now I'm going to make Major play croquet, since he won't play tennis."

"I'll play croquet," says Major. "Croquet doesn't make you sweat, so it's in line with my leisure agenda."

I lie back and look at the stars again.

What a magical boy. A boy with lemons in his pockets. A boy in flip-flops, who needs a haircut. Who says "butthole" to my mother, to correct for the rudeness of saying "weenies." A college boy, or a nearly college boy, who kissed me tonight, and might kiss me again.

We are going for a boat ride.

23.

MOST EVERYONE HAS left the lawn and I am heading back into the house when I spot my father down on the end of the dock. He's with the dogs: Wharton, McCartney, Albert, and Uncle Dean's Lab, Reepicheep. He is bent over, doing something in the moonlight, wearing a dark sweater over his white clothes.

I turn and head down there. I haven't forgotten the

photograph in my mother's jewelry drawer, and it is rare to get him alone. I want to ask him about it.

He's pulled up a loose board. "Needs repair," Harris says when I get close. "This thing has rusty nails sticking out of it." He sets the board down on the edge of the dock. "I'm sure it's not the only one. I should probably have the whole thing looked at."

I'm not interested in his real estate maintenance, but I glance at the old board in pretense. "It's warped," I say.

"There are lots like that. The storms we had this spring really did a number on the island." Harris sits down in one of the two Adirondack chairs we have stationed on the dock. His glass of whiskey, ice melting, rests on one arm. "Did you have fun tonight?"

"I did."

"Your mother got cross with me because I didn't hunt."

I nod. It's a typical dynamic between the two of them. "She wants all her work to be appreciated with full participation."

"I appreciate it. I just don't need to look for lemons like a schoolboy." He chuckles. "Dean went all-out hunting. He's kissing up to her after bringing all those guests."

"Is she going to forgive him?"

"Dean does whatever he wants in the moment and charms people later. That's his modus operandi," says my father. "They always forgive him." Albert comes up with a tennis ball in his mouth and drops it. "Okay, you beasties," Harris says to the dogs. He stands up again with the ball. "You ready?"

They are.

He winds up, pretends to throw it, laughs at their confusion.

Then he really throws it, and all four dogs hurl themselves into the ocean, paddling urgently toward the ball. Harris looks at me. "They are indefatigable," he says. "It never ceases to amaze." The dogs come out and he throws the tennis ball again.

"Can I ask you a question?" I say.

"You may." He winks, to take the edge off correcting my grammar.

I planned to ask him about the photograph, but I stop myself before the words come out. To ask will be to force Harris into a vulnerable position. *Your wife has a secret.*

If he knows she keeps the photo, I can't imagine he's happy about it, whether it's Uncle Chris or an old boyfriend. And if he doesn't know she keeps it, he'll hate that he didn't know. Either way, he'll lash out.

I press my lips together. "Never mind," I tell him.

"Drop it!" Harris says to Albert, who has come up the ramp with the tennis ball.

Albert drops it.

"Good dog." My father snatches the ball and holds it high, waiting for the others to come out of the water and pay attention. "You sure?" he asks me. " 'The wise man doesn't give the right answers, he poses the right questions.' "

"I think it was the wrong question."

"Claude Lévi-Strauss," he adds, explaining the quote. "Anthropologist."

All four dogs are waiting now. Harris throws the ball and they leap into the water, swimming and panting.

He puts his arm around me. "You did well tonight, with the lemon speech," he says. "Did me proud."

24.

THAT NIGHT, I take one of the sleeping pills I stole.

I take it because I am curious.

I take it because if I don't take anything, I'll likely get up in the middle of the night sweating, thirsty, and disoriented. That happens a lot. And I like the feeling I get from my painkillers, so I want to save those for when I'm awake.

I take it, too, because the events of tonight have me especially keyed up—my mother's photograph, seeing Yardley and George, the kisses with Pfeff, the plan for tomorrow, the conversation with my father. Energy buzzes through me, but I am also bone-tired. I want to turn myself off like a light.

I am careful. I do not take the sleeping pill with anything else. I have not had any alcohol.

And it works. I fall into sleep, fast. It is dreamless.

I do not know yet that it will take me some years and two stays in rehabilitation clinics to stop taking pills.

I do not know that this habit will make me drop out of college. Or that even after recovery, I'll always drink a little more than I should, to fill the gap where once these pills consoled me.

I don't know yet that I'll regret drinking so much, and the way that habit has made me a lazy thinker. It clouds my judgment and makes me a more selfish, dimmer version of the person I might have been. I don't know yet that I will wonder, in my forties, whether my son Johnny is dead partly because I am such a drinker.

I don't know any of that.

I just sleep.

25.

LET ME TELL you another fairy tale. It is not a famous one. I first read it in our family's copy of Grimms'. And I read it to Rosemary again, the summer I am seventeen.

This is my version.

The Stolen Pennies

ONCE UPON A time, a man went to visit a friend. This friend had several children and a wife.

On the day of the guest's arrival, they all sat down to a meal. As the clock struck noon, the front door of the house opened.

In walked a girl of about ten years old. She wore a white dress and no shoes.

No one in the house paid any mind except the guest. They all just kept eating.

The girl walked silently past the family at the table and into the next room. She did not look around. "Who is that child?" asked the guest.

The family told him they saw no one. They returned to their meal.

After a time, the child walked back out, past the family and through the front door.

"Who is that child?" asked the guest again. "The one with no shoes?"

But again, the family saw no one.

The next day, at precisely noon, everyone was eating together again when the front door opened. The girl walked in. As before, she walked silently past the family and into the next room.

No one else saw her.

This time, the guest followed. Through a crack in the door, he saw the child on her knees, scratching with her fingernails at the floorboards. She became frantic, digging. He feared she would injure her hands.

The guest told his hosts what he was seeing. He described her tangled hair, her round face, the mole on her chin.

Now they revealed what they had hidden from him during this strange, tense visit: one of their children had died four weeks ago, of a sudden illness. She was a ten-year-old girl with tangled hair, a round face, and a mole on her chin.

The parents went into the next room. They wrenched open the floorboards where the ghost child had been digging and found two pennies.

And now the mother knew the story. She had given the money to her daughter so that the girl could give it to a beggar who was asking for food in the street.

The girl had pocketed it.

"She probably wanted to buy zwieback cookies," said her mother. "So she kept the pennies for herself."

The ghost nodded.

"I will donate this money now," said the mother. "It will help someone in need. My daughter should not worry or feel sorry any longer."

When the guest turned to the corner where the ghost child had been standing, she was not there anymore. She was at rest in her grave.

THIS IS MY story. I am the guest.

I am the one who can see the ghost of a ten-year-old girl. Rosemary has come back to get my help as she searches for rest.

100

The guest is the truth-seer, the truth-speaker, the one who can see and acknowledge the pain, thereby absolving the family. So that is me.

I mean, I would like to be the guest.

But let me be honest.

If I am telling this story right, really telling it the way I need to, I am not the guest, after all. In this story, the story of the stolen pennies, I promise you,

I am the

ghost.

26.

PFEFF DOESN'T SHOW up at the dock at eleven.

I busy myself with the boat. I check the anchor and the life vests. I make sure there's gas. I have a shopping list from my mother and a cooler for the ice cream she's asked me to buy in Edgartown.

Did he change his mind? Or did he forget?

My father taught us not to wait for latecomers. "Better three hours too soon than a minute too late" is one of his favorite quotes. It's from Shakespeare, The Merry Wives of Windsor. Not that I've read it, but Harris told us.

I leave at 11:10.

It's stupid, it's silly—but tears prick my eyes as I start the boat and pull away from the dock. I've been stood up.

I want to be the kind of girl a guy would remember to meet. The kind of girl that boys will wait hours for.

Penny's boyfriends always wait for her. Lachlan and the boys she had before him. They come to her tennis matches. They stand outside her classrooms so they can go to lunch with her and save her a seat at assembly.

Anyway. I won't think about it. I'll buy soap and sunblock at the drugstore, plus magazines for us all to read on the beach; I'll get fudge at Murdick's; a new beach umbrella to replace the one that's broken. I'll buy myself a strawberry milkshake and drink it looking at the boats in the harbor.

It doesn't matter.

It was just a kiss. Two kisses.

Kissing is nothing to a boy like Pfeff, who has no doubt kissed a million girls, even gone to bed with them. He was just caught up in a moment last night. I was caught up in the moment, too.

I shouldn't care. I don't even know him.

I am motoring past the Tiny Beach when I hear my name over the roar of the engine. "Carrie!"

I slow down and squint. Pfeff is ankle-deep in the water, wearing board shorts and a hooded sweatshirt. Waving his arms.

I cut the motor.

"I just woke up," he calls. "Is it too late?"

I am not sure I want to see him at all anymore. Every word he speaks will remind me: He isn't interested. I'm not worth waking up on time for.

"Carrie!" he calls again. "Hold on! I'm coming."

He runs forward, diving into the gentle waves.

He is swimming to the boat. In his hoodie. His freestyle is strong but messy. I'm farther out than he thinks.

I watch him for a moment, taking it in. Pfeff is putting forth a lot of effort. To get to me. He's nearly out of the cove, so I restart the boat and move slowly toward him.

"You're making bad choices," I tell him, when he hauls himself up the ladder.

"That is a thing I do pretty often," he says, shaking his head to get water out of his hair. "God, this sweatshirt weighs a ton."

He pulls it over his head, along with a soaked T-shirt.

I do not know where to look. He is so close to me. His shoulders are tan. He has just a little hair on his chest. He wears a thin chain around his neck with a dog tag hanging at the end of it. "Thank you," he says. "For not just driving away when I was making that long-ass grand gesture." He leans in, soaking wet and naked from the waist up, and kisses me lightly on the cheek, right by my jaw. His lips are very cold. "Okay, let's motor."

A kiss. But not a kiss. I don't know what to make of it, so I pretend I barely remember last night. Like I've kissed a thousand guys. Kissing in the moonlight is just how I spend my average Friday evening and nothing means anything in the morning.

I drive toward Edgartown.

Pfeff leans over the edge of the boat, wringing out his shirt and sweatshirt. "We're going to have to buy me shoes," he says. "I left my flip-flops on the shore."

"Do you even have a wallet?" I ask.

"I do." He unzips the pocket of his shorts, pulling out a blue canvas wallet, thoroughly soaked. He opens it to reveal several wet twenty-dollar bills and a wet bookshop gift certificate. "Oh, harsh." He refolds the wet paper and returns it to his wallet.

We have to yell to converse with the boat going fast, so we don't talk much after that. It's nearly an hour to the Vineyard. By the time we tie up at the dock, Pfeff is dry and his clothes are back on.

"Hey," he says, touching my arm as we walk up the dock into town.

"Yeah?"

"I'm—ah—I'm sorry I slept so late. And made you think I wasn't coming."

"Doesn't matter."

"Okay." He smiles at me. His dark eyes are merry. "Let's shop. Are you ready? I love shopping."

27.

IN EDGARTOWN, THE sidewalks are brick. The buildings nearly all white shingle. Picket fences line the streets, draped with climbing rose vines. You can walk from one end of town to the other in ten minutes.

The shops are either old and practical—a tiny drugstore, a hardware shop, a "package store" that sells liquor—or quaint and touristy, selling housewares, wind chimes, books, and candy. There are several ice cream parlors.

First, we go to a beach shop. There's pop music playing. The walls are full of bathing suits with cutesy phrases on the butts (*The Vineyard Is for Lovers*), *Jaws* T-shirts (the movie was filmed up-island), inexpensive beach towels, kites, and sun visors.

Pfeff talks to the girl behind the counter, asking about sweatshirt sizes. She looks like a college student. Bored. A few years older than we are. "Do you think I'm a size medium?" he asks. "I might be a large." And before she can answer, he adds: "Oh, and while I have you, tell me something. 'Kay?"

"Sure."

"I'm a person who makes bad choices, apparently," Pfeff says. "Actually, I knew that before today. And the thing is, I made the bad choice to pack for my visit here—well, I'm not staying in Edgartown, we're on this island out"—he points toward the harbor—"over there somewhere. Anyway. I wonder where a person would go to buy underwear in town. Is this even the sort of place where a person can buy underwear?"

"Yes," says the girl. "We have underwear here."

"I already know where to go," I tell him.

But Pfeff ignores me, and I realize he's not really concerned about getting the information. He wants to have the conversation. "Okay. Where are the boxer shorts of Edgartown?"

She directs him to the shop.

"And what about socks?" asks Pfeff. "Will there be socks?"

"There will be socks," she tells him. "But we have socks here."

She shows him socks with little seaplanes on them, with maps of the island on them, gulls, lobsters, and whales.

Pfeff buys one of each. "These are totally exciting socks," he says. "I'm like, set for life with these socks." He shows me the pair with lobsters. "Ooh, do you think they have shrimp?" He turns to the girl. "Do you have shrimp socks, as well? Or crabs? I will buy all the crustacean socks you have on hand. I mean, one pair of each. I'm not going wild or anything."

She only has lobsters. No other crustaceans.

"Crawdads?" asks Pfeff. "Clams?"

She says clams are mollusks, and also they don't have clam socks.

"Thank you anyway," says Pfeff. "I like to be very thorough about this kind of thing."

He pays with a credit card, buying not only socks but flip-flops that he wears immediately, a Vineyard T-shirt to replace his damp sweatshirt, and two pairs of cheap and deeply silly mirrored sunglasses. "Do I look like *Top Gun*?"

"Tom Cruise does not have mirrored lenses," I tell him. "He has normal ones."

"No way," says Pfeff. "They are totally mirrored. I swear."

"You look nothing like Tom Cruise anyway." Though he does, a bit.

"I can dream," says Pfeff. "Let me dream. You get to walk all around looking like a fashion model or whatever. You don't know how it feels to be a regular human."

I flush. It's a cheap and generic compliment. And it's not true. But I like hearing it, anyhow. "Shut up," I tell him. "Are you hungry, or do you want your boxer shorts first?"

"I didn't eat breakfast," says Pfeff. "Because I made bad choices."

WE GET LOBSTER rolls, Cokes, fried clams, and fried pickle chips. We eat them sitting on a bench by the harbor. Then Pfeff buys underwear. And an argyle sweater that makes him look "like a grandpa, but in a good way."

In the bookshop, he wants to buy presents: Armistead Maupin for Major, Stephen King for George, and a medical thriller for Yardley, because she wants to be a doctor. He's surprisingly well-read. "I read a lot of popular stuff," he tells me. "But stuff we have to read for school makes me fall asleep." We go upstairs to the sci-fi section and he finds several fat paperbacks to add to his pile.

As we head back downstairs to the front room of the shop, Pfeff sees someone he knows: a petite girl with long black hair, Asian American, dressed in ratty jean shorts and a soft plaid shirt. She carries a huge tote bag that looks like it's made of wicker. Her face is round and gently sunburned. "Sybelle," Pfeff whispers, like it's a big secret. "That's Sybelle."

She turns. "Oh my god, Pfefferman. Are you following me?"

"Ha. What's it been, like a year?" He turns to me. "I haven't seen her in forever. I'm not following her. Carrie, Sybelle. Sybelle, Carrie. Sybelle and I did this Canyonlands outdoorsy thing together last summer. Like a program where they took us in the wilderness for three—no, maybe four weeks. I nearly died, actually, multiple times."

"You are not a mountain man," says Sybelle.

"There was belaying and stuff like that," says Pfeff. "I still have scars."

"Do you have time to go get ice cream?" asks Sybelle. "We could catch up."

"Definitely," says Pfeff. He pays for the books with his gift certificate. "I'll meet you at the dock, 'kay, Carrie? Won't be long. I just haven't seen Sybelle since I like, fell off that cliff in Utah."

"Sure," I say, faking a smile.

"Are you sure you're not following me?" says Sybelle.

"I'm not even on this island," says Pfeff. "I'm on a whole different island, really."

He hands his bags to me. "We had the best shopping day, didn't we?"

"I literally bought nothing," I say.

And they are gone.

28.

I DROP THE bags in the boat.

I run my mother's errands.

It doesn't matter. It doesn't matter.

I don't even know him.

I buy a strawberry milkshake. It tastes like all the summers past. The same milkshake I drank when I was three, when I was nine, when I was thirteen. The same white cardboard cup.

I lean against the boat. My hands get cold. My lips.

I dig my sweater from my bag and put it on. Stupidly, self-consciously, I run a comb through my hair and put on lip balm.

And I wait for Pfeff.

From three-fifteen till four. Then four-thirty.

I could leave, like I did this morning. But we never set a precise time we were meeting. So he isn't late.

And if I leave him, someone else from Beechwood will have to motor back to collect him at some other time. Or I will.

And does he even know the phone number at Goose? I don't think he does. Are Harris and Uncle Dean even listed in the Cape Cod phone book? Maybe, but maybe not.

If I strand Pfeff, he will be angry. And I'll lose my chance.

So I wait. And in waiting, I have to admit that I want this boy, with his broad shoulders and his broken nose, with his excitement about everything. I want a boy who would swim to the boat in his hoodie, who would kneel in front of my mother, who buys lobster socks and presents for his friends. Who kisses the way he kisses. Who calls me clever and impressive and beautiful.

He went off with Sybelle three hours ago.

I take a codeine and wait for the pain to go away.

I am cold. And bored. I climb into the boat and sit on the floor, protected from the wind.

The codeine kicks in. At some point I find a pay phone and call Tipper, telling her not to wait for supper.

THE SUN IS setting when Pfeff arrives on the dock. "I am so sorry," he says, starting the conversation from far away as he walks in my direction. "We rented bikes. There's this area you can bike to, it's not far, where there's water on both sides of you." He climbs onto the boat and pulls on his sweatshirt. "Ocean on one side and some kind of pond on the other. It's so beautiful. You have to see it."

I have seen it. Many times.

I don't reply to him. I just untie the boat.

"Did I make you wait?" Pfeff says. "I hope not. We got so far out on these bikes and then it took forever to get back, and then we couldn't remember which bike shop we rented from, it was the stupidest thing. We rode around town and none of them looked right. You would think the bikes would have stickers on them, but they don't. And we didn't have our receipt. And anyway, then we were starving and I knew I should get down here, but the pizza place with the slices was right there and I thought I'd just shove two slices in my mouth, like, as I walked, and that would make me a much better companion on the boat ride back, but it turned out we had to wait for a new pizza to come out of the oven."

"Bite me, Pfefferman."

I am surprised to hear this come out of my mouth. I had planned to be bouncy and relaxed, and to pretend I had only just arrived at the boat myself.

"What?" Pfeff looks surprised.

"Don't even start."

"Okay. I *know* I made you wait. An unforgivably long time. But it was a really complicated situation, Carrie!"

"What?"

"Sybelle and I. On that Canyonlands trip, we were . . . Anyway, it ended badly, you know? I—I screwed everything up. And then she was here! After a whole year of probably hating me. And she was being so nice. I felt like I was finally forgiven for being such an idiot a year ago, and I thought maybe us hanging out together today sort of made up for everything. I didn't know how to say 'No, Sybelle, I have to meet Carrie at the dock.' Because I was in the middle of a whole forgiveness thing with her."

I steer the boat into open water, then turn on him. "You're just a dick," I tell him. "There's no explanation you can give that will make you not a self-involved, inconsiderate dick."

"You don't understand," says Pfeff. "It was—"

"I understand that you don't care about anyone but yourself," I snap. "That you'll happily make a person wait five hours for you and keep a whole island's worth of people waiting on sup-per so you can tell yourself some girl you dumped thinks you're excellent now. In fact, I thought about it, and everything you did, all day, was to basically make people think Pfeff *is excellent.* Flirting with salespeople. Complimenting people. Buying gifts. But you don't actually care about anyone. You only care about the idea of your own specialness, and not anyone else's actual experience."

"Carrie," he says. "I'm sorry."

"Just stay away from me," I say. "Don't even talk to me."

29.

WHEN I GET back to Clairmont, Luda has finished the supper cleanup. Tipper, Harris, and Uncle Dean are on the porch, laughing and drinking nightcaps.

I eat a chicken sandwich in the kitchen and talk to Penny and Erin, who join me at the big wooden table. The evening has turned chilly, and Erin's black turtleneck sweater looks out of place in our kitchen, as do her dark eyeliner and the lipstick on her full, pretty mouth. But she seems comfortable. She is shaving small pieces off a chocolate cake left over from supper, eating with her fingers. Penny's wearing an old blue sweater that belongs to our father and drinking peppermint tea.

"You kissed Pfeff?" says Penny. "Last night? Why am I only just now hearing about this?"

"You were still sleeping when I left this morning," I say. "How was I supposed to tell you?"

"You were supposed to find me last night and tell me this stuff immediately," she says. "That's your duty as a sister."

"You were busy," I say. I tell them the story of the day in

111

Edgartown—the shopping, meeting Sybelle, waiting for five hours, then arguing.

"What a weenie," says Erin, tilting her heart-shaped face thoughtfully.

"Vile," says Penny. "Making you wait like that. Was she pretty?"

"Who?" asks Erin.

"Sybelle. The girl was called Sybelle, right?"

"Yeah," I say. "She was very, very pretty. She had a sunburn, though."

Erin has an analytical way about her. She furrows her brow and dissects whatever is the subject of discussion. "Do you think he was like, sleeping with her?"

"In Edgartown? In the daytime?" I hadn't thought of that.

"I don't think they were biking that whole time," she says. "There's no way."

"Where would they even . . . ?" I ask. The idea spreads cold inside my chest. I was jealous because Pfeff spent the afternoon with Sybelle and she used to be his girlfriend. It hadn't occurred to me he'd *slept with her* while I waited for him at the dock. Honestly, it hadn't really occurred to me that anyone slept with *anyone* in the middle of the day.

"At her house, duh," says Penny. "She's staying there. She's got to have a bedroom."

"So you think the whole bike story was a lie?" I ask. "He knew about the road with the water on both sides, though."

"Beach road." Penny reaches out and takes the knife from Erin's hand. She slices herself a piece of cake. "Yardley says Pfeff gets around," she adds. "She says he's like, always got someone."

"You'd get around with him," says Erin to Penny.

"Shut up. You know I would not."

"Major asked if I wanted to take the kayaks out," says Erin. "Did I tell you?"

"No."

"Well, he did. Do you think he's into me?"

"No," says Penny again.

"I'm asking Carrie," says Erin. "Carrie, do you think Major could be into me? Because of the kayak idea, or whatever else, like if you noticed him looking at me?"

I have finished my sandwich, and take the plate over to rinse it in the sink. "Are you into him?" I ask Erin. "Because my opinion is that he would be lucky to get anywhere near you."

"I don't know," says Erin. "I like red hair."

"Major is gay," says Penny.

"He is not." Erin widens her eyes.

"He told me he was. His parents are like hippies or something, so they're fine with it and he's just open," Penny explains. "So be into him all you want, but it's not going anywhere."

Erin looks skeptical. "Major confided in you?"

"It wasn't like, a secret," says Penny. "It's just a thing he mentioned."

"Apropos of what?"

"Apropos of nothing. He told a story about a guy he used to go out with. And then when I asked, he said his mom is super spiritual and meditates and everything—and 'love is love,' that's her philosophy."

I didn't know that about Major. I have never met anyone else who is openly gay.

"Well, I'm glad you two are so cuddly," says Erin. "Maybe you should go in the kayaks with him. Be best friends."

"Oh my god, Erin," says my sister. "Finish your cake and let's go to sleep. I think I got too much sun. I'm wicked tired."

Erin laughs. She stands up and turns to me. "Pfeff spent the afternoon boning that girl," she says.

30.

WHEN I GET to my room, Rosemary is there, wearing her cheetah suit. She is petting Wharton, who is curled up on the rug, tuckered out after a day of running around with the other dogs.

The suit was given to Rosemary on her ninth birthday by one of her friends. Basically, pajamas with feet, the kind we used to wear as kids. But it has a tail and a hood with ears. When she was alive, Rosemary wore it all winter, to sleep in. Now she's waiting on my bed, with the hood up. The shiny fabric is worn thin at the elbows. "Hi!" she says brightly. "Wanna watch *Saturday Night Live?*"

"What?"

"It started at eleven-thirty. I checked the TV guide."

"We can't do that," I say. "People are down there."

"They're watching it without me?"

"Mm-hm. Bess is. And Tipper and Harris are still on the porch."

"But I've never seen it."

"Buttercup," I say. "We can't go join them. Can we?"

"No." She heaves a sigh, then lightens her tone. "I'm not here to hang out with Bess, anyway. Just you, you, you."

I start changing for bed.

"I would like to see it someday though," she goes on. "I don't think I should be dead and never know what everyone is always talking about."

"'Kay. We will try to make that happen."

"Next week?"

"Sure. We can try."

"All right. Want to play Kings in the Corner?"

Ugh. I have so many emotions churning through me, because of the trip to Edgartown.

"It's a short game," adds Rosemary.

I can't pretend to enjoy a card game. I just can't. "I'm beat," I say. I put on an old tank top and pajama pants.

"Just one round? I'll let you win."

"No, buttercup. Let me brush my teeth and I'll snuggle with you."

I take a Halcion and braid my hair loosely. I open one of my windows wide and turn on the fan. When I finally get in the bed, Rosemary turns her back to me and I spoon her fuzzy cheetah self.

She breathes slowly. We listen to the fan whir in the window. We can hear waves hitting the shore.

Rosemary's hand grows limp beneath mine. She seems to be falling asleep.

"You know what would make this better?" she says softly.

"What?"

"If we were watching *Saturday Night Live*," she says.

"You're terrible," I say. "I thought you were sleeping."

"Picture it. Snuggle snuggle, plus TV."

"Not happening."

"'Kay, not that," she says. "Oh. Know what else would make it better?"

"What?" I wonder if she is trying to tell me what she needs. Why she's here. Haunting me.

"If Wharton got a cheetah suit."

I laugh. "Wharton dressed as a cheetah?"

"She would love it," says Rosemary. "She wants to be a cheetah."

"All three dogs in cheetah suits."

"No, no. Albert and McCartney don't want to be cheetahs. They don't have any aspirations."

"Big word."

"You taught me that in Scrabble."

"I did?"

"Mm-hm. Oh, wait. I have a better idea."

"Better than Wharton in a cheetah suit?"

"Yes, better."

"Okay. Don't keep me waiting."

"If you had a cheetah suit."

"That would be a definite plus to this situation," I tell her.

"So go get one."

"Now?"

"Yuh-huh."

"Okay," I say. "I'll just go down to the dock, start up Guzzler, drive an hour—no, wait, Edgartown will be all shut. I'll have to go another hour to the mainland, then get a taxi, go to a twenty-four-hour K-Mart somewhere on Cape Cod, and buy a cheetah suit, right?"

"Yup."

"Then I can come back and snuggle with you. It'll take five hours, but that's okay."

"It'll take six hours," says Rosemary. "But it'll be worth it."

"The double-cheetah-suit snuggle," I say. "I can't wait."

"Oh, you know what would make this even better, even better?" she asks.

"Go to sleep."

"No, seriously."

"What?"

"If we were playing Kings in the Corner," says Rosemary.

"That is not happening," I say. "We are sleeping now."

"You're sleeping," she says. "I'm a cheetah. I barely need to sleep because I'm the fastest animal that lives on earth."

"And what you like to do is play Kings in the Corner?"

"Yah-huh," she says. "With other people in cheetah suits."

"You mean other people who are cheetahs," I say, beginning to drift off.

"Yup, that's it."

31.

EACH NIGHT THE boys are here, my parents fixate more and more on colleges and their expectations for me. "Amherst has a great history," my father says, glancing to be sure I'm paying attention. "Robert Frost taught there. Lived there, too. A great poet." And quoting: " 'But I have promises to keep / And miles to go before I sleep.' "

The boys contribute gamely to this line of conversation. They ask Harris about his time at Harvard, his sports, hijinks he got into with the members of his house. Tipper contributes with cute college-days anecdotes and asks the boys about their plans of study. Harris points out subjects that sound interesting and activities I might want to join. He muses on what schools take women's softball seriously.

I take codeine to get through these evenings. It is better to be medicated. I don't want to feel the full force of what my parents want from me.

I already know what it's like to live in a dormitory. I know the grand library and the fifteen-page paper. I'd rather go to nightclubs and wander through museums and have an ugly walk-up apartment with some friends. I want to find someone to love and wait in line with on a cold night to see pieces of strange theater. I think I'd like the hustle of a city that's dirty and chaotic and poor and wealthy, that's chic and strange, where people are different from me. Maybe I'd like to make something with my hands.

Although Tipper spends her days making piecrusts and peeling asparagus, for me, she wants college. A life of the mind and achievement. She is unmovable.

I walk a path of my parents' making. I walk it the same way I walk the wooden walkways they've made that stretch across Beechwood. I do not see how to step off.

If I exit the walkways into the bushes, under the trees, or onto the sand—it doesn't matter.

I am still on their island.

PFEFF ACTS AS if we never quarreled, and I act as if I never cared. We hang out in the same room, but we don't really speak to each other. The situation is tolerable.

Night after night at Goose, the boys turn the music up loud. R.E.M., Prince, and the Talking Heads. We play Scrabble, or poker for pennies and dimes. One night we watch Ben-Hur and another, Mary Poppins. The living room is cluttered with bags of chips and empty cans. When the night air is warm, the boys run fearlessly down to the Tiny Beach and throw their bodies into the black night water.

Some evenings, Penny and Erin come to Goose, as well, but they have taken to walking the island's perimeter path together, smoking clove cigarettes that Erin brought with her and talking endlessly. "We're doing the walk-and-talk," says Penny, shaking her head when one of the boys asks her if she's coming to Goose.

One evening, about eight days after Pfeff and I went to Edgartown and argued, we are in the sea, up to our chests. Me, Pfeff, Yardley, George, and Major. The night air is muggy and the waves gentle.

George: "Let's play Sausage."

Yardley: "Oh, not again."

Me: "What is it?"

Yardley: "The stupidest game. We played it the other night after you went home."

George: "Stupid is the joy of it."

Pfeff: "I'm in."

Major: "I'm in."

I am conscious of Pfeff's body in the water. He trails his hands across the surface, making small waves. My eyes are drawn to the definition of his shoulder muscles, the line of his neck.

George: "Loser is the person who laughs. Or gives an answer that's not *sausage*."

Major: "All right. Yardley, you're it. You have a new gentleman companion. Oh yay: he has an eight-inch . . ."

Yardley: "Sausage."

George: "What comes out of a dog's butt?"

Yardley: "Sausage."

Me: "They used to build log cabins out of logs, but now they build them out of . . ."

Yardley: "Sausage."

Pfeff: "Plop plop." He jumps up and down in the water, ridiculously.

Yardley: (laughing) "Oh my god."

Pfeff: "Ha! Got you."

Yardley: "Why are you plopping? You were supposed to ask a question with the answer *sausage*."

Pfeff: "I know. But if you laugh, you lose. Or if you say something that's not *sausage*. Right?"

Yardley: "Plop plop. You're terrible."

George: "Accept defeat, Yardley!"

Yardley: "Okay, Carrie's turn."

I glance at Pfeff. I don't want to glance at Pfeff. I don't want to be thinking about him, and the way his neck felt under my hand when he kissed me, and the way his lips were surprisingly

120

soft. I don't want to think of it, but I'm nearly naked in the water and he's only four feet away, and I can hardly think of anything else, even though he's an inconsiderate dick and I'm not interested.

Me: "Sausage."

Major: "I have one. You go swimming and it feels like there's a ton of water in your ear. You shake your head, you know, like you do. And what comes out?"

Me: "Sausage."

Yardley: "You shoot a wild boar and take it home. What do you do next?"

Me: "Sausage."

Pfeff: "Beans!"

Yardley: "Pfeff, you are so random."

Pfeff: "Toothpaste!"

George: "Okay, let's see. You have a baby and you need to change its diaper . . ."

Yardley: "George. The baby one is the same as the dog one."

George: "No, no. It's totally different."

Yardley: "You can't do the *same poop joke* over and over."

George: "If it makes Carrie laugh or break into speech, then it counts for the game. That's the only measure."

Yardley: "Disagree. Then we could just be having a Make Carrie Laugh contest."

"Sausage," I say, very seriously.

"You have to mix up the poop jokes with other things," says Yardley. "Otherwise they lose their tang."

"Artichokes!" yells Pfeff, as if he has just thought of the most brilliant thing.

I laugh.

Pfeff swims closer to me as the others continue the game. His hair is wet and there are water droplets on his cheekbones. He comes so close I could kiss him, easily.

"I made you laugh," he whispers. "You have to admit it."

32.

LATER, AS I'M heading to bed, I pass the open door to Penny's room. She and Erin are passed out on Penny's twin beds, an empty bottle of whiskey on the floor. I think about leaving them there, but I know Tipper will walk by the room on her way upstairs.

I shake them gently till they wake and make them clean their teeth and drink tall glasses of water. I give them each two Tylenol. They drink and swallow obediently, and when they try to flop back onto their beds in their clothes, I pull pajamas from Penny's dresser and make them change. "I don't even wear pajamas normally," Penny argues, slurring her words. "I wear a tank top and my underwear. Mother's going to know something's up."

"Be a credit to the family and wear the pajamas," I tell her.

"I looked at Mother's secret photograph," she says.

"Shush, Penny." I don't want her talking about that in front of Erin.

"You wanted to know what I think! You wouldn't have told me about it otherwise," says Penny, slinging her arm around my shoulder.

"Be quiet."

"I think it's Daddy in the picture," Penny goes on. "And I think she scrapes a little piece of his face off every time she's mad at him, because he's so bossy. So it's like, she goes up there and gets it from the hiding place and goes scrape scrape scrape. It's how she gets her fury out."

"It's not Harris," I say. Though it might be.

"She has like a ritual for how she gets back at him, like when he doesn't pay attention to her."

"That's not even the same as what you said before."

"Think about it." She yanks off her shirt and bra, buttoning the striped cotton PJ top over her naked body. "You happy?"

"Pajama pants, as well," I say. "Be good."

"Mother should see a psychiatrist," says Penny, falling onto the bed once her pajama pants are on. "It's not normal to scratch out your husband's face."

"You are unbalanced right now," I say.

"Me?" she says. "I'm not the one high on pills all the time."

I freeze.

I didn't know she knew about the pills.

I didn't think anyone knew about the pills.

"That's not true," I say.

"Yes it is," she says. "Now go away. Erin and I are very fatigued and also drunk. So bye."

33.

DESPITE THE LATE nights, Major and Pfeff, sometimes with George and Yardley, have begun taking Guzzler out very early.

Not every day, but pretty often. I find out a couple nights after we play the sausage game, because Major invites me. "You coming to the Early Morning?" he asks.

"What's that?"

It is after dinner and Major is sitting next to me on the big blue couch in Goose. On his lap is a large bowl of pretzels mixed with Lucky Charms. His arms are skinny and sunburned. His black jeans have holes in them. "We go out in the boat in the morning with coffee," he says. "We swim and commune with nature."

Pfeff is on the floor in front of me. He is wearing George's seersucker blazer and a U2 T-shirt, plus Nantucket-red shorts. He has been making merciless fun of the movie (*Mary Poppins*) and also singing along and making up his own lyrics.

> *Kill your elders! Step in time.*
> *Wag your weenie! Step in time.*
> *Take no prisoners, do some crimes.*
> *Know your math facts! Step in time.*

Stuff like that.

"We go very gently and slowly," he says now, about the early-morning boat ride. "Because of our hangovers. But it really is maximum beauty."

Major nods. "Gently and slowly is the kind of boat ride I need."

"I learned to make coffee," puts in George, who is squashed into a big armchair with Yardley. A couple of weeks on-island have relaxed his style—his red plaid shorts look worn and dirty.

His hair is no longer the crisply cut beige cap it used to be. "We swim, or just laze around. I used to go fishing with my dad, you know? It's like that. We get a jump on the day, doing nature stuff."

"I didn't want to go at first," says Pfeff. "But now I'm into it."

"That's why they like, all have to pass out after lunch," teases Yardley. "You come into Goose, and Pfeff's like, snoring on the couch. Major's asleep in the lounge chair. And George is facedown on the bed with his shoes still on."

"I sleep very cutely," says George. "It's a documented fact. So there's nothing to make fun of."

"You could come tomorrow," says Pfeff, to me. He turns and looks at me hopefully. "It would be fun to have you." He smiles and I can't take my eyes from the soft curve of his lower lip.

"You could, too," Major says to Penny and Erin. They have just joined us after their "walk-and-talk."

"Ugh, early morning anything is not my idea of fun," says Erin.

I don't like Pfeff, but I want to kiss him again. I want to feel clever and impressive, to stroke my fingers along his warm neck. I remember the healing thrill of his kiss, like cold water and raspberries, dispelling the taint of my malformed, infected jaw. I'd like to feel that again.

He's just said he wants me there, in the early morning. Me, especially.

"I'll go," I say. "What the hell. Tell me what time."

34.

IT IS 6:15 a.m. No one is awake in Goose Cottage.

I call hello, but there is no answer.

I have already had coffee with my mother and Luda, but still, I put on the coffee maker in the guesthouse, mostly to have something to do.

I feel young and overeager, being there on time. Maybe they didn't mean today.

The coffee machine finishes its cycle. I pour some into a mug and add milk and sugar. I skim a newspaper from four days ago.

Eventually, Pfeff wanders in, shirtless, rubbing his eyes like a child. His pajama bottoms are low on his hips. "Hey, Carrie. Morning," he says. "Oooh, coffee. I'm so happy now. Did you make it?"

"Yah-huh."

"That's big-time excellent."

I can't stop looking at him. I hate him, but I also wish he'd just come close to me, lean in and touch my hair. Maybe he'd whisper, "Can I kiss you? I really want to kiss you," and I'd kiss him for an answer. I could run my hands down his strong back and touch his gently freckled shoulders. I'd feel his lips on mine, so gentle but also urgent, and he'd taste of black coffee.

126

I could go to him, I think, shaking myself. I don't have to wait.

But I cannot tell how he'd respond.

Maybe he's with Sybelle, wrapped up in the drama of their reunion.

Maybe he thinks I'm just a kid, a foolish girl who threw a tantrum over nothing, over a short wait.

Maybe he didn't like kissing me at all.

So I do nothing.

I don't stare at

his naked chest or

his strong hands around the coffee cup. I don't look at

his cheekbones outlined in morning sunlight or

the way the muscles of his shoulders ripple when he pulls open the fridge.

I pay no attention to

the way he folds a piece of toast around a hunk of cheese and eats it hungrily,

how he likes to lift his coffee cup with both hands,

how he sucks his finger when he burns his hand on his second piece of toast.

No attention.

THE EARLY MORNING boat excursion ends up being just me, Pfeff, Major—and Penny, who turns up on the dock at the last minute, holding a warm strawberry sheet cake with a tea towel and wearing a bikini and an old plaid flannel shirt that belongs to Harris.

"Erin wouldn't get up," she says. "Lazy wench."

"Is that cake?" asks Major.

"It's just out of the oven," says Penny. "I might have stolen it."

"Doesn't Tipper want that for after supper?" I ask.

"I dunno," says Penny, shrugging. "She wasn't in the kitchen."

We motor out, Pfeff driving. The boys have towels and thermoses. Penny and I share my thermos of coffee. Or rather, she takes it from me without asking, drinks half of it, and sets it down between her feet.

When we get out a ways, Pfeff cuts the motor. "This is it," he says.

And we sit. Feeling the glow of the early sun. Watching some seagulls overhead. Beechwood seems far away.

"It's kinda boring," says Penny, after a few minutes.

"Well," says Major. "It helps when you're high."

Penny slaps his leg. "Are you *high*?" she says. "Like right now, before breakfast?"

"Maybe," says Major, laughing.

"Just a little," says Pfeff. "To better appreciate nature."

"So this is a wake-and-bake situation," says Penny.

"It just—everything seems so much brighter." Pfeff grins.

"God, they're delinquents," says Penny.

She stands and shrugs off her flannel, then jumps into the sea. Major pulls off his sweatshirt and does the same. "Oh hell," he shouts when he surfaces. "So cold."

"It always is," says Penny. "It's the stupid ocean, city boy."

I watch them paddle around for a minute.

"You going in?" asks Pfeff.

"Too chilly this morning."

128

He nods. We sit in silence. "Hey, Carrie," says Pfeff, finally. "Can I tell you a story?"

"Yeah. All right."

"Well. Once upon a time, Baby Lawrence Pfefferman, that's me, was given his dad's name, which was his grandfather's name. So I'm Lawrence the third. And they called me Lor, 'cause my dad was Larry and my grandad was Lawrence. And that was the idea, you see? That I would be like them."

"Okay."

"So. Lawrence the first went to Amherst and became a lawyer. And Larry went to Amherst and became a lawyer. And when Baby Lor got big, they wanted him to go to Amherst."

"And become a lawyer."

"Well, they're open to a few other professions. But that's the general idea."

"Why are you telling me this?"

"Well," says Pfeff, "you've made it pretty clear that you think I'm a butthead."

I shrug. I do think that. But I still find him magical, and funny. I still want to touch him any time he's this close to me.

"There are extenuating circumstances," he adds.

"Did Sybelle tie you up so you couldn't get to the dock in Edgartown?" I ask. "Because 'I decided to spend the afternoon fornicating in a historic landmark house' is not really an extenuating circumstance."

He laughs. "That's not it. I just— Look. I'm a bogus student."

"So?"

"I don't like school. I want to—I don't know, I want to travel. I'd like to go to Mexico or Italy, and learn the language, and just meet people. I would get off on eating some nice food, hanging out with friends. It's not that I don't want to work. I don't mind work, actually. Last year I bussed tables at this burrito bar on weekends, and the days were long, and people yelled at me, but I was into it—the scene at the restaurant, the rush of customers."

At this point, Penny climbs wetly up the ladder, followed by Major. "Oh my god," she says. "You don't need to be high for that to be an amazing start to your day." She grabs a towel and turns to me. "I feel like Supergirl now. Or Wonder Woman or whatever. Can I have your sweater?" I take it off and give it to her. She puts it on, wraps her towel around her waist, and picks up my thermos of coffee. "Why are we not doing this early morning thing?" she asks me. "Why did we have to wait for these bozos to think of it?"

"I need breakfast, now," says Major. "Can we go back?"

"Oh!" Penny is delighted with herself and grabs the strawberry sheet cake, covered in foil, from its resting spot.

"Penelope," says Pfeff. "I think I love you. Quite a lot, actually."

"Don't call me Penelope," says Penny.

And just like that, I hate him all the way again. *I think I love you.* Does he really have to make every single person adore him? Does he have to flirt with everyone, including my sister? *Quite a lot, actually.* Is he trying to make me jealous?

I ignore Pfeff for the rest of the boat ride. We unwrap the pan and cut slices of cake with a Swiss Army knife. Vanilla batter with swirls of strawberry jam and small chunks of hot strawberry. Sticky. Fragrant. We eat and then motor back, Pfeff driving.

I think about our half-finished conversation. Poor little rich boy, Lawrence the third, you think it makes you special that you don't want to go to college and you liked your summer job? You think feeling that way makes you one of the people? You imagine you're unique because you want to travel and bum around drinking beer? Everyone wants to travel. No one wants to go to college.

But then—people do want to go to college. At least, the people I know. My friends at school do. Major and Yardley and George do. And I am sure lots of people want to go who cannot.

But I don't.

I want what Pfeff wants. To make things. To work. To see more of the world.

And unlike him, I've never done it. I haven't had any job, ever. I haven't left my family for the summer like he is doing now. I certainly haven't worked long hours in a burrito bar or fallen off a cliff in the Canyonlands while in the middle of a torrid love affair.

We arrive at the family dock. Tie up. Penny and Major race each other up to Clairmont, where no doubt people are gathered now, eating breakfast on the front porch.

I am last to climb out of the boat, because I'm collecting the empty cake pan that no one thought to take. When I look up, Pfeff is waiting for me.

"Carrie." The wind whips through his T-shirt. His hair is in his eyes.

"What?" I try to sound neutral, uninterested.

"You can tell I'm a fake, right? I feel like a fake all the time," he says. "You can see through me."

"Because I called you a dick?"

"Maybe." He looks at his feet. "I just—I'd like someone else to know the truth. Besides my parents. And I feel like you kind of already know. You look at me like you can tell what a liar I am."

I wait.

"I didn't get into Amherst," he says finally.

"But you're going," I say. "Right? With Major?"

"Yeah. But I didn't get in, because it's really hard to get in, and my grades suck, and mostly I partied my way through high school. Actually, I didn't get in *anywhere*."

He is looking down, kicking the old board with the nails sticking out of it that Harris still hasn't replaced. He pokes his sneaker into the gap in the dock where the board used to be.

"So my dad made a phone call," he goes on. "Or something. I don't know. He made a couple calls and maybe made a big donation to the school, and suddenly, I had a letter saying I was in off the wait list."

"Wow."

"But I was never *on* the wait list," says Pfeff. "And I was ashamed, you know? Ashamed of having messed up so badly that nobody wanted me. And I didn't want to take the spot they were offering. But my dad had done whatever he did, and it had been months and months of my parents being—well, really pretty angry at how I messed up the college process."

"So you're going."

"Yeah. I'll show up at Amherst, and I'll be just like every-body else. There's no stamp on my forehead saying 'Loser.' I'll just go."

132

"It'll be like it never happened," I say.

"Just an ugly thing in my past that nobody knows about," Pfeff says, looking up and smiling devilishly. "Except you. You know, now, what a terrible person I am." Suddenly he seems delighted with himself, instead of ashamed. "Okay, Carrie? You're the keeper of my secret."

35.

"WHO'S THE MAN in the picture?" I finally ask Tipper, late that day. Penny's theory about it being our father, outrageous as it is, makes the asking seem more urgent.

I have come to my mother's room when it is nearly the six-o'clock cocktail hour. She likes to change her clothes after cooking, to put on something fresh for the evening.

I have been meaning to ask her about the picture, but I have hardly seen her alone. She is always with Luda in the kitchen or with Harris on the beach, or else with Gerrard discussing plantings and repairs to the houses. She is also off-island more than anyone, shopping for food.

"What picture?" she asks now. She is inside her walk-in closet.

"The one of you and the man with no face," I say, sitting down on the bed beside Wharton.

Tipper comes to the door of her closet. She is wearing a black cotton shirtdress and looks severe. "When did you see that?" she asks sharply.

"When I put your pearls away. It was sticking out," I add, though that is untrue. "I thought it might be of Rosemary."

A spasm crosses her face. "Well, it's not."

"I know that, now."

I have given it some thought, and I doubt the man is Uncle Chris. Or Harris. I'm guessing instead that he is Albert Holland, Tipper's first-year college sweetheart. I've been told how he took her to dances and football games, and how he once got his a cappella group to sing "Zing! Went the Strings of My Heart" outside her dormitory window.

I want to know why the face is scratched out, and why she hides it in her jewelry drawer.

My mother goes back into her closet. I hear her rustling clothes and moving hangers. "Did you ask your father about it?"

"No."

"Is that the truth?"

"I didn't ask him."

"Well, don't."

"Why do you hide it?" I ask. My hands begin to shake.

Tipper doesn't answer but she returns to the room, this time in a blue skirt and white blouse. "Carrie."

"What? We never talk about anything," I say. "We never talk about Rosemary, or my face, or Uncle Dean's hookers, or his divorce, or the people with their houses flooded, or the people who have AIDS, or Uncle Chris. We never talk about any of it. We just pretend it's not there."

"I don't know half of what you're on about."

"Rosemary is *gone*," I blurt. "She's gone, but her spirit is here with us and there's not even anything in her bedroom anymore. Don't you think she'd want her storybooks here? And her stuffed lions? And her games? She wouldn't want her whole life shut up in the attic like it never happened, like she didn't matter."

Tipper softens a bit.

"You don't even want her," I say, beginning to cry. "She came to you and you didn't want her. How can you not want your own daughter? How can you walk away from her like that when you're the mother? How am I supposed to know you're here for me, like if something went wrong, if I needed help, when Rosemary went to you and you sent her away?"

"Carrie, you're not making any sense."

"Yes I am. You know I am."

"Rosemary's not here," Tipper whispers. "We all wish she were, but I don't know what you're talking about when you say I sent her away."

I look at her. Her brow is knitted with concern for me. "You don't?"

"You're— I think you're imagining things. Something's muddled."

"You don't remember Rosemary coming to you? To your bedroom, at night, this summer?"

"No, sweetheart."

She's forgotten. Or she thinks it was a dream. Or she's lying. "You never want to talk about her," I sob. "About anything. Everything's off-limits. I don't even have my real face anymore, I don't even know who I see in the mirror, and people are dying, and suffering, it's all in the news all the time. But we never mention it. I don't know how to even process it, their lives, my life, Rosemary." I flop facedown on the bed, weeping.

Tipper pats my arm, then strokes my hair like she used

to when I was young. "It's true, I don't like to talk about hard things," she says. "But I have reasons for that."

"What are they?" I sniff.

"It's better, I think, to move on. To look forward."

"But—"

"We can't change what's in the newspaper, so why obsess about it? And we can't change the past, so why dwell on it?"

"But then we never—" I don't have the words for what I want. "We're all in the dark," I say finally.

"Dredging up old hurts doesn't make things better," says Tipper. "There's no point in wallowing."

"But then life is just lemon hunts and party games and colleges and what's for supper. Books we've read and plans for taking the sailboat out."

"It's joy," says Tipper. "I aim to live a joyful life, Carrie. And I think you should, too. I think maybe you've lost track of that, a little."

My parents always have some phrase that makes the way they choose to live seem the best of all possible choices.

A joyful life.

Better three hours too soon than a minute too late.

Never complain, never explain.

Don't take no for an answer.

Take care of things when they need taking care of.

I sniff and wipe my cheeks. I want Tipper to be happy with me. I cannot help it. I love her. She is my mother.

She wants me to stop asking about the photo. She wants me not to be sad.

But now is my chance to get an answer. To one question, at least. If I back down and stop complaining, if I back down

136

and try to live the joyful life, the chance will be gone. "Who is the man in the picture?" I ask again. "I wish you would just tell me."

Tipper sighs. She goes to the jewelry drawer and pulls out the photograph.

36.

"DO NOT TELL your sisters about this conversation," she warns.

I nod.

"Do not tell your friends, or mention it to *anyone*," she adds. "Your father already knows." She runs her fingertip over the picture.

"He is the person who scratched the face out," I say, realizing.

"Yes." She hands it to me.

Suddenly, I feel special.

I am the only one of her children my mother is going to tell. I am the one she trusts with this secret. Because I am the eldest, perhaps. Or because we spent time together, alone, when I was sick after my surgery. Or because I am trustworthy. And I was bold enough to ask.

She looks at me kindly for a beat and says: "Daddy is not your biological father."

I can only stare at her. My mouth drops open.

She takes a deep breath and goes on. "The man in the

photograph was named Buddy Kopelnick. And—I'm sorry, Carrie. I should have told you a long time ago. Or maybe I shouldn't be telling you now. I honestly don't know what to do. Your father loves you very much. Harris, I mean. He loves you. And he's never wanted you to know."

"Buddy Kopelnick was my father?"

She shakes her head quickly. "No, no. Harris is your father. He is your legal father. His name is on your birth certificate."

"But . . . I wasn't his baby. Is that what you're saying?"

"We were married when I got pregnant. Harris wanted you to be his and I wanted you to be his, so we agreed that you would be his. Once you were born, we agreed we would never talk about it." My mother wipes her eyes like an actress in a movie. "Some part of me has always wanted you to know," she says. "Buddy was a good man."

"Who was he?"

"He was a boy I went with in college," she says. "But in those days—well, Buddy was Jewish. My family didn't want an interfaith marriage. A mixed marriage. Nowadays, no one would think much of something like that, would they? Or not many people. Attitudes have changed so fast. Erin is Jewish, isn't she?"

I nod.

"Well. You know Daddy loves to tell the story of how he proposed to me four times before I said yes."

"Um-hm."

"I didn't say yes because he finally bought a ring," Tipper says. "Though that's the story I always tell. I said yes because I finally understood that I could never marry Buddy. Marrying

138

Harris meant I had to stop dithering, stop thinking about it, stop wishing things were different. I chose my future, and once I chose, there was no going back."

"You loved Buddy."

"I loved Buddy," says my mother. "But I love your father now, too. I grew to love him."

I remember what she said when she let me wear the black pearls. Harris bought them, she'd explained, for their second anniversary, when she was pregnant with me. It *was a very meaningful gift*, she said. *Things weren't easy then.*

"So you kept on with Buddy while you were engaged to Harris," I say, understanding. "And after you were married."

She nods.

"And when you got pregnant, you knew the baby was his."

"Your father had been in London," she says. "For three weeks. He was looking into buying a press there, something like that. I hardly recall the whole story. But he'd been gone a long time."

I do not know what to say.

I wish I had never asked.

"I wanted to be pregnant," my mother says softly. "I wanted you so much. I was just confused, very confused, in the first years of my marriage, about who I loved and why I had gotten married. And when I realized I was having a baby, I also realized that I didn't want to leave your father. I had chosen him already, and even if I had said yes for some wrong reasons, I was married. There was every hope that I could make something good of it."

She glances at the clock and goes over to her dressing table, talking as she puts on delicate, almost invisible makeup. "My girlfriends advised me not to tell. All of them did. But I knew I didn't want to live with a lie between me and Harris. I had to take whatever consequences were coming, right away. That was the only way we could move forward."

Moving forward. Always a value of theirs. "That's when he gave you the black pearls," I say. "That was the tough time you were talking about, when you were pregnant with Buddy's baby."

She nods.

"And Harris scratched the picture?"

"Yes." My mother puts a thin black headband on, to keep back her hair.

"What happened to Buddy?" I ask.

"He's gone," she answers. "He got sick. I heard about it from some college friends."

I turn my face down into my parents' bedspread. I know I should not cry. Or yell. Or do anything else that will make Tipper upset with me. I am overwhelmed, suddenly, with the idea that my position in the family is conditional.

Harris has to love Penny, and Bess. He had to love Rosemary. They are Sinclairs. They are his blood.

But he does not have to love me.

37.

TONIGHT, WE ARE to play Who Am I after supper. Drinks are always at six on the Clairmont porch, with the meal at seven. It's fine to be as late as six-thirty, but after that, someone will begin to wonder about you. Nibbles are crackers with cream cheese and fish roe, a bowl of dark green olives, some pecans toasted with sugar and rosemary.

My father and Uncle Dean are leaning against the porch railing when I get downstairs, holding drinks in fat, clear glasses loaded with ice. George and Yardley are on the sofa. Both of them have drinks as well.

"Are we getting booze?" I ask Yardley.

"Apparently," she says. "Apparently if someone with a weenie asks your father if it's okay to drink alcohol, then the answer is yes."

Harris laughs. "George is my guest," he says to Yardley. "No one is driving. And he asked very politely."

George raises his glass. He's slicked his beige hair down neatly and wears his seersucker blazer.

"Does that mean I can have one?" I ask.

"I think yes," says Yardley. "I don't have a weenie and I got one. Since George did the asking, so politely."

"Watch your language," says Uncle Dean.

Harris makes me an old-fashioned, which is what they're all drinking. It's a sugar cube dissolved in water, some ice, a splash of aromatic bitters, a glug of Jim Beam, and a sliver of orange peel, twisted so the oil drops into the amber liquid. He gives me instructions for future reference as he makes it, then hands me the glass. "I draw the line at Penny," he tells me. "Penny, Bess, and Erin are sticking to soft drinks."

"That's arbitrary," says Yardley.

"It's always arbitrary," says Harris airily. "Most rules are arbitrary, but we still need them. Otherwise, we'd have anarchy."

I drink the whole drink in four gulps, even though it tastes like fuel.

Harris Sinclair is my father. And he is not my father.

This is my porch, has always been my porch. My yard, my beach. My island.

And yet only because of my name. Not my blood.

Harris greets Pfeff and Major as they arrive. They eagerly accept cocktails and descend on the nibbles. Erin and Penny come down, wearing each other's shirts, with wet hair. Penny looks different in a sleeveless black turtleneck.

Harris asks Major if he's got a girl back home in New York. "I bet you do, right?"

Major looks at his shoes.

"Or maybe a couple?" Harris presses.

"No, actually."

"Ah, well. You'll do great at Amherst. Smart women there. They'll give you and Pfeff a run for your money, I'll bet."

George touches Harris's shoulder. "Mr. Sinclair."

"Harris. Call me Harris."

"Major—" He turns and asks his friend, "Can I say this?" And when Major nods, George says, "Major plays for the other team."

"That I do," says Major.

A shadow passes over my father's face, so quickly I don't think the others catch it, though Penny and I do. We are alert to his slightest displeasure, always. Harris is embarrassed to have mistaken Major, and he's angry at George for telling him he's wrong in front of other people. If you must correct Harris Sinclair, you do it privately.

Also, he's not happy with Major now. My father isn't

142

comfortable with homosexuality. Neither is my mother. Their catchphrase on the subject is "live and let live," but they tense up around the topic like it's dirty. Like it's something they don't want us to know even exists.

"Well," Harris says awkwardly. "Live and let live."

He begins talking college sports with George.

I make myself a second old-fashioned and let my head spin.

I want to grab Penny and tell her about Buddy Kopelnick, but she is talking to Pfeff, and I mustn't tell her anyway.

The pressure of my secret is behind my eyes, behind my whole face.

OUR FAMILY OFTEN plays Charades, Celebrities, and Dictionary—but Who Am I is a new game. Tipper, who arrived before supper looking wan and distracted, has now gone into her hostess mode. We have eaten and Luda is clearing.

Tipper guides us into the living room. She has attached thick white cards to safety pins. On each card is written the name of someone famous in royal-blue ink. She pins a card on the back of each individual. We do not know what our own cards read.

She has asked Harris to explain the rules. "Hear ye, hear ye," he announces in a resonant voice. He is reading off a pad of paper. "We are now a group of extremely famous people," he says. "We are so famous, even Tomkin will have heard of most of us." Laughs all around. "But—sadly, we all have amnesia."

"Why do we have amnesia?" calls Uncle Dean.

Harris goes off-script. "Let's see. Traumatic brain injury? Yes. We have all hit our heads, and while we remember how to walk, talk, and eat, we none of us remember who we are." Back to the script. "All right. Your mission for the rest of the evening is to discover your own identity. You'll find tea and coffee on the sideboard, booze on the cart, plus chocolate-covered strawberries, orange cake, and shortbread cookies. Eat your fill. And while you're eating, find out who you are on this great earth. Except! You must not ask. You don't get to ask questions like *Have I been president?* Or *Did I write a book?* Instead, you've got to talk to people as naturally as possible, and your job is to tell your friends about themselves. Give them clues. So you might say, " 'I hear you like jelly beans,' if someone is President Reagan. Or 'I loved your latest novel.' "

"Does the president like jelly beans?" asks Tomkin.

"Yes, he does," says my father. "Now, when you've figured out who you are, step to the deck and see Tipper about it. If you end up wrong, she'll send you back in."

I EAT THREE shortbread cookies and pour some Jim Beam into a teacup when the adults aren't looking. I want to stop my thoughts circling around Buddy Kopelnick. The two old-fashioneds haven't been enough to do it.

As the game begins, Tomkin bounds up to me, grinning. "I saw your tag!" he says.

"I saw yours," I tell him. He is Walt Disney.

"I'm glad to meet you because I love you a lot," Tomkin says.

"You love me?" I drink from my teacup. The straight bourbon burns the roof of my mouth.

"Oh, yeah." He does some kind of motion with his hand that I can't interpret. "You're the best."

I tell him *Mary Poppins* is pretty excellent, even when you've seen it ten thousand times.

"What?"

"*Mary Poppins.*"

"You're not supposed to tell me who I am! Didn't you listen to the rules?"

"That's not who you are." But Tomkin is distracted by the plate of orange cake Tipper has just handed him. He wanders off, shoving forkfuls into his mouth.

I drink from my teacup again. The room blurs.

"Did you have a chocolate-covered strawberry?" says Erin, who is Cher. "Oh my god, you have to."

"I like your hair," I tell her.

"Penny did it," she says, touching a braid.

"No, your person's hair."

I drink more from my teacup and let the edges of the world go soft. George and Yardley stand in front of me now, holding hands.

"I'm thinking my guy is some kind of serial killer," says George, who is Charlie Chaplin.

"How come?" I ask.

"Everyone hates him. I mean, me."

"I hate him with a passion," says Yardley. "Pfeff hates him. Major hates him."

"You're very talented at what you do," I tell George, meaning Charlie Chaplin. "You, maybe not so much," I say to Yardley, who is Kermit the Frog.

George complains that he doesn't know the name of any serial killers, so how can he possibly figure this out?

Yardley laughs.

I drink from my teacup.

Yardley tells me, "White looks very good on you."

"I'm wearing blue."

"No, on your person. It looks good on your character."

"But who am I?" I say. "Tomkin loves me."

"No telling," says Harris to Yardley as he walks over. He pats me on the back. "You finding yours hard?"

"A little."

"I know I'm Beethoven," he says. "But I'm pretending to be puzzled to please your mother."

I drink from my teacup.

Tipper is next to me now, looking concerned. She is not playing the game, just supervising. "You okay, Carrie?" she asks. "You look— Well, Daddy gave you a cocktail or two, didn't he?" She points to my teacup. "That tea is decaf. Do you want some coffee?"

"Yes, please."

"I'll get you one."

She bustles off. The room tilts. I walk over to Major, who is sitting on the couch, alone. He leans forward obligingly so I can read the sign on his back. He is Paul McCartney. "I love your accent," I tell him.

"Pfeff called me a disgrace."

"Oh, no," I say. "You're just a little mushy, that's all."

"Does that mean I'm not Hitler?" says Major. "I've been worried I was Hitler."

"Not Hitler," I tell him.

Uncle Dean sits down across from us. "I am obviously Sherlock Holmes, but I don't want to be the first person to go sit outside." He grins at Major. "I heard you on the radio this morning."

Suddenly, I am no longer on the couch but leaning against the bookshelf. "Are you a little drunk?" Pfeff is saying to me. "Is that possible?"

"Show me your sign," I say.

"I just showed it to you."

I don't remember. He shows me his back, apparently for the second time. He is Pablo Picasso. "Do you mean my character is a little drunk or do you mean I myself am a little drunk?" I ask him.

"The latter," says Pfeff. "But whatever. So am I. Oh, here's a question."

"What?"

"How do you feel about your sister now?"

"Penny?"

"No, I'm talking to—" Pfeff gestures to the card on my back. "The person you are tonight."

And now I am sitting with Bess, squashed together in an easy chair. "Yardley told me white looks good on me, too," says Bess, who is Marilyn Monroe. "Do you think she's saying that to everyone?"

"No," I tell her. "Just you and me."

"Okay, are you ready? Here's a clue," Bess says.

"Ready."

"I like your little green friend."

"My what?"

"Your little green friend."

I drink from my teacup. It is nearly empty. Tomkin climbs

on top of me and Bess, sitting on our joint laps. "You don't know who you are yet?" he asks me.

"No."

"But you're the best guy!"

"What about me?" says Bess. "Am I the best guy, too?"

"I have no idea who you are," says Tomkin. "But you're a lady."

And then I am with Penny, over by the stereo, and Tomkin and Bess are at the dessert table, eating shortbread. My cup is empty, so I set it down on a windowsill.

"Apparently I have a lot of sex appeal," says Penny, who is Elvis Presley. "You have sex appeal as well, I should say."

Her face is blurry but I force myself to focus.

"Are you drunk, Carrie?" she asks me sharply.

"No." I force myself to look at Penny directly—and reel back. We didn't sit near each other at supper. This is the first time I've been close to her since she came down in Erin's black turtleneck.

Her pale cream hair shines against the dark shirt. And she is wearing the black pearls.

38.

I REACH OUT and touch them at her neck. "Those are Tipper's."

"I asked if I could try them. You got a turn. All her other stuff is so old-lady."

"She let you wear them?"

Penny shrugs. "Sure, whatever. Tomorrow I think we should go to the Vineyard and do some crimes. We could see an afternoon movie and go to the arcade, or whatever. Something different. You, me, Yardley, and Erin?"

How could Tipper let her wear the black pearls?

"Well," says Penny, ignoring my silence. "Up to you. Oh, and your father is not your father."

"What?"

"Your father is not your father," she says again. "Hope that helps." She reaches out as Erin walks by. "Erin, I'm very sexy, right? Major told me I'm very sexy."

She and Erin go off together.

I grab Bess. "Penny just said to me, 'Your father is not your father.' "

"Yeah?" Bess adjusts the strap of her dress. "Was it helpful?"

"What did she mean?"

Bess shrugs. "Did you see she's wearing Mother's black pearls?"

"Yes." I lean against the bookshelf to steady myself.

"I'm going to see what Mother will lend me," says Bess. "I mean, the black pearls are probably the coolest thing she has, but girls at school are wearing these long ropes of white pearls, like costume jewelry. Do you think Mother has anything like that I can wear?"

"No." I shake my head to clear it. "What did she mean, 'Your father is not your father'?"

"God, Carrie. Chill. I don't know. I didn't see the second movie."

I have to get some air.

I RUN OUT to the porch and down the lawn. When I am some distance from the house, I reach around, breathing hard, and pull the Who Am I card off my back.

Luke Skywalker.

Tomkin loves him. He looks good in white. Yoda is a little green friend. He has sex appeal. Bess didn't see the second movie. His father is not his father.

Penny knows nothing. But Tipper let her wear my pearls, the pearls that tell the story of Buddy Kopelnick, and an unwanted pregnancy, and a husband who forgives his unfaithful wife.

She let my sister have the pearls that tell the story of me.

I realize: my weak jaw, my malformed teeth, now restructured into beauty . . . my father wanted to fix me so that I looked like him. He erased the Buddy Kopelnick in my face, telling me I had no choice.

I am drunk. I throw myself into the tire swing, spinning, careening, letting the swing whirl my body into something approximating the chaos I feel inside.

Buddy, Rosemary
Codeine and Jim Beam
Pfefferman, Kopelnick
My father is not my father
My face is not my face
My sisters are not my sisters
She gave the pearls to Penny

I spin, and cry, feeling I have lost my place in this small world I've always lived in, sobbing until my body feels like it can't possibly sob anymore.

I let my feet touch the grass. The swing slows to a stop.

Pfeff stands on the lawn, his hands behind his back. He looks like a statue, his skin almost blue in the moonlight.

"Go away," I say. I don't want him to see me crying. "Please just leave me alone."

"Carrie."

"What?"

He steps toward me. "Are you okay?"

"Obviously not."

"All right, then."

I turn away and wipe my eyes, though there's no hiding my distress. "I can't explain," I say. I don't want him seeing me like this, drunk and raw and illegitimate.

"So don't explain," he says in a whisper.

"It's not your business."

"Okay."

"Just 'cause you told me you didn't get into Amherst doesn't mean I'm going to share all my secrets with you." Words spill out of me, the bourbon loosening my tongue. "So will you please go away?"

He keeps standing there, his eyes in shadow.

"Why are you guys even here, still?" I ask petulantly. "You came for like, a short visit, and you've been here ages. Don't you have anywhere else to be?"

"I think you know why we're still here."

"No. You're just here, and still here, and still here." My head is dizzy from spinning. Fogged from all my tears.

"Think about it, Carrie," Pfeff says softly.

"Is it the Ping-Pong table? The shortbread? The parlor games?"

"Very funny."

"Yah, that's me. A never-ending river of joy and laughter."

"But you know the real answer," Pfeff says. "Why am I still here?"

"I told you to leave me alone," I say. "I'm not having the best night and I'm in no shape to guess riddles."

"You don't need to guess," he says. "The answer is right in front of you."

39.

PFEFF GRABS THE tire swing with one hand, and
   reaches for me with the other, and
   before I know it, he is kissing me. I am
   light-headed and his lips taste like
   orange cake and he needs a
   shave. He's tall and bends down to reach me.
   Pfeff traces his
   fingertip along my
   neck and pulls away to say:

"Please come with me. To my room. Okay? Please, Carrie."

He kisses me again.

"Please," he says. "Please."

I GO
with him
back to the heady dark softness of
his room
in Goose Cottage.
We take off our clothes,
listening to the crash of the water outside and the chirp of
the crickets, our
skin salty, our
breath uneven,
codeine and Jim Beam
running through my system.

40.

"I AM WORRIED," says Rosemary.

"About what, buttercup?"

She is waiting for me when I get back from Pfeff's room, very late that night, long after everyone in Clairmont is fast asleep.

No one else ever sees Rosemary. Not since that first night, when Tipper told her to stay away. When I've been hanging out with her and someone else comes along, Rosemary just leaves. She vanishes so quickly I almost think I imagined her in the first place.

She doesn't know how she does this trick, just like she can't really say where she sleeps when she isn't here, only that it is "soft there," warm and dark.

"I'm worried," she repeats, "that you'll do something terrible."

"Things with boys aren't terrible," I say. "I know they seem weird when you're little."

"I don't know how to say it. I'm just worried."

"Don't be."

"You smell like alcohol."

I go into the bathroom, brush my teeth and take a Halcion. My lips are swollen from kissing. My body is alive to the cold of the water and the brush of the towel.

"I love you," she says, through the door.

I open it and come back to my room. "I love you, too, Rosemary."

"Can we make bracelets?" she asks.

"Oh my god, buttercup, it's the middle of the night."

"I really want to," she says, wiggling in anticipation, stamping her feet lightly.

I absolutely do not want to make bracelets. I want to lie on my back and feel the Halcion slide through my veins and think about Pfeff, and the dark of his room, and everything that happened between us. His lips on my neck.

Rosemary is too young to understand. She doesn't want me to grow up.

"I can't be a child with you forever," I say gently.

"That's not it."

"I think it is, buttercup. You know I love you a million loves. I am so lucky you're here. But ghosts come back to their houses because— You're a ghost because something's wrong, yes?"

She nods.

"How can I help you feel better?"

She pouts. "I just want to make bracelets."

I am trying to be kind. But the challenge of helping my sister come to terms with the end of her life—it's a lot. I love her so much. I try to be nurturing, consoling—and I will try every time I see her, until what? She finally feels safe? Knows she is beloved? Feels that she has really said goodbye?

"Please, buttercup," I say. "Go to sleep."

"Can I lie down next to you?" she says. "Just for a little."

"M-kay," I say. I change out of my dress.

Rosemary wants a cup of water.

She asks me to braid her hair before bed.

The Halcion begins to work.

She's hot and wants to lie on top of the blankets.

She doesn't like the whir of the fan.

The drug is dragging me down into sleep, and when I set my head on the pillow, finally, I drift off to the sound of my sister singing gently to herself.

"Hey hey hey hey."

41.

PFEFF PULLS ME into the Clairmont mudroom and presses his mouth to mine. Then he takes a drink from his cold can of Coke and touches his icy lips to the hot skin of my neck.

He tells me I smell good.

He tells me he wants me.

He finds a place to set the Coke down so he can touch me with both his hands, and when it seems like I've kissed him so much my knees will buckle, he releases me.

We take the sailboat out, just the two of us, and spend a sunny afternoon completely alone, our bodies intertwined on the warm wood of the deck. As I run my fingers along the skin of Pfeff's bare back, I am awestruck at the magic in the world. I am allowed to touch him, to thread my fingers in his hair, to skim his earlobe with my thumb. It is like a miracle, that two people can find each other so perfectly imperfect. That we can see the uniqueness in one another, celebrate it, communicating through touch. Blindfold me and I'd recognize the feel of his hands on me, the scent of his neck, the curve of his shoulders under my palms.

At night, when we are all "watching the hell out of *Bedknobs and Broomsticks*" (as Pfeff puts it) for the second time, I touch his leg. My fingers tingle on the fabric of his jeans. We sit there for ages, like that. Eventually, he slides his arm around my shoulder, in front of everyone. I feel so warm, so accepted. We snuggle, we spoon.

Another day, when everyone is packing to leave the Big Beach, heading to take showers and dress for supper, Pfeff hangs back. "Stay here with me," he whispers as I'm picking up a tote bag. "Stay here with me a while longer."

We watch the others disappear and then get back in the water. He takes off my bikini top gently, and presses his chest up against me underwater. We kiss in the gentle rise and fall of the salty waves. It is slippery. Disorienting. I wrap my legs around him.

I want to tell Penny about Pfeff. I mean, she does know—everyone knows. Bess asked if he was my boyfriend, and Yardley said, "I'm not surprised."

But Penny hasn't said anything. I want to talk to her, tell her how he kissed me at the tire swing, what it's like to be with him, all the details. She wants to know, I'm sure.

But she is always with Erin.

Of course I could talk to Bess. She would be eager to hear. But I have been growing apart from my sisters over these weeks I've been with Pfeff.

My father is not my father.

I am forbidden to tell this secret, but I am sure Penny and Bess can feel it wedged between us.

I miss them, but I do not know how to go back to jelly beans and sparkler parades.

On Tipper's annual Picnic Night, we eat fried chicken and mustardy potato salad down on the beach, sitting at card tables draped with blue cotton cloths. Candles flicker in cloudy white glasses. There are cold slices of watermelon and ears of corn wrapped in foil, oozing with butter and fresh-ground pepper. Harris builds a bonfire and we toast marshmallows on long sticks, smashing their blackened bodies into sandwiches with dark chocolate and graham crackers.

Bess, Penny, and Erin get in the water, floating together on the rubber raft the boys bought in Edgartown. I sit by the fire with Yardley and George, Pfeff and Major. I lean against Pfeff and gaze into the flames. His arm curls around me.

George and Major are telling about the summer camp they went to for years. They had bunk cheers.

> You gotta get in the car
> You gotta step on the gas
> You gotta get out the way
> And let Thunder Bunk pass!
> We say,
> Ooh, ah, look at that booty
> Ooh, ah, ain't it fine
> Ooh, ah, look at that booty
> Ooh, ah, ain't it fine.

"Sounds sexist to me," says Yardley. "The counselors taught you that?" She is leaning back with her hands in the sand, her legs stretched in front of her.

"It wasn't about girl booties," says Major, his hand on his chest in mock offense. "It was about our own booties."

George nods very seriously. "Definitely our own booties."

Yardley shakes her head. "Yah, right."

"We slapped them," says Major. "We slapped our own eleven-year-old booties."

"That's how we know it was our own booties," says George.

At that, Yardley demands they do the cheer for her with the motions. "I want all accompanying gestures," she insists. "Dance moves, whatever. I need to see this."

"Not with your dad down here," says George, tilting his head at Uncle Dean.

"And not with Harris," says Major. "That man is not sure about me, I'm telling you."

"Aw, who cares about Harris?" says Yardley.

"I do," says Major. "That guy scares me."

42.

LATE THAT NIGHT, there is a tap on my door. I have just finished reading a story to Rosemary.

I go to the door, and when I turn to look over my shoulder before opening it, Rosemary is gone.

Pfeff leans against the doorframe, wearing an ancient blue cable-knit sweater and jeans, panting slightly. "Can I come in?" he asks.

"What are you doing here?"

"Quick. God, you look so pretty. Someone's going to find me in the hall and kill me."

I let him in.

"I was thinking about coming up here, the whole time at the bonfire," Pfeff whispers. "I couldn't think about anything but touching you."

I feel like Rosemary is still here.

Pfeff presses me gently up against the wall and leans in. His lips touch mine and heat spreads through me. He puts his hand on my lower back and pulls my body against his. As always, I am overwhelmed by being close to him. I want to touch him and make sure he's real and feel the strength of his arms around me, run my hands over his chest.

But Rosemary is here. Or not.

She might be.

I have had that feeling a lot lately. That she might be in my room, watching me, when I can't see her.

"No," I tell him. "Not here."

"I just risked getting murdered by your dad," he whispers.

"I know," I say.

"It was very heroic."

"Yah-huh."

"Has a guy ever risked his life for you? No, don't answer that. I'm sure lots of them have. But I made it to the top of this fortress tower thing where you live. You have to let me stay."

"I can't. Not now, not here."

"Please. No one will know. I'm extremely stealthy."

The Halcion I took earlier begins to release into my system. I can feel it, like honey in my blood.

I don't want to be with him like this. I could fall over. Or fall asleep. "You have to go," I whisper.

He kisses my neck. "Please. I don't want to go home."

I am too sleepy. Too drugged. And there's Rosemary.

"I love that you risked getting murdered," I say. "That is a truly romantic gesture. But go."

I open the door.

"Please, Carrie. Please."

"No, I took a sleeping pill. I can't."

"Please?"

"Bye." I push him out.

He goes. But then he stands on the other side of the door and whispers, "Can you hear me?"

"Yes."

"Are you mad?"

"No."

"Are you a tiny bit mad?"

"No."

"Then why did you kick me out?"

"Go to bed, you big goof," I tell him. "We can go boating in the morning. Alone, just you and me. Okay?"

"Okay. I'll set an alarm," he says. "For six. Will you set an alarm?"

I am dizzy with sleep. My veins feel heavy, my thoughts thick. "Yes," I tell him. "I will."

43.

ROSEMARY DOESN'T SHOW up again that night. She is absent for several days, in fact, but one morning she wakes me at seven o'clock by bouncing one of her stuffed lions next to my face.

We play Scrabble. I let her win.

She is still hungry after her potato chips, so I go downstairs and bring up a bowl of sliced watermelon and some warm banana bread.

Then we thread brightly colored plastic beads onto jewelry string to make bracelets. The colors used to be organized, but the set is old and they're pretty much jumbled together.

Rosemary sorts them. She is a slob, but she does love color coding, like Bess and Tipper. While she works, I read her another story.

I want to tell that story to you now, because—well, like

the other fairy tales, it may help you understand this difficult thing I am trying to say, the part of my life that I cannot yet put into my own words.

Mr. Fox

ONCE UPON A time, Lady Mary longed for love.

She lived with her two brave brothers in a house of their own, but she believed in love and wished for a husband.

When Mr. Fox came along, Lady Mary felt the days had grown brighter. Mr. Fox was clever and amusing, handsome and adoring. If he sometimes seemed careless, that was no matter. He told her she was beautiful, clever, and impressive. He wanted her to be his wife. Lady Mary loved him and she accepted his proposal.

No one knew where Mr. Fox came from, but that was no matter, either.

"Where shall we live when we are married?" Lady Mary asked Mr. Fox.

"In my castle," he said.

A castle sounded good to Lady Mary.

But Mr. Fox did not invite Lady Mary, or Lady Mary's two brave brothers, to visit his castle, even as weeks went by.

That was a little strange.

One day, Mr. Fox was traveling on business of some sort, so Lady Mary went in search of his castle. She had to search long and hard, but at the end of the day, she found it. The building was made of stone, tall and majestic, with a moat and crenellations and all that good castle-y stuff.

Lady Mary walked across the drawbridge and found the gate open. She entered the castle and went up a long flight of stone stairs. There was no one around.

She continued, looking into rooms and running her fingers along the walls, imagining her future life as mistress of this immense place. Oh, the fun they would have together! She relished the thought of their nights alone in the dark, and their bright sunny mornings of laughter.

On the top floor of the castle, at the end of a very long hall, Lady Mary found a closed door. It was made of steel, larger and wider than an ordinary door. A shudder went through her as she stood before it, but she pulled it open nonetheless.

Inside was a long corridor. It was filled with bones and the dead and bloody bodies of women.

Trophies. That was what women were to Mr. Fox. Objects of pleasure and then disgust, to be silenced and kept in a closet for memory's sake while he went in pursuit of the next.

Lady Mary turned and ran, but as she reached the ground floor of the castle, she heard the front door begin to open. She hid herself up in a cupboard and held still, barely breathing. Looking out.

Mr. Fox came home.

He was dragging the body of a young woman, dead as could be. He stopped in the entryway and dumped her on the hard stone floor. The woman wore a heavy diamond ring on one finger. Mr. Fox tried to take the ring for himself, but it stuck.

In fury, he drew his sword and cut the dead woman's hand off.

Then he dragged the body up the stairs.

Lady Mary scooped up the hand and ran home as fast as she could.

The next day, they were to be married. Before the ceremony was a breakfast. Mr. Fox, Lady Mary, her two brothers, and their guests all sat down together at the table.

"I had a terrible dream last night," Lady Mary announced to the company.

She told the story of her visit to Mr. Fox's castle. She told them of the closed steel door, and of the corridor behind it, filled with bodies. She told them of the dead woman, whose hand was cut off for the sake of a diamond ring.

"It is not so," said Mr. Fox. "It was only a dream, my darling."

163

"But it was so," said Lady Mary, and she held up the severed hand for everyone to see.

At once her two brave brothers drew their swords. They cut Mr. Fox into a thousand pieces.

"MR. FOX" IS my story, just like "Cinderella" was.
  I am Lady Mary,
  longing for love,
  enraptured by a new romance,
  protected by her siblings.
  And Pfeff,
  he is Mr. Fox.

BUT MAYBE I am Mr. Fox, too.
  We can argue about it in hell.

PART FIVE
Mr. Fox

44.

IT IS LUDA'S night off. After supper, Tipper asks Yardley and me to help clean up.

The boys, Penny, and Erin disappear back to Goose, with Bess trailing them. My father and Uncle Dean pour themselves nightcaps and begin arguing. Something about financial ethics and business associates—nothing interesting. Tipper shoos them outside and they take themselves to the Big Beach. Tomkin goes into the Clairmont den to watch television.

Yardley and I are to help with the dishes, the dirty counter-tops, and so on. Tipper gives us aprons and Yardley grumbles as she straps hers on.

"I do this every night of my life, young lady," says my mother merrily. "So get used to it. When you have a family, there's no alternative."

"I think I'll be in the operating theater," says Yardley. "My husband will feed the kids while I'm sewing up someone's chest cavity."

"My kids will eat in restaurants," I say.

"Okay, ladies," says Tipper. "We'll see how that goes down when you have two little ones in diapers."

"Oh, my children won't wear diapers," says Yardley. "They won't poop at all. They'll be completely hygienic and they'll never smell, or I won't even have them."

"You're very good company," Tipper answers. "But I need

you to put on the rubber gloves and make some progress in that sink."

When we are finished, our hands smell of bleach and our cheeks are flushed from the heat of the kitchen. Yardley and I leave my mother, who brings her glass of wine over to watch TV with Tomkin.

By now, the others have been at Goose for at least an hour. As Yardley and I head in that direction, we run into Uncle Dean and Harris, coming from the Big Beach. There is tension in the air.

Harris doesn't look at me but claps Yardley on the shoulder as he passes her. "Done," he says. And keeps walking.

Dean looks at his daughter. "Lotta fuss about nothing," he says.

"I don't think so," she tells him.

"You want to come talk about it?"

"Nope."

"Yard, come on."

"Carrie and I are going to Goose."

Dean shakes his head. "Harris has a stick up his you-know-what."

"Yeah, well. You put it there," she says, and walks on.

"What was that about?" I ask when Dean is out of earshot.

"Oh god. I should tell you the whole thing. Do you want to hear?"

"Sure."

"We can sit out here," says Yardley as we step into the Goose Cottage garden, which is mostly in darkness. Light shines from the living room. The grass is littered with beer bottles and Ping-Pong balls. We can hear music thumping inside, Peter Gabriel's "In Your Eyes."

I'm heading to flop onto the grass so I can learn why

Yardley's mad at her father, when she grabs my hand suddenly. "Oh no," she says.

I turn to look where she is pointing.

45.

AGAINST THE PING-PONG table, in the shadows, Penny is kissing Pfeff.

They are wrapped around each other, her hand in his hair. He has pulled her loose linen shirt up and his fingers are touching her pale pink bra.

They do not seem to hear us, they are so lost in the ecstasy of one another.

My sister.

And Pfeff.

46.

I FREEZE.

"Do you not hear us come in the gate, you assholes?" shouts Yardley. "We're literally right here. Me and Carrie."

"Damn," says Penny, whose back is against the table.

Pfeff turns around, pulling away from her. His eyes grow wide. His lips look swollen, the way they get from kissing.

I cannot face the two of them.

I cannot speak.

My throat closes, and a ball of hot fury and pain barrels into my head and pushes out through my skin.

It melts my face.

My features ooze like wax,

sliding down my bones,

dripping onto the boards beneath my feet.

I cover my face with my hands, feeling like that's the only way to keep my flesh from

pouring onto the walkway as it melts,

everything agony.

Yardley puts her hand out to me, but I turn and run, bursting through the gate and down the walkway into the dark, dark spaces of the island.

THE IMAGE OF Penny's hand in Pfeff's dark hair—it makes me sick.

To think that he's kissed me all those times and had me up in his room, and told me his secret about getting into Amherst, and touched me so softly and urgently; to think that he made me feel clever, insightful, beautiful, impressive—and all the while, he'd have rather had Penny.

She is prettier than I am, no doubt. Even if beauty is subjective, even if beauty standards change over time, she is prettier than I—to everyone. Always. Even though I had my damned jaw broken and reconstructed.

Even though.

It doesn't matter that I understand how Pfeff feels about college, or that I can see he's a faker and call him on it, or that I'm good at speaking in front of people, or that I make him laugh.

It doesn't matter that I feel things deeply and think about the world beyond Beechwood. Everyone loves Penny best. They love her best

because how her eyes fit into the sockets of her skull,

because of her extra quarter inch of cheekbone,

because of her creamy, silky hair, and

the line of her jaw and

the slight menace of her white canine teeth.

People will love Penny best even though she

doesn't care about them, or

because she doesn't care, even though she's

not much good in school and is

careless of everyone's feelings. Even though she

cannot cook like Bess does, and

does everything sloppily, and

never puts herself out for anyone,

people will still love her best.

I could hack off my own heel with a butcher knife (I have hacked up my mouth already); but it would not be enough to win me love, because still the blood would

seep into the glass slipper,

telling the world I am worthless,

while Penny slides easily into that shoe,

puts her hand in his, and

takes him

from me.

47.

I WAIT FOR Penny in her room with the light out, sitting on her bed with my knees pulled up to my chest.

She comes in with Erin behind her.

Of course, Erin.

They flip on the light and Penny startles to see me there. "Erin," she says. "Could you give us a minute?"

"I've got nowhere to go," says Erin. "Your parents are downstairs. I'm not hanging out with them by myself."

"Go back to Goose," says Penny.

"No, thank you," says Erin. "You two talk in Carrie's room, or take a walk or something."

I don't know why Erin is so huffy with Penny, but I say, "A walk is fine."

I do not want to have this conversation in my room, because of Rosemary. I don't know what she might overhear.

Penny grabs a jacket and stomps downstairs as if she is the one angry with me.

I follow her.

We avoid Tipper and Harris by going out the mudroom door and head for the perimeter path.

Now that we are alone, I do not know where to start. We walk in silence for a few minutes.

"I want to know how you could do that to me," I blurt finally. "I would *never* do anything like that to you. Never."

"I wasn't doing it *to you*," says Penny.

"You were," I say. "You knew I was with Pfeff. You knew it, and you chose to ruin the one good thing I had, I don't know, just because you could? Because we never had a heart-to-heart about it? Because I haven't been hanging out with you so much? Why?"

"I—"

"Or does it make you feel powerful to kiss a guy when you know he's with someone else? Or do you hate me for some reason?"

"That wasn't it," she says. "Neither of those."

"What was it, then? Because it was the meanest thing I feel like you could possibly do to me." I feel the exploding heat of rage and shame in my face again, the melting sensation of my features. I am

ugly. I am

unlovable. Penny

doesn't love me enough to

leave Pfeff alone. Pfeff

doesn't love me enough to

be true to me.

"Why would you do that, Penny?" I ask. "What have I ever done to deserve being treated like that?"

Penny sighs. "I mean, you irritate me, yes. It's really irritating, how you act."

"What do you mean?"

"Even now. Mooning over him, making yourself so vulnerable, letting everyone know how you feel at every possible moment of every day. It's a lot to be around."

I am stung.

"But that wasn't it," she goes on. "Not really."

"What was it, then?"

"I don't want to get into it."

"You just ruined my—you ruined everything for me," I say. "I think you owe me an explanation."

"If it was that easy for me to ruin it," says Penny, "it couldn't have been very strong."

She is right.

She is right.

But also, it was three weeks of happiness. I wore his T-shirt. He kissed the palm of my hand. "Sometimes things are fragile," I snap. "That's why they're valuable."

She shrugs. "I'm just saying, if he went off with me, he wasn't really with you."

I grab her arm and shake her. "Stop it," I say. "He *was* with me. He was. And you knew it. Don't tell me you didn't know it."

She sighs again, heavily. "I knew it."

I go on. "The question isn't why did Pfeff do what Pfeff did. The answer is obvious. It's because you're beautiful, and you get whatever you want, and everyone wants you. The question is, why did *you* do what *you* did. To me." The perimeter walk is windy and cold. Our hair is whipping around us.

"I didn't do it to you!" cries Penny. "I told you that already."

"Well, I feel like you did!" I shout. "I feel like you went behind my back and kissed my boyfriend, and I don't see how you can possibly say you didn't do it to—"

"I did it to Erin," she yells. "Okay? To Erin."

"What? Why would Erin care?"

"Don't be stupid," says Penny.

"I'm not. I—"

"Figure it out."

"I can't. I don't— Why would Erin care?"

"She and I are together," Penny says. "Okay? I mean, we were. We— It started just at the end of the school year, when she stopped going out with Aldo, and I was never all that interested in Lachlan, and then I—well, I've had feelings for girls for a long time," she finishes. "A very long time."

I reel. I am stupid.

I never thought.

Penny goes on. "I know Daddy and Mother will be just—ugh."

"Not the best."

"Not the best. And I like boys, too. I think. Maybe not. I don't know. I don't want to disappoint them. The parents. I can't deal with all of it." She tries to catch her hair, which is whipping around her head in the wind. She pulls most of it back and snaps it into an elastic she has been wearing around her wrist, making her face look suddenly severe. "Don't tell Bess."

"I won't."

"Don't tell anyone," she goes on. "I haven't told anyone. I don't even know if I'm— I don't know yet, is all. And Erin, when she first got here, everything was great, and it was like, this beautiful secret romance, but then, I don't know. The newness wore off, maybe. For her. Or she was just goofing around or experimenting or something. She isn't into it anymore, is what I'm saying, and we had this fight about whether she should go home tomorrow. She wants to go home and then be just friends at school, like we used to be, and have boyfriends and all that. And I wanted to make her want to stay, you know? Like if I kissed somebody else, she'd get jealous, and then she'd realize that she cared, and then she'd stay." Penny wrings her hands. "I hoped that, anyway. Or maybe I wanted to hurt her."

"Sounds like you."

"Or maybe I wanted to tell myself I like guys. If I could just like guys, everything would be easy. Nothing that happened with Erin would even count, at all. Part of me was thinking that. You know? Like, it's not too late to just be a straight girl. I should just like a guy instead. Easy to do."

I know I should tell her she's perfect just the way she is.

I should tell her it's beautiful to love whomever she loves. Because it's true.

I should tell her I'll back her with our parents if she ever wants to tell them.

But Penny has just betrayed me. "Maybe that's a good idea," I say sharply. "But you didn't have to like Pfeff."

"There's no one else here!" cries Penny.

"Then you shouldn't have been with *anyone*," I say. "You should have thought, Carrie watches out for me. Carrie loves me. Carrie always my back. She's loyal, that Carrie. She's a stand-up person. And even though I can throw her over and crush her heart and take her boyfriend, even though I can do it, I'm not going to. Because she's my sister and I don't want to hurt her. Because there are some lines you shouldn't cross. Some things that once you've done them, you can never, ever take them back, and I actually value my relationship with my stand-up, loyal sister more than any of the other stupid stuff that's going on in my head right now. You should have just been a halfway good person, Penny. Why is that so hard? That's not even a high bar for being a good person. Everyone knows this rule. It's very basic. Don't kiss your sister's boyfriend, because if you do, you're a goddamned asshole."

Penny chokes with sobs, not hiding behind her hands like I would, but just letting the tears run down her delightful, delicate face, her mouth curled into a grimace of agony. "I'm sorry," she says.

It strikes me as a bit theatrical. Penny is performing her agitation. Standing in the moonlight for maximum drama.

"I don't care that you're sorry," I snap. "I care that you did it. I won't ever forget that you value me so little. Not ever."

I turn and run down the walkway, leaving her alone.

48.

I SLEEP LATE the next morning. Rosemary doesn't wake me. I haven't seen her in some time.

I wonder if she is sulking.

I am sore and headachy. My skin is clammy. I don't remember going to sleep last night.

When I go into our shared bathroom, Bess is curling her hair—teasing it and spraying on hair spray.

"Go swimming and it'll all be straight again," I tell her.

"That doesn't matter. I'm practicing," she answers. "So I can be good at it when I get back to North Forest. If I can wash it the night before and then get my routine down to ten minutes in the morning, I'll be able to—" She breaks off and puts the curling iron down. "Oh, Carrie, about last night."

"I don't want to talk about it." Not to Bess. Bess is shallow, aspirational, trying to be older than she is all the time. She'll offer sympathy when what she really wants is gossip.

She clutches my hands. "I told Penny not to talk to Pfeff so much. I pulled her aside, and I was like, Carrie's going to be mad when she gets here and what are you doing? I think she had too much to drink, though. She wasn't thinking straight, and you know, he's very cute. I'm sure she didn't mean to."

I free myself, squeeze the toothpaste, and begin to brush my teeth.

"She had like three beers in an hour," continues Bess. "I counted. And I bet she wishes she never went outside with him and—"

I spit and rinse my mouth out. "She knew what she was doing."

"It was only kissing," says Bess. "Not anything more, in case you're wondering."

I stop and look at her. "Were you watching?"

"I was using the upstairs bathroom," says Bess. "And I looked out the window. I couldn't help but see them on the lawn. And then you came, and—"

"Ugh." I bang into my room and begin pulling on clothes.

Bess follows me. "I'm trying to say sorry."

"You don't have anything to say sorry for. You didn't do anything," I snap. "Except spy on people and meddle in their business. But you're not sorry for that, are you?"

Bess. Our martyr. The virtuous sister. She stands for a moment as if in shock, then stamps her foot like a child. "You're mean," she says. "You think you're the only one who has any feelings, don't you?"

"What?"

"Carrie got sick, Carrie's in love, Carrie misses Rosemary, Carrie's crying in the middle of the school carnival, or the middle of a family party—like you're the only one who's sensitive,

178

when really, you're just the only one who's a *complainer*. You know that?"

I stare at her, open-mouthed.

"You think I don't know you're taking pills?" Bess goes on. "We share a bathroom. And you're obviously looped out of your mind half the time. I can't believe our parents haven't noticed. You're falling apart, Carrie, and it's hard to even sympathize with you because you don't care one ounce about me. You never think of me, never talk to me. You basically try to get rid of me, any time you can. So no. I actually don't care if Penny kissed your boyfriend. I can't believe he even liked you in the first place."

49.

WHEN BESS LEAVES, I take a long shower. I clean my room and fold the clothes in my drawers.

I don't want to see anyone. Ever. Maybe I'll stay up here for the rest of my life, medicating myself and talking to Rosemary, safe in my room where no one can hurt me.

But eventually I get hungry.

I run a comb through my hair and put on clothes.

In the kitchen, my mother is folding napkins into neat squares. She makes me toast with apricot jam while I fix myself coffee. If she notices my swollen eyes, she doesn't comment. "I need you to do a boat run," she says as I sit down to eat.

"'Kay. How come?"

"Gerrard is busy with the bush guy."

"What's a bush guy?"

"Putting in my new bushes," she says. "Snowball viburnum and honeysuckle. I told you about it."

"Do you need shopping?"

"Luda will do the shopping on the Vineyard. I need you to take people to Woods Hole."

"Oh. Who's leaving?" I don't want to take Pfeff.

"Erin needs to go home," she says. "And so does Yardley."

"Yardley? I thought she was here all summer."

"Well, she changed her mind."

"How come?"

"She didn't say. Just came to breakfast and said she needs to go back to the mainland and would I arrange transport. And that was just after Penny told me Erin was leaving, too." Tipper laughs bitterly. "I think we've been good to that girl. Weeks of sand and sun, meals, everything anyone could want. And now she's leaving with no notice, as if she doesn't even like it here."

"I thought you didn't want to have so many guests anyway."

"The boys," my mother says. "The boys are a bit much. Erin is fine. Quiet as a mouse and keeps Penny occupied."

My head hurts from the pills and all the crying last night. And the fight with Bess. "I'm sure she's grateful. She probably just feels like she's stayed too long."

"Then I haven't been a good hostess," says my mother. "No one should ever feel they're anything but welcome here."

I would actually love to get off the island. Away from everyone. "I'll take them," I say. "I'll tell Erin how much we loved having her. It'll be fine."

Tipper hugs me. "You're a good girl," she says.

180

I MEET YARDLEY and Erin at the family dock at noon. Tipper has packed them Brie-and-sun-dried-tomato sandwiches. They each have a container of sliced nectarines, another of salt-and-peppered cucumber, and a wax paper packet of ginger cookies. I hand them their brown paper sacks and they hold them like schoolchildren.

Erin will catch the bus home. She got a ticket by phone, which she can pick up at the ferry terminal. Yardley's mother is sending a car and driver for her.

Uncle Dean and Tomkin come down to the dock right after me. Tomkin hugs Yardley and says goodbye. Dean silently loads the boat with both girls' bags.

"Sweetie," he says to his daughter, almost jocular. "I'm gonna tell you: I think you should stay."

"No thank you."

"Things will settle down. You'll understand. Nothing's that bad."

"Not gonna happen," says Yardley. "Carrie, could you start the boat, please?"

I do as she asks and we pull out into the water.

"Bye, Yardo!" yells Tomkin. "See ya soon."

"Bye," she calls. "I'll miss your ugly little face a lot, you know."

THE SUN IS strong overhead and all three of us put on sunglasses. I am filled with curiosity about Yardley's situation, but I'm also spent. My painkillers are kicking in and my muscles feel weak and droopy. I am cried out. My fury at Penny and Pfeff is at a low ebb, though it is slowly rebuilding in my gut.

So I drive, and let my thoughts run.

I know why Erin is leaving. However she feels about Penny—scared of commitment, scared of being gay or scared of coming out, bored, ambivalent, or just not in love—she must be angry about Penny and Pfeff. Nothing's keeping her on this island if she doesn't want to be here.

But what about Yardley? Why isn't George with her? Why is she so mad at her father?

I could easily crawl into the shell of my own misery and never find out. It's none of my business, and I certainly have enough to keep my mind occupied. Our family believes that silence shows respect for someone else's interior life. I could pretend it's perfectly normal that she's leaving midsummer, and Yardley would probably appreciate it.

But I reach out. Without Bess, without Penny, without Rosemary (really), and now without Yardley, there will be no one on Beechwood who is my ally. Yardley and I have been every-summer compatriots. We have shared probably one hundred bags of potato chips, read the same books squashed together in the hammock. We have paddled kayaks together, sung campfire songs, picked berries on the Vineyard. We have built imaginary worlds and hunted for lemons.

I gesture that she should stand by me at the wheel. "You want me to drive?" she asks.

I put my arm around her. "I don't want you to go."

"I can't stay."

"Why not?"

Erin can probably hear snatches of what we are saying, but not much. The motor and the wind make conversation impossible from one end of the boat to the other.

Yardley sighs. "So you know when you asked me about that photo? Of your mom and the guy, whatever, from a long time ago, with the face scraped off?"

Buddy Kopelnick. "What do you know about it?"

"Nothing, not that," says Yardley. "But what I said to you, remember? When you asked, during the Lemon Hunt?"

"You said not to get involved." But now the conversation comes clear. I can see Yardley's face that night, lit by the moon, her yellow floral dress, her hands gripping a wicker basket with a large yellow bow. "You said something like, let the stupid grown-ups deal with their emotional garbage and their illegal stuff. Something about shady guys coming over."

"Yeah," says Yardley. "That's it."

"Is that what this is about? Why did I not even remember that till now?"

"You were dealing with your own worries; it's fine."

"What shady guys?" I ask.

"Yeah, exactly. 'What shady guys?' is the question. The thing is, once that came out of my mouth, once you asked me about the family and stuff they might be hiding, that changed everything. I heard myself say those sentences aloud, I was just like—what did I mean, 'illegal stuff'? I kind of knew what I meant, but I had never actually spoken to anyone about it. I was just like lalalalala, if I look the other way and think about something else, this isn't really happening."

I nod.

"But you—the thing about you, Carrie, is you're willing to say things. You ask questions. Everybody else wants it all swept under the rug. When I said that to you, about illegal stuff, I was like, Oh. Okay. There's something bad here."

"What?"

"My dad—the way he makes his money." Yardley shakes her head. She takes a moment. "He's like a money guy that no one ever suspects because he wears a suit and went to Harvard, but he does like all kinds of financial stuff for these white-collar criminal people."

"My god."

"I made this friend in sixth grade," she says. "Jenny Neugebauer. Jenny used to come to my house, sleeping over and all that. We were friends for years, 'kay? But at the start of tenth grade, she disappeared. She never called, or wrote. Like, *poof!* Gone. All she is to me now is a sweater she let me borrow that I never gave back." Yardley sniffs and glances at Erin before continuing. "People at school said Jenny's mom lost all her money, like her business went under and completely ruined her. So Jenny had to go live with her grandparents in Florida. Anyway, I miss her. I never got to say goodbye. And then I went to the library in Edgartown a couple weeks ago," Yardley goes on. "I had been thinking about what I said to you. I wanted to look up some people my dad works with. Business friends of his who have been over for like, pork chops and applesauce. They ask me how my classes are going, you know. And when I looked them up—it was very bad news."

"Like what?"

"One guy invested in all these small businesses and then deliberately undermined them so they failed. He made money off of ruining these people's lives. Now he's left the country to escape going to prison. Like, he's an actual fugitive from justice. My dad is his financial advisor."

"Wow."

"Yes. And one of the people that guy ruined on purpose? Was Jenny Neugebauer's mom. It was a documented fact. In the newspaper."

"You think your dad knew about it?"

"Oh, for certain. And another friend of his—this couple he advises—they were indicted for embezzlement. My dad is way deep in, no question. His list of client friends is full of seriously disgusting people."

I don't know what to say.

Yardley goes on: "The thing is, Jenny Neugebauer—my dad knew her. He knew her mom, too. I mean, I know I should care about *all* the people he's been screwing over, and all the laws he's been helping people break, but when I saw that name—Miriam Neugebauer—written down, that's when I really got it. He doesn't care who he hurts if he's making money. If he's having a good time. He likes a bit of danger, probably, or he likes the feeling of getting away with stuff. And these clients are making him rich."

"Ugh."

Yardley sighs. "He's a good dad. Stupid annoying, a lot of the time, and he drinks too much, but a good dad. Like, he's horsing around with Tomkin in the water all the time, and making steaks on the grill, and seeing us every weekend when we're at Mom's. He takes us places." She wipes her eyes and sniffs. "And now I basically don't want anything to do with him. So I told Harris. Last night."

"What did he say?"

"He got very serious. He said that if everything I said about Dean panned out—that he planned to cut ties."

To Harris, family means the good name of the family. They are one and the same to him. You must be *a credit to the family* or he wants nothing to do with you.

When I think about it later, I see that this thinking is compromised. My mother's family money is dirty—earned by the exploitation and enslavement of people. But Harris can imagine that money washed clean, because it came into the family so very long ago. Then there is dirty money like his own, earned by hard work but also by the exploitation of nonunionized and vulnerable workers. But he can imagine it's clean because it's legal, and he cares very much about freedom of the press.

Dirty money like Uncle Dean's? He cannot imagine that money clean.

I cannot articulate any of these thoughts, nor even think them clearly when Yardley is talking to me, but I feel the force of the situation nonetheless.

This is the last summer we will be together.

"I'm so sorry," I say.

"My dad still thinks it'll blow over. He tells me I don't understand how he does business." Yardley takes a deep breath. "But I don't want his college money and I don't want his spending money and all the money just seems, whatever, tainted to me, basically. It's toxic. That's the money he paid for this shirt with, and ugh." Yardley wipes the hem of her shirt as if it's filthy. "I told Harris before supper," she goes on. "And then I told my dad that I told Harris, and he was all, 'Honey, don't worry so much,' and I was all, 'I'm leaving.' And then we all ate, and I was going to tell you, but then we were cleaning up with

Tipper and then there was the thing with Penny and Pfeff, and then everyone was all worked up."

"Who was worked up?"

"Bess, of course. And Erin. And George, actually. Major didn't care. Sorry about Pfeff, by the way, but I did tell you to watch out." She pokes me and smiles through her misery. "I completely did tell you to watch out."

"You did."

"Pfeff's a bastard and I hate him and he sucks and I'm never speaking to him again, in case that's any help. And I told Penny off, as well. I called her the b-word and the f-word and a lot of other words. It was pretty cathartic."

I feel tears and rage rising behind my eyes. "Let's not talk about it yet," I say. "I don't want to cry."

She pats my shoulder and returns to her own problems. "So I dragged George away and I told him I needed to leave in the morning. I said I didn't want anything to do with my dad or his money ever again. And do you know what George said?"

"What?"

"He thought I should sleep on it! Sleep! He said maybe I didn't understand the whole picture. And I told him, 'Yes, I do. And what's more, Harris understands the picture. Harris is cutting ties.' And George said he just thought maybe there were circumstances I hadn't considered, and I shouldn't do anything rash. In other words, he said exactly what my own dad said."

"That's garbage."

"So I said he was being terrible, George was, and I said that he should back me up. And George was like, 'Let's be rational about this, Yardley. You don't know that your dad has done anything wrong.' And I said, 'Do you not love me if I walk away from my money?' And he said, 'Yardley, that's not it. You're not thinking straight.' And I said, 'I think you're not my boyfriend anymore.' "

"God."

"Yeah. And then apparently we had to have about two hours of crying and talking and him saying I was being unreasonable. I said I'd take him back if he'd come with me in the morning when I left and not question me. Like, he didn't have to agree with me, he just had to come along and keep his mouth shut. But George said it was impossible for him not to say what he thought. And I was like, 'I can't believe you care about my money,' even though actually, I can totally believe it. Then I didn't want to sleep in Pevensie with my dad and I didn't want to sleep in Goose with George. So I packed up my stuff and brought it down to the dock in the middle of the night. I slept in the den at Clairmont and talked to Tipper in the morning."

WE PULL INTO the dock at Woods Hole. I help Erin and Yardley with their bags. Yardley's car is waiting for her. We hug goodbye.

There is more to say, but we don't say it.

I will miss her very much.

She is gone in minutes.

I walk Erin to collect her bus ticket and wait at the depot with her in silence.

50.

THE NEXT DAY, Gerrard drives Uncle Dean and Tomkin off the island. They will not be back.

Many years later, I will learn that my father paid for Yardley's college when she would not take Dean's money. And that he engaged our family lawyer, Richard Thatcher, to help buy Dean out of his half of the island property.

Pevensie will lie empty for some years.

When I marry William Dennis, my father will clear some land and build a house for me. William and I will name it Red Gate, for its dusty red picket fence and trim.

Around the same time, Harris will tear down Pevensie and rebuild on its foundation, naming the new house Windemere. He'll give Windemere to Penny, who marries Sam Easton around the same time. For Bess, marrying Brody Sheffield a year later, our father tears down Goose to build Cuddledown.

Eventually, it will seem to me and my sisters as if Windemere has always been there, at the north end of Beechwood Island.

We won't even feel the echoes of Pevensie, won't ever think about what might have been. We will forget to miss Tomkin and Yardley, forget that their children would have run down the walkways with ours.

51.

ON MY RETURN from Woods Hole, I go to my room, pretending to have a headache. I stay there through the evening. Tipper brings me supper on a pretty tray.

She tells me the boys have asked to stay a few more days despite Yardley's absence. They need time to make arrangements for the rest of their summer. "None of them want to go home to their parents," she says. "They imagine themselves independent here, though of course it's Luda doing their laundry." George and Major might work as last-minute August summer camp counselors, she says. "At that camp they used to go to." They're making calls. Pfeff will probably go visit some cousins. "I know you'll miss him very much," she tells me. "I hope you feel better soon so you can enjoy your last days together."

It is the first time she's mentioned Pfeff to me.

She thinks we're still together.

I nod and don't correct her. I can't tell her what's happened. I can't be the complainer Bess accused me of being; can't tell on Penny. I can't be my messy, miserable self when my mother wants her "good girl."

And I do miss Pfeff.

I think: Maybe he will come to my room any minute and beg my forgiveness. Maybe I will be able to forgive him. Maybe he will say he loves me and have a reason for what he did. He will listen to me, truly listen.

But he does not come.

I also think: Penny will knock on my door for certain, ashamed and sorry and ready with a real apology and promises of loyalty. Bess will come, worried and loving. She will take my side and cheer me up with frivolities and cookies she's baked.

But another day goes by.

I stay in my room.

I want to talk it all out with my sisters, have them be righteous on my behalf, have them hate forever the person who betrayed me, have them hate forever the person who accused me of being selfish, have them make me laugh and distract me.

But maybe we were never that kind of sisters.

And they are the ones who have done me wrong.

So I return to thinking about Pfeff. He must want to talk. How could he tell me his secrets and undress in front of me and hold my hand and tell me how much he wants me—and feel no remorse for his betrayal? It is impossible. We are enmeshed.

Time after time, I put blush on my cheeks, comb my hair, and walk out my door to go talk to him. I feel I can't rest until I hear what he has to say about it all.

Time after time, I stop at the top of the stairs and return to my room.

It doesn't matter, I tell myself.

But it does.

I spend my time reading novels and talking to Rosemary. She wants to paint her nails, try Bess's curling iron. She makes up a song about scones.

> Scones are worse than muffins
> Scones are worse than English muffins
> Scones are blobs of dough
> Let's make a law against scones

She teaches me a "famous dance" that she claims cheerleaders do. I pretend to be joyful for her, through my fog of misery over Pfeff and Penny, Yardley and Uncle Dean, my father and Buddy Kopelnick. I want to show my sister how much I love her. Help her be at peace. I love that she is here, but it doesn't seem right that she should haunt me forever. She must be searching for a way to rest. And yet I don't know that I really want her to go, even if that's what's best for her. Right now, she is all I have.

THREE DAYS AFTER Yardley's departure, I have had enough. It is afternoon and I am cooped up in this hot room, sweltering and festering while Lor Pfefferman lives free and easy. There is a clambake tonight, down on the beach. There will be corn on the cob and potatoes cooked in the fire. Clams and lobsters, melted butter. Strawberry shortcake up at the house afterward.

This is my home. Pfeff doesn't get to eat my strawberry shortcake without facing up to what he's done.

I go downstairs, my hands shaking. I will not hide any

longer. I'll talk to him, and then I will hold my head high and take my place in the world of this island.

52.

THE KITCHEN IS empty except for Luda, who is wiping down the inside of the fridge.

No one is in the living room.

Outside, Bess shucks corn on the steps. I ignore her as I go past.

From the walkway, I can see Penny and my parents down on the Big Beach, building the fire for the clambake.

I head to Goose.

I want an explanation. I deserve one.

I want Pfeff to understand—really understand—how much he hurt me. I want to see his regret and his shame.

The boys aren't at Goose, they're at the Tiny Beach. Major is lying on his abdomen in the sand, reading the Armistead Maupin book Pfeff bought for him. George and Pfeff are in the water.

I stand at the bottom of the steps, looking at the scene. I feel righteous and shy.

They do not notice me at first. There are sizable waves today, which is unusual in the cove. George and Pfeff are throwing themselves onto boogie boards like little boys.

Major looks up from reading. He's wearing a black T-shirt and dark blue swim shorts. His forehead and nose are white with sunblock. "Hi, Carrie."

"Hi."

"Do you want a sandwich?" he asks. "We have tuna with that crispy lettuce and also roast beef and Havarti on Portuguese sweet dough."

"No thanks."

"Tipper said you had a wicked headache."

"It's gone now."

In the water, Pfeff sees me. He looks directly at me, picks up his boogie board, and heads back out to find another wave. He calls something to George I can't hear.

"I thought I'd talk to Pfeff," I say.

"Good luck with that," says Major. "I mean, the guy will talk your ear off, but I'm guessing you want him to listen."

I walk past Major and down to the water.

Pfeff sees a wave he wants to ride—and turns in my direction. He looks surprised to see me, as if he'd already forgotten I was standing on the beach.

He turns away again. Says something to George.

George waves at me. "You feeling better?" he yells. His square white teeth form a smile.

"Pfeff," I call. "Can we talk?"

Pfeff doesn't turn around.

"Pfeff!" I call again.

"What? Hi." He turns and smiles. "You gonna swim?"

"What?"

"Come swimming." He runs a hand through his wet hair and comes a little closer. I cannot believe he's asking me to go swimming. Like I'm an acquaintance. Like nothing bad ever happened.

"I was hoping we could talk."

George, now a bit farther out than Pfeff, ducks under a wave. When he comes up, he swims, putting some distance between himself and the conversation, seeming occupied with the water and his board.

Pfeff has come close enough to talk but stays knee-deep in the water. "I don't want to discuss anything," he says.

"Well, I do."

"Look," he says. "I'm impulsive. I make bad choices. That's who I am. You knew that from the beginning."

"Will you please come out so we can have a conversation?"

"I kiss a pretty girl in the moonlight with no warning," he says. "I forget to set alarms. I forget to pack my socks and underwear. I don't do my schoolwork."

"I just want to know—"

Pfeff interrupts me. "There's nothing else for you to know. I said I don't want to talk. I'm sorry you got upset, Carrie, but I told you the truth up front. I'm going to college in four weeks. This is like, a surreal, enchanted summer that I stumbled into, and I never pretended it was anything else."

"It's not a surreal, enchanted summer," I say. "It's my life." How infuriating that he's standing there in the water and I can't reach him without getting my pants wet. "I think you owe me an explanation."

"I just gave you all the explanation you're going to get," he says, holding his board in front of his body like a shield. "I make bad choices and you always knew that."

I want to scream in frustration. Or hit something. I want Major and George to take my side. I want Pfeff to break down in tears and explain why he's a terrible person. I want him to be penitent and ashamed of himself. I want him to rush at me and scoop me into his arms and kiss me passionately and ask if I'll forgive him. I want to slap him across his self-satisfied face.

Pfeff turns and flops onto his boogie board. He swims toward George.

I think he'll turn back, regret how he's acting, but he does not. He swims out, and out. As if I don't exist.

I bite my lip to keep from crying. I turn and walk up the staircase that leads from the beach.

Back at Clairmont, I tell Luda I'm skipping the clambake and head to my room. There, I take double my usual dose of Halcion, hours before the sun goes down. I change into pajamas and sob until the drug knocks me out completely.

53.

I WAKE FROM Halcion sleep at one a.m. Bess is opening my door.

"Go away," I tell her.

"Carrie."

"Go. I'm sick."

"No," she says. "We need you."

"What for?"

They used to always need me. "We need you" to help us condition our hair, to build a fort, to explain our schoolwork, to give advice about a boy, to give advice about clothes, to watch Rosemary.

But they haven't needed me in weeks and weeks.

"Just come," whispers Bess. "I wouldn't ask if it wasn't important."

She is holding her hands to her chest, twisting them together.

I sit up. My head is fogged. "Are we going outside? Do I need shoes? A flashlight?"

"Yeah," she says. "You need all that."

QUIET AS COTTON, we go downstairs. Outside via the mudroom door. Along the walkways to the family dock.

I can see the outlines of the sailboat and Guzzler, black against the moonlit sea.

Bess turns and puts her finger to her lips.

PART SIX

A Long Boat Ride

54.

PENNY STANDS IN the water, near where the dock meets the shore. She is knee-deep. I can see her shoes on the sand.

She is washing her hands and face, getting her loose white shirt and jean shorts wet, scrubbing her cheeks urgently.

"Penny," I call softly. "You okay?"

"No, no, leave her," says Bess.

"But you brought me down to—"

"That's not why we need you."

She takes my hand and leads me to the end of the dock. The first thing I see is that missing wooden board, moved from where my father left it. It lies crisscross in our way, the nails poking through the wood in a sharp row of three.

Coming off the nails are several human hairs.

We step over the board, and there, at the end of the dock, lies a body.

I stop.

"He's dead," says Bess. "We touched his neck. And his wrist, looking for a pulse. We checked and double-checked."

I step a little closer and kneel down.

It is Pfeff. Someone has bashed his head with the board.

His shirt is off. It's a plain gray T-shirt and lies crumpled nearby. His belt buckle is undone, and his jeans are unbuttoned, pulled partway down on his hips along with his boxers.

He's wearing sneakers. His socks have small red lobsters on them.

I touch his wrist myself, not knowing what else to do. There is no pulse.

He is beautiful and pitiful in death, his features calm instead of animated.

"We have to call the mainland. Get an ambulance boat. And maybe the police," I say.

"No," says Bess.

"Who could have done this?" I ask. "How did you find him?"

"I didn't," says Bess. "I didn't find him."

55.

OH.

Oh.

She killed him.

She kneels down next to me. "He left Goose with Penny tonight. I saw them go. They said they were going for a walk. But they were, you know, touching each other during the movie—we have *Fletch* from the Edgartown library, remember? And partway through, they left. It was George and me and Major left at Goose. And they were nice enough, but they think I'm just a kid. And Major was like, 'Don't give Bess the whiskey, it'll be too much for her.' And that was true, but I didn't like to admit it. George was upset about Yardley leaving, but I could tell he didn't want to talk about it in front of me, and it was really, really late, and—I wanted to know if Penny was making out with Pfeff, to be honest. I didn't think it was fair to you, even though you said it was none of my business, and even though we were in a fight, so I—"

"Bess," I interrupt. "How did Pfeff die?"

Penny comes walking up the dock, dripping water. "He and I— Don't be mad, Carrie."

I am furious.

Penny knew how I felt, she knew how broken her betrayal made me feel, she knew because I told her, and still—none of that mattered in the face of her need to be wanted, to be the prettiest girl in the room, to make Erin jealous, to be the straight girl my parents wanted, to kiss a boy she thought was hot—all of that mattered more than I did.

Maybe some part of Penny can tell I am only half her sister. Maybe she loves Bess in a way she can never love me. Maybe that's why she could do this to me a second time.

But a boy is dead at my feet and Bess has said "We need you," so I swallow all my rage and listen to Penny's story.

"We came down here to fool around," she says. "Well, at first to sit on the dock and like, kick our heels against the wood and look at the water, but then we started kissing and all of a sudden, he was like, on me." Penny kneels down next to Pfeff's body. "And I guess he expects stuff from girls. Like he's had a lot of experience or doesn't think sex is a big deal. He took his shirt off and he was like, tugging my pants down, and his pants down, and I was like—oh my god, no. I barely know him and we aren't going out, and I just thought we'd mess around a little. Here he was, like, forcing himself on me. I said no, and he just kept saying 'Please. Please, Penny, please.'" Penny is crying, and she wipes her nose with the back of her hand. "And I got confused by the 'please,' you know? But I still said no, this was all I was doing—but stupid, stupid, I let him kiss me again. Then he just seemed on automatic, somehow, just going ahead even though I'd said no. I was thinking how do I get out of this? And I said no a third time and he kept saying please and I wished I could be anywhere in the world but here, only I couldn't figure out how to leave. Then Bess came and hit him on the head with that board."

Bess nods. "I should have pulled him off, or even just shouted, but I was running down the dock and the board was just there, and I picked it up. I wasn't thinking."

Penny pets Bess's hair. "You saved me."

"But he's dead now," moans Bess. "He's dead and it's my fault."

"He wasn't going to stop," says Penny. "He's a fucking rapist."

We stand in silence for a moment. I am immobile, unable to move or speak, the situation is so overwhelming.

Bess turns to me. "What should we do?"

56.

I COULD SAY, "Let's ask our parents' advice."

But our parents are not easy people to confide in.

I could say, "Let's wake the boys."

But we'd be throwing our lives into the hands of Pfeff's friends.

We could call the police.

But I do not want to expose Penny to the terrible things people say about a girl who has been nearly date-raped.

She shouldn't have been alone with him.

She wanted it. He was cute. She wouldn't have gone there with him if she didn't want it.

She accused him after the fact, to save her sister. She's a slut and a liar.

And Bess. I must protect her from whatever happens to fourteen-year-olds who kill someone with rusty nails and an old board. An investigation. A trial. Some kind of juvenile home. Or even if she gets acquitted, even if Pfeff's death is understood as morally justified by a jury, the exposure will be awful.

Oh, sure, Harris would pay for her defense. He would uphold her good name to the end. But when people know you are capable of killing someone—well, you're no longer a credit to the family. Let's put it that way.

The decision doesn't feel like a decision at all. It feels like the only path.

I am choosing my sisters. I am choosing their safety. I am the protector and I can see the best way to protect them. I failed to keep Rosemary safe and I will not fail Bess and Penny, even if it means we must do terrible things on top of the terrible things that have already been done.

"Bess," I say. "Go to Clairmont, really quiet, and get—I'm going to give you a list of things to get there. Okay?"

She nods.

I think for a moment and then run through it. "A bottle of whiskey. A bathing suit for each of us, plus a cover-up—shorts and T-shirt, whatever. Sweatshirts, too. Spray cleaner and a roll of paper towels. And take some food from the pantry—like Pop-Tarts or whatever is easy to carry. Got it? Say it back to me."

She does.

"Be absolutely silent. Get a tote bag for the stuff. Use one of the beach bags in the mudroom. You clear?"

"I'm so sorry," she snivels.

"Keep it together," I say. "Don't panic. Go."

Bess turns and heads down the dock to the house.

"Now, Penny, go to Goose, but don't go in until you're sure all the lights are off. Everyone has to be asleep. Peek in and be sure no one's passed out in the living room. Then make coffee. Doesn't matter if it's bad coffee. Just make it, first thing you get there. You know how to make coffee?"

"Yeah."

"Wait. Before you go inside, get the sand off your feet and put your shoes on. Squeeze out your wet shirt. I don't want you dripping water in that house or tracking sand."

Penny nods.

"Okay, get four beach towels. Four. And then go up to Pfeff's room. Can you do that?"

She nods again.

"On tiptoe, you hear me? Peek in there and make sure the bed looks slept in. If Luda was in there cleaning this afternoon, his room will be neat. Mess up the bed. Get it seriously messy, like pull the sheets out at the bottom. 'Kay? Then mess things up a little more, throw some clothes on the floor. Get one clean shirt for him. Doesn't matter which one. Get that, and the four towels. Fill four thermoses with coffee, and come back."

"What do I do if George and Major are still up?"

"Wait outside till they go to bed. Don't let them see you."

206

"Why don't I go to Pevensie? Nobody's there."

"We want Pfeff's bedroom how we want it. And we need his shirt. Also, we need the towels and the thermos cups to be from Goose. Tipper and Luda know everything that's in all the houses."

"What are we doing?" asks Penny. "I don't know what we're doing."

"We are taking care of things when they need taking care of," I answer. "Like Harris tells us to."

57.

MY SISTERS ARE gone and I am alone on the dock with Pfeff's body.

I cannot stop to feel sad or shocked. I just act. I pull off my sweater and wrap Pfeff's head in it. His wound is not large or particularly bloody, but I don't want to risk getting anything more on the dock than what we have to clean up already. It's awkward, putting the sweater on his head and tying the arms loosely, but I am relieved when it's done. I don't have to look at his face.

I put my arms under Pfeff's and pull him toward Guzzler. His jeans snag on the ragged boards of the dock. I have to set him down and pull up his pants. I refasten his zipper and button. I buckle his belt.

Then I move him a second time, getting him to the edge of the boat, sitting him against its hull. I climb in. I reach over, grab him under the arms again, and pull his body onto the seat. I lay him down and get out.

I take the loose board to the beach by the foot of the dock. I kick off my shoes and roll up my pajama pants. I wade in and I wash the board, forcing myself to touch the sticky, hairy nails, rubbing them clean.

Bess comes back with the bag of supplies. I spray the board with cleaner and rinse it again in the ocean. Then I give the cleaner to Bess.

She takes the paper towels and my flashlight. She scrubs the dock, going over each board, looking for signs of blood or hair.

Meanwhile, I collect several large, heavy rocks from the beach, lugging them to the motorboat and setting them carefully inside. Then I load in the rest of Bess's supplies. I check the bag she brought. "You forgot the whiskey," I say, alarmed.

She looks up from scrubbing the dock. "I didn't—I didn't know what to take," she says. "The bar cart was confusing. Like, is bourbon whiskey? Is rye?"

"So you brought nothing?"

She nods. That is so Bess. If she's not sure she's doing something perfectly, she won't do it at all.

"I need the whiskey" is all I say. "Where's Penny?"

"I don't know."

"I'm going up to Clairmont."

"But—"

I don't give Bess the chance to complain about being left alone with Pfeff's body. I walk up to the house as quickly as I can. I enter through the mudroom, being careful not to make a sound. There are cases of hard liquor in the cellar. I should have told Bess to go there, instead of to the bar cart.

I have to flip a light on in the basement—Bess has my flashlight.

And when I do, Rosemary is sitting in an old wicker rocking chair.

58.

SHE IS WEARING leggings and one of my T-shirts. It is much too big for her. Her feet are bare. "I just woke up," she says. "I wasn't like, sitting here in the dark for a long time."

"You scared me, buttercup," I say.

"Your pajama pants are wet. What are you doing?"

"I'm—" I can't tell her what I'm doing.

"Why were you swimming in pajamas?" she asks.

"Rosemary."

"What?"

"Why are you here?"

"I don't know!" Her face crumples. "I sometimes wake up and come see you, is all. I've never come to the basement before." She looks around. It's a big room with a low ceiling. Everything is neatly labeled. In the harsh overhead light, it seems bleak. The corners are still dark and the paint on the walls is cracked. "I'm scared."

I kneel in front of the rocking chair and hold her hands. "It's just a creepy basement, 'kay? All basements are creepy. If we go upstairs, it'll seem just like any other night, with Tipper and Harris sleeping at the top of the house and flowers on the kitchen table and good food in the fridge and the moon shining in the windows."

"But why are you up?" she asks. "Why are you down here? Why are you wet?"

Oh god. I want to console her. I want to help her to feel at peace. But I cannot cuddle in the middle of the night when I am covering up a murder.

"I woke up," I tell her. "I went down to the water for a bit to think. Then I thought I might—well, I'm not proud of this, but I thought I might drink some wine to help me go back to sleep."

"Don't drink wine all by yourself in the middle of the night," says Rosemary, appalled. "It's how you get alcoholic. Even I know that."

"You're right," I say. "You're totally right. Why don't we go upstairs together, super quiet, and I'll take a bath and you can—I don't know. Do you want to read or make another friendship bracelet?"

Rosemary nods.

"Come on, buttercup. Should I pick you up? I'm not sure I still can, but I'll try."

She reaches up and I lift her. Her legs wrap around my waist. We shut the basement light and walk slowly, slowly up the stairs to my room on the second floor.

I turn the fan back on, to mask any sounds from the dock area. The curtains are drawn.

I set Rosemary down on my bed and kneel before her. My heart is drumming and my hands are shaking, but I want to make her feel safe and loved, despite what I'm going to do next.

"Do you remember when you and Tomkin made the biggest sandcastle? Far up the beach so it wouldn't get washed away? We ringed it with rocks and decorated it with shells."

"Um-hm."

"Mother let you bring cups and mugs down to the water so you could mold lots of different-sized piles. And you were so proud."

"We have a picture of it," says Rosemary. "In one of the albums."

"Yes. That was a good time. Think about that. It was such a good day."

Rosemary begins to cry softly.

Oh, not now, little one. Don't need me now. "Why are you crying?"

"I'm not going to make a castle again," she says. "I'm never going to make another one."

"Oh, love. We could make one."

"I'm not going to see Tomkin again, either," she says. "I saw him for the last time, and I didn't know it was the last time."

"You could see him," I say. I don't want to tell her Tomkin won't be coming to the island again.

"No," she says. "I am just here to visit you. And Mother, but she doesn't want me."

"But maybe if you visited him, you'd feel better. Tomkin would play with you. He's much more into board games than me, and you could teach him to weave the bracelets."

Rosemary shakes her head. "I only come to this house. And you. I told you that already." She wipes her nose on the hem of her shirt. "It's what happens. I'm not the boss of it. I'm just here."

I snuggle her. Her sobs slow down. She sniffles a few times.

I think of Bess, down on the cold dock with a dead body.

And Penny—where the hell is Penny? Is she back? Did she get what we need?

"I'm going to run my bath," I tell Rosemary. "And get out of these wet pajama pants."

She nods. "Okay."

"Just hang out, and I'll be back in a little bit. I gotta warm up, and I need the bath to make me sleepy."

"Um-hm."

I grab a clean pair of sweatpants and an old pink sweatshirt. I go into the bathroom and shut the door. I run the water, but I don't put the plug in the tub, and I don't run it hard, because I don't want to make any noise that would wake our parents.

I put on the dry clothes, shove my feet back in my sneakers, and ease open the connecting door to Bess's room. I tiptoe through it and run downstairs. I throw my damp pajamas into the laundry and grab a bottle of whiskey from the basement. Then I run as fast as I can to the family dock, leaving my sad, isolated, needy ten-year-old ghost of a sister waiting for me to come back.

I feel worse about this betrayal than anything else, really.

59.

BESS IS ON the dock. "Where's Penny?" I whisper when I am close enough for her to hear.

"She never came."

"Did you look for her?"

"Nuh-uh."

"Why not?"

"You didn't tell me to."

"Did you get the boards clean?"

"I went over them twice."

"What did you do with all the paper towels?"

"They're in the tote bag."

"Good. We can burn them later. Stay here."

"Where are you going?"

"To see what's keeping Penny."

"Should I come?"

"I said stay here."

"I don't want—I don't want to."

"Just stay."

I leave her and head to Goose Cottage. I am reaching a hand out to the gate when I hear "Carrie."

Penny is crouched in the bushes, just off the walkway. I kneel down by her. "Are they still awake?"

"They were. They went upstairs finally, and it took forever, but Major's light is off now."

"Is George's off?"

"It was when I checked. His room is around the back of the house."

"How long does it take people to fall asleep?"

"Not that long, I don't think. They were drinking beer earlier."

We walk around to the back of Goose. George's light is still off, but the bathroom light is on.

"Is someone in there?" whispers Penny. "Or are they just wasting electricity?"

"Probably wasting."

We go back to where we can see Major's window. We sit down on the walkway to watch. And Penny, who hasn't ever really cared how I feel,

who thinks only of herself—

selfish,

beautiful

Penny—

reaches out to

take my hand

like she did when we were kids.

She used to reach for my hand

when Harris was mad at us,

when we had to recite poems for Nana and Grandpa,

when Tipper was late to pick us up from dance class,

while we sat together on the boat and saw Beechwood Island emerge from the empty expanse of the sea.

We hold hands now, and wait.

There are footsteps on the walkway and Bess comes into view.

"You're supposed to be with Pfeff," I whisper.

"You took forever," she says. "I got worried."

"It's okay. The boys weren't asleep. But I'm pretty sure they are now."

"If I help, we can get in and out faster," Bess says. "I'll go upstairs and do his room." She tucks her sunny hair behind her ears with resolve. "It'll be easiest for me."

That is true. Bess can mess up Pfeff's room without recalling the smell of Pfeff's neck, the curve of his cheekbones, the way he looked in that one sweater, the way he dog-eared the pages of books. She won't care about his Edgartown socks, or the pillow where he laid his head at night.

"Good," I say. "Penny, you get beach towels and thermoses. I'll make the coffee."

And we go.

It feels almost like slow motion, the three of us silently entering Goose, separating as Penny goes into the pantry, Bess begins her stealthy climb of the stairs, and I open the cabinet where the coffee can is stored.

Penny lines up four thermoses on the counter. She finds a beach bag, still full of sunblock and warm, unopened cans of Coke. She shoves four towels into it. She grabs my arm and whispers, "Do we need a bathing suit?"

"Bess got them."

"For him. A bathing suit for him."

"No," I say.

"Why not? He would have one on."

The coffee begins percolating through the machine and into the carafe. "No."

"But—"

"Listen," I say. "Do you want to take his pants off and put a suit on him?"

Her face pales.

"I don't, either," I say. "And we really don't need it. We're gonna weight him down and nobody's ever going to find him. Not in a million years." I don't feel anywhere near as certain as I make myself sound.

"Okay," says Penny. "I trust you."

We stare at the coffee maker as it hisses and the pot fills.

Bess comes down the stairs. Gives us a thumbs-up.

When the coffee is ready, we pour it into the thermoses, cap them, and head out. I grab a bag of potato chips on the way out the door.

60.

WE ROW GUZZLER away from the dock. Me on one oar, Penny on the other.

We don't want any noise from the motor.

It is two-thirty a.m. now. Lights in all the houses are out, except the ones George and Major left on in Goose.

When we are a good ways out to sea, we pull in the oars and I start the engine. The air is cold and the water looks black. After a bit, we can no longer see the land, and it seems as if the black of the sky is the black of the sea and we are afloat in the middle of nothingness.

When we are truly far out, so far out that it seems impossible Pfeff's body could ever wash to shore, I cut the motor. I drop the anchor.

We unwrap Pfeff's head. I do not think anyone will ever find his body, but if they do, my sweater should not be on it.

The skin of his face is cold. I shut his eyes.

We remove his sneakers and his lobster socks, putting the

socks into the shoes, like he would have left them if he'd gone swimming.

We take the rocks I collected on the beach and shove them into his front and back pockets. It is a horrendous operation. His skin is clammy and hairy. The rocks do not go in easily.

We are worried there is not enough weight to make him sink, so we roll his pant legs and tuck smaller stones into the rolls.

"I still think he should be in a bathing suit," says Penny. "If anyone finds him. We should have brought one."

"That won't help when he's weighted with stones," I explain. "We have to weight him, and once we weight him, it'll be obvious what happened to anyone who finds him."

"These stones won't be heavy enough. He's not going to sink."

She's right.

"The anchor," I say.

We pull it up. It's on a chain attached to yellow nylon rope. We use the Swiss Army knife, the same one we used to cut the strawberry cake that first Early Morning, and work the blade through the nylon. Then we tie the rope tight around Pfeff's waist.

Penny stops abruptly and covers her face with her hands.

"What's wrong?" I ask. Though of course, everything is wrong.

"We shouldn't do this."

"Let's just finish it."

"I can't."

"You can."

She lifts her eyes to me. "We should go home now and tell everyone the truth. It's not too late to change our minds."

"No."

"They'll understand. We'll tell them—I don't know what we'll tell him, but we'll call the police and—"

"Penny." I try to speak softly. Calmly.

I explain to her and Bess what will happen to the person who killed Pfeff.

I explain what will happen to Penny, as well.

"He's dead," I say. "He was not a good person. We have to just get through this and wish it never happened. We will lie about it extremely well and then we will just forget it. Never think of it. Never talk about it. And it'll basically disappear."

"I can't forget it," says Penny.

"You can. Like you did Rosemary."

Penny looks at me, stricken. "I didn't forget Rosemary."

I stare at her.

"I didn't," she insists.

"It seems like you did."

"I think about her every single day."

Bess nods. "I . . . This sounds weird, but I kind of pray to Rosemary. Like she's an angel or something. Before I go to sleep. I like to think she's looking over us." She shivers. "But not now."

I sit with this for a moment. They do not ever talk about her. Not one word since Penny and I were up in the attic, and when I yelled at Bess. "I can't tell that either of you thinks about Rosemary for even a second," I tell them.

"Mother and Daddy don't like to talk about her," says Bess. "It's too much. I try to, you know, respect them that way."

"I don't like people knowing my feelings," says Penny simply. "It feels too naked."

"So we can do this," I say. "We are good at it."

"What?" asks Penny.

"Acting. We have been pretending everything's okay all year, and we will keep pretending everything's okay. We know how. It's the family way. And after a time, it will be okay. Understand?"

They nod.

"We just have to get through this next part and the rest will be easy in comparison. *No way out but through.*" I quote my father's motto.

Bess holds the anchor.

I take Pfeff's shoulders.

Penny takes his legs.

We lift him and step onto the seats. The boat tilts with our weight, all on one side, but we do not lose our footing.

We drop Lor Pfefferman into the sea, the anchor around his waist.

We watch his body sink.

" 'Of his bones are coral made,' " says Penny, quoting Shakespeare. " 'Those are pearls that were his eyes.' "

61.

I TURN ON the motor and we move away. Soon we cannot tell where Pfeff lies, and we stop the boat again.

We change clothes—into the bathing suits and cover-ups that Bess brought.

We put our sweatshirts on.

We use a lighter, stored in the motorboat for our parents' cigarettes, to burn the paper towels that Bess used to clean the dock. We toss the burning papers into the air and watch them disintegrate to nothing, tiny orange sparks settling on the sea and then extinguishing.

I open the bottle of whiskey and we pass it around in silence. It is about 3:45 a.m.

We lie all three together under a rain tarp on the floor of the boat. But it is hard to sleep.

"Remember when that friend of Mother's took us all camping?" says Bess.

"Um-hm," I say, though I don't, really. I have a fuzzy memory of hot dogs cooked on sticks and a bright yellow backpack filled with supplies. That's about it.

"I was like, only three," Bess says. "We all slept together under a blanket like this. I was way too young to go camping."

"You peed the bed," says Penny.

"Did not."

"Oh, you totally did," says Penny. "I woke up with Bess pee all down my leg. I had to go to the creek and wash in this freezing, freezing water, and our bed was all pee-covered and we had to put everything in a black plastic bag to bring it home to Mother to wash."

"Who was that guy?" asks Bess. "Why did he want to take us camping?"

"Beats me," says Penny. "But he gave Carrie this bag of mixed jelly beans, I remember. And he said 'Share them with your sisters,' but he totally put her in charge of them. She

220

would dole them out two at a time, like she was queen of the jelly beans."

"Buddy," says Bess. "That was his name."

"How do you even remember that?" says Penny sleepily.

"My brain is more powerful than you know."

"Buddy Kopelnick?" I say, understanding.

"Maybe," says Penny.

Buddy Kopelnick took us camping. Took me camping.

"Kopelnick?" asks Bess.

"Yeah, that was his name," I say, remembering more now. "We had the hot dogs on sticks. He put the ketchup on a paper plate and we all three dunked our hot dogs in there."

"It was supposed to be just you," remembers Penny. "Because you were the oldest. But then I pitched a fit and Mother said I could go. And Bess pitched a fit, and so we all went."

"That's not like Mother to let some random dude take us camping," says Bess.

"He was an old friend," I say.

I try to recall Buddy's face, but it isn't there. His whole self isn't really there. I can remember the hot dogs and, now that she told the story, Penny washing her leg and yelling about it. She was wearing sky-blue athletic shorts, and her dirty white sneakers sat on the shore of the creek beside her. I remember keeping the pink jelly beans for myself, too, and doling out green and black to my sisters, since I didn't like them. Bess extending sticky palms, asking for more candy.

His face won't come up, though. It is like he never existed for me. Buddy Kopelnick is only a scratched-out face on an old photograph.

Bess and Penny have stopped thinking about him. They are tipsy, singing "What Shall We Do with a Drunken Sailor?"

They're doing just as I asked them to. As we Sinclairs always do.

Pretending. Lying. Trying to have a good time.

WHEN THE SUN comes up, we drink the coffee from three of the four thermoses. We eat the potato chips.

I tell them about Rosemary and me, that time we had the potato chip breakfast when she was alive.

Bess wants to drink more whiskey, but I say no. We have to be sober and smell of seawater and coffee when we get back.

Instead, we pour some of the coffee from the fourth thermos into our own cups. Into "Pfeff's" thermos, a tall one, we pour a large amount of whiskey, leaving room at the top so it looks like he drank at least half. We have no idea how fingerprinting works, and we should have put Pfeff's mouth and hands on the thermos, but it's too late now, so we wipe it with a beach towel and plan to say it fell in the water with the lid on. That's the story of why his prints aren't on it. If anyone asks. But there's probably no police record of his fingerprints, I tell my sisters. So it likely doesn't matter what's on the thermos.

We eat the Pop-Tarts.

We toss the whiskey bottle into the ocean.

With a towel, we wipe the boat seat where Pfeff lay. Then we spray the towel with cleaner, soak it in the ocean, and wring it out, stretching it to dry. We take Pfeff's blood-stained gray T-shirt, my sweater, and everything any of us have worn this past night and wind them together into a tight ball around a large stone. We sink the ball. It goes down slowly, but it disappears.

"Rest in peace, good gray top," says Bess.

"Rest in peace, best jean shorts," says Penny.

"Goodbye, pink sweatshirt," I say.

It is more than any of us said for Pfeff when he went under. But there is no use pointing that out.

When we are certain the boat is irreproachable, we go swimming, wetting our hair and swimsuits. Later, when we return to Beechwood, our cover-ups will be convincingly damp, and our towels, too.

We leave one towel, Pfeff's towel, neatly folded. We crumple the shirt we took from his room and put it on the floor of the boat next to his shoes and socks, like he took it off to go swimming.

We wipe our prints off the spray cleaner and toss it into the sea.

We are so far out we can't even see land, but the compass guides us as we head home.

It is 6:48 in the morning when we pull up to the island.

62.

WE TIE UP the boat and leave it a mess. We run up the dock.

Tipper, Luda, and Harris are in the Clairmont kitchen, which smells of coffee and cinnamon rolls. They are startled as we burst in.

We girls all talk over one another. Penny cries. Bess cries. I cry.

We went out to do an Early Morning with Pfeff, we explain. It was one of these adventures we'd been going on, to enjoy the sunrise.

Pfeff brought the coffee and

we brought snacks and it's

true

we thought Major and George were coming, but they weren't there. We don't know why. It was Pfeff's idea and maybe he forgot to tell them. Or maybe they just slept in.

Anyway, we went out, like usual, except this time, Bess got to come.

And Pfeff was acting funny, like maybe he was

drunk.

He was zigzagging the boat and being

wild,

and it's

true,

it seems impossible for someone to be

drunk at six in the morning, but we are pretty sure he was, because he was like, singing and being weird.

We tried to get him to eat some breakfast, but he said no,

and when he stopped the boat, we all went swimming, like we usually do.

We should probably have tried to make sure Pfeff didn't swim, because of course you shouldn't swim when you're

drunk,

and we really are very careful, usually, but we weren't thinking. Well, it's

true

Carrie did say "Don't go in, Pfeff," but he just laughed and jumped in anyway.

Then we were swimming and he went kinda far away from the boat, really far, but he was laughing and everything was fine and then Penny got out of the water.

She was leaning over the edge talking to Bess when something went funny with the anchor. The yellow nylon thing, the rope that goes down to the chain part of the anchor, that was like, all frayed, and Penny heard a *flop* sound and she was like,

"Oh my god, I think the rope just broke."

Carrie and Bess got out of the water to look and we pulled up the anchor and it wasn't even there anymore. The rope had broken.

We were all busy with that and we were worried you'd be mad at us for losing the anchor, Daddy, even though it wasn't our fault, but it's

true

that we hadn't checked the cord was strong and we do know you're supposed to check the cord is strong every time you weigh anchor, but anyway, it's

true

we were totally distracted and when we looked up, we couldn't see Pfeff.

We called him and called him, and we looked all around, and he just wasn't there.

He went under.

We couldn't find him.

We started the boat and we went around, looking for him and looking, and calling, but he wasn't there.

225

It could have been a

shark, because you know how people talk about

sharks in the water, even though we've never seen one,

or it could have been just that he was

drunk

and he choked on some water, or breathed it in, and we

don't know, he went under.

We called and called and looked and looked, and

finally, we came home, to you,

Mother and Daddy.

We're so scared.

63.

TIPPER WANTS TO ring the police, but Harris isn't sure. He says he doesn't want them involved. He says it is a family matter.

Tipper counters that with an accidental death you have to call the police. And they could search for Pfeff. Maybe he's still alive.

"He's not alive," I say.

"He could be," says Tipper. "Clinging to a buoy or trying to swim ashore."

"He was nowhere," I say. "We looked."

"I don't want police on the island," says Harris.

"Darling, please," says Tipper. "We have to do right by that boy."

In the end, my father agrees and Tipper rings the police—but it is three hours before their boat arrives, and even Tipper has to admit that Pfeff would have swum to shore by now if he had any hope of doing so.

She is somber as we meet the police boat at the staff dock. It unloads two Martha's Vineyard officers in uniform. Both are ruddy white guys. One is burly and young, a buffalo of a man. The other is wiry, weathered, and quite a bit older, more of a python.

They assure us that a team is looking for Pfeff at sea. They ask us questions about where we were anchored when he died.

We lie.

They accept coffee from my mother. They say they do not need to talk to Major and George, Luda or Gerrard, but they speak briefly to my parents and interview me, Penny, and Bess separately.

My sisters and I all know our story.

I sit down with the officers in the dining room. My skin feels sore from fatigue but I force myself to look them in the eyes.

What time did you take the boat out?

"Five-thirty." I know my mother's alarm rings at 5:45.

That's awfully early.

"We wanted to catch the sunrise." I looked the time up in the morning paper.

Still, that's early for teenagers, yeah?

"It's a thing we've done before," I say. "You can ask George and Major. But the truth is, sir, we planned this particular morning extra early, thinking my little sister Bess would sleep through and not come with us. She's always wanting to do things with the older kids, you know? A tagalong."

The early start time was supposed to be a deterrent.

"Yes, sir."

But she came.

"She did."

Your mother tells me you were with this boy, Lawrence. That he was your boyfriend.

"She said that, sir?" Penny, Bess, and I have agreed on this story. "I would never call him a boyfriend. But yes, there was something between us. A summer fling. It was his idea to go boating." This is part of our story—that Pfeff and I weren't serious. And that he'd wanted to make things up with me and asked me to go out on the boat. We hope this will be enough to convince George and Major.

So you met up at five a.m.?

"Five-thirty. My sisters and I brought food from the big house, and Pfeff—I mean, Lor, Lawrence—he brought coffee and towels and stuff."

Tell me what happened after that.

I tell the story we told my parents. How he seemed drunk. I shouldn't have let him swim. It could have been a shark. "Do you think he drowned?"

Could be. Drowning is surprisingly silent and swift. We have several drownings a year in these parts.

"It was like he disappeared. So fast."

People go under in sixty seconds or less. A lot of them never wave or yell for help. There's a physiological response that stops them.

"We didn't hear anything. But we were busy with the anchor. The string to our anchor broke."

The officers write something down about the anchor.

"He was drinking," I add. "I'm not positive, but pretty sure. Maybe something in the thermos."

Mm-hm. We have a team looking for the body now.

"Will you send divers?" We have told the officers that Pfeff drowned in a different area from where we left him, nearly an hour's boat ride away, but still—I'd like to know.

Yes, miss. A team of divers.

"Oh gosh. And how long does it take?"

Couple days.

"Will you tell us if you find him?"

Sure thing.

And they let me go, for now.

We'll need to talk to you again later. Don't be afraid. This is all standard procedure.

Additional team members arrive on the island. They are in plain clothes. They seem to be here to search Guzzler. I stand in Rosemary's old room and watch them from her window.

They photograph everything. They look at our bags and boxes of half-eaten snacks. Our piles of damp towels and Pop-Tart wrappers. I watch as they open every thermos. They smell the contents. They pick up Pfeff's T-shirt, shoes, and socks. They look at the cord for the missing anchor.

Harris comes down to see them, followed by the dogs. He talks for a minute. And as he heads back toward the house, I notice something:

The board is missing.

The board, which I sprayed with bleach cleaner and washed in the sea.

I know I placed it back where it had been lying all summer. I know I did.

But it is not there anymore.

64.

I WANT TO ask my sisters where the board is, but Penny, Bess, and I have agreed that we absolutely will not confer with one another this day. We know it will be tempting to talk about our situation, but someone could overhear us. It is not worth the risk. We cry and let our mother comfort us. We tell the story, individually, to Major and George.

When the day is done, the police leave. Later, they telephone my mother. They say they have had no luck yet finding a body, but divers will go back out tomorrow.

Pfeff's parents have been notified.

Major and George have made plans to leave Beechwood tomorrow.

We eat a somber supper indoors. Tipper puts out place mats and wineglasses. She and Luda serve a simple linguine with meat sauce, followed by a salad and a cheese plate.

We are mostly silent as we eat. Bess cries a little. Penny says, "Oh please, you knew him the least of any of us," which makes Bess cry harder, until she has to leave the table.

George, wearing a suit jacket and with his hair slicked to the side like a businessman's, tries to make conversation with my father, while Major wears a black T-shirt and stares miserably into his plate, swallowing almost nothing.

Later, Penny and I walk down to Goose. We offer to help the boys pack. Tipper asked us to. It is our responsibility to make them feel better.

George and Major don't care about their packing. They plan to leave it all till the last minute and do it willy-nilly. Instead, they ask if we want to put on a movie. The four of us huddle on the couch under old cotton blankets and watch *Mary Poppins* yet again.

Halfway through the movie, Bess joins us.

"I'm sorry I was a witch to you at supper," says Penny, surprisingly.

Bess nods. "It's just a lot."

"It is a lot," says Penny. "We have to take care of our Bess." She beckons, and Bess squeezes in between me and Penny.

"It's a sister sandwich," says Bess.

"Yah, yah," I say. "You okay?"

"I'm okay."

"You want a beer?" asks George, who has gone over to the fridge. "Pretzel mix?"

"Just a Tab is cool," says Bess. "And the pretzel mix. Yeah."

George mixes small pretzels with a bag of chocolate chips, Frosted Mini-Wheats, and a bag of tiny marshmallows. "I really learned to cook on this trip," he deadpans as he sits back down and gives Bess her Tab.

We all stick our hands in the pretzel mix and eat it in salty-sweet handfuls. Major turns the movie back on.

It is good not to have to speak or pretend, but just to watch and forget.

When it's over, the boys toast Pfefferman. "A funny man, obsessed with his weenie, a lackadaisical tennis player," says George, raising what is probably his third beer. "A friend since the sixth grade, the 'mayor' of the Germantown Friends School, interested in everybody, a terrible outdoorsman but an okay sailor. Pfeff was not scared of sharks, even though he should have been. He made me laugh a million times, and for that, I'm forever grateful. Pfeff, my man, I hope you're happy up there. May the beer be cold and the women blond for ya."

Major stands up. "Pfeff, you were a butthead, but you knew it, and you made us love you for it. Not a lot of people could do that. You wore some incredible socks. To be honest, I wasn't sure about this summer, when George decided we'd all come here. I didn't know much about you besides what I just said. But we had some good talks, Lor Pfefferman. I think we would have gone our separate ways at Amherst, but here on Beechwood we had dance parties and midnight swims. And we had those good Early Mornings, waking and baking, appreciating that water and the sunrises. I'm glad you got one more Morning in, and that if you had to go, it was because of something as badass as a shark attack. Rest in peace, Pfeff."

They look at me like maybe I want to say something.

I stand. I have not dared to drink, for fear of loosening my tongue, or taken a codeine, for fear of dozing off after my sleepless night. I raise my can of Coke. "To Pfeff. He was a flirt, sometimes a cad, but also a dreamer. A charmer and a great finder of lemons. Always forgiven his trespasses because of his awesomeness. We wish him well in the big sleep."

The words feel sour coming out of my mouth, though some of them are true. There is so much about him that I cannot say.

He was capable of rape.

He was cruel. False-hearted. Untrustworthy.

"Penny," says George. "You want to say something?"

Penny looks choked. She shakes her head.

Bess, always one to do whatever is "right" in the moment, stands up in her stead. I am worried about what she will say. She looks drawn and exhausted. Her hair is flat and dirty, and she's huddled in her warmest sweater and an old pair of jeans. I reach out and squeeze her hand.

Don't confess.

Don't break.

Be strong.

"I'm glad I got to know you, Pfeff," Bess says. "Thanks for the laughs at supper, and for the time you brought us cold sodas on the beach, and for catching sand crabs with Tomkin. Thanks for being so nice to our mother. Rest in peace."

She sits down.

George makes popcorn in the microwave, and since none of us knows what to do next, we start another movie. *Fletch.*

Not long into it, Penny and Bess fall asleep. Penny's head drops onto my shoulder.

A while later, George pauses the movie to go use the bathroom and I turn to Major. "You didn't like Pfeff so much, did you?" I ask.

Major hesitates for a minute, his face flushing. Then he shakes his head. "Since you're asking, no. I mean, I'm sorry and shocked that the guy is dead, but no."

"Why not?"

"All the back-and-forth with you and Penny, for one. That's just low. Though I guess you forgave him."

I nod. "He made a pretty stellar apology," I lie. "When he got around to it."

"But he had this attitude," says Major. "Like everything belonged to him; it was all his for the taking. Some gay jokes. Jokes about my parents' spiritual practice. Like, who makes fun of people's religion? Since when is that okay? I mean, the guy was all the good things I said, too. But underneath, like down deep, I don't think he thought about anybody else. Nobody else was really a person to him." He shrugs. "They were just toys."

George returns, but we don't watch the end of the movie. I rouse Bess and Penny and the three of us hug them and say

It's all such a shock,

it's terrible,

we can't believe he's really gone,

we're so sorry your trip ended this way,

we've loved having you,

come back to Beechwood anytime—

though we know that they will never be back.

AS PENNY, BESS, and I walk through the night to Clairmont, I tell my sisters, in a whisper, about the missing board. Their eyes widen.

Penny says she didn't move it.

Bess says she didn't move it.

"It was stupid as hell to move it. Do you understand?" I say. "If someone finds it, hidden, that will look suspicious. It has literally been sitting in the same spot since the Lemon Hunt. If the police find it in the basement or under your bed or something, it will be so, so bad."

"Duh," says Penny. "That is why I didn't touch it."

We both look at Bess. She shakes her head earnestly. "I don't have it," she says.

"Did you used to have it?" I ask. "Did you do something with it?"

"I told you, no. I haven't even been on the dock."

There is nothing for us to do but go home and go to bed.

I am scared to see Rosemary again, after the way I left her, and after all that my sisters and I have done last night and today. But she does not visit me, and the Halcion knocks me hard into the dark.

65.

WORKERS COME AND rip apart the dock. They stack the rough, worn boards in a pile on the sand and eventually cart them away.

They rebuild in the same shape, a little wider, with bright new wood. They do repairs here and there on the walkways, fences, and steps. They fill the island with the sounds of their tools.

It takes four days.

My mother and Luda clean Pevensie from top to bottom. They ship all Tomkin's and Yardley's things to their mother's address and Uncle Dean's things to his place.

Harris says only one thing to me about Dean's departure: "He and I are no longer seeing eye to eye."

Privately, Tipper says that the rupture "was unavoidable and your father is completely in the right."

Gerrard has been upset over Pfeff's death. He is a sensitive person, and the second drowning in two years has made him want a job on the mainland. He takes his leave of us kindly, and will not be back.

I haven't seen Rosemary. I cannot bear that I hurt her. I left her alone when she most wanted me. Abandoning her has probably undone everything I did all summer to try to make her feel loved and secure.

I don't know how to mend it. I am both afraid to see her—and longing to.

The day after the dock is finished, Mr. and Mrs. Larry Pfefferman come to the island. Tipper offered to pack up Pfeff's things and ship them home, but the search for the body is ongoing. Pfeff's parents want to come out and talk to the police. My mother felt she should host them.

Harris picks up the Pfeffermans at Woods Hole. The rest of our family waits for them on the new dock. We introduce ourselves and say how sorry we are.

Mr. Pfefferman is fat in a wide, square way, as if his body has grown into the shape of a boxy business suit. He has his son's thick hair and wears wire-rimmed glasses. His wife is Italian-born. She speaks with an accent and wears a slim-fitting black summer dress and heels. Her hair is that monochromatic brown that comes from dye.

Bess's lips quiver when she says hello.

Penny looks at her feet.

I look the Pfeffermans in the eye and think, *He was hurting my sister.* Then I course-correct: *He was drunk in the early morning.*

He swam too far from the boat. We weren't looking and he went under. We searched and searched.

Tipper puts the Pfeffermans in Pevensie. Goose is still a mess after the hurricane of the boys.

Bess, Penny, and I agree that we will never be alone with Pfeff's parents. We will speak to them as little as possible. It is Luda's night off, so we offer to help Tipper with supper. She is making mini-quiches for nibbles, something she only does for best company in Boston. Bess, a much better cook than Penny or I, rolls and cuts out the quiche crusts and lifts each one into a baking tin. There will be lamb chops, potatoes, and a lettuce-and-mint salad. A blackberry slump with soft-whipped cream for dessert.

The supper is quiet. Harris talks about his publishing company. Tipper and Mrs. Pfefferman discuss cooking and cardiovascular exercise, and Tipper says "what a pleasure it was" getting to know Pfeff. "He was such a polite boy."

After we eat, and once Bess and Penny have excused themselves to watch TV in the den, Pfeff's mother takes a photo album from her bag. It is large and covered in a faded fabric printed with storks, like she got it at her baby shower.

I stand to leave the room. I don't want to be near the Pfeffermans any longer than I have to, or see pictures of the little boy who grew up to think a girl's body belonged to him just because he said please. But as Mr. Pfefferman goes out on the porch to smoke, Tipper grabs my father's hand. "Harris, stay and see the pictures. They lost their boy." She turns to Mrs. Pfefferman. "We lost our little girl, too," she says. "Last year. We lost our Rosemary in the same ocean."

I cannot move.

We lost our little girl. Not since the funeral has anyone said that. Not since the funeral has my mother shown me that she feels the loss. Even when I brought it up, she only said *Rosemary's not here. We all wish she were.* Then she went on to talk about not dwelling on hard things and living a joyful life.

But here she is, bringing up the subject.

"Did you?" says Mrs. Pfefferman, her hand on her throat. "Oh, Tipper. I am so sorry."

"No, no. It was a long time ago. Pfeff—I mean, Lor—he was just here. You've had a terrible shock. I don't mean to talk about myself."

My father puts his hand on Tipper's shoulder. I'm not sure if he means to console or quiet her.

"It is the worst thing in the world to lose a child," says Mrs. Pfefferman. "They are meant to outlive us."

"She was so little," says my mother, choked. "She loved to swim. We let her swim and no one was watching her. I don't think I'll ever forgive myself."

"We miss her every day," says Harris. "That never goes away."

"You miss her?" I blurt.

"I do."

I stare at his face, as familiar and weathered as always, but now etched with grief he almost never shows.

"I can't believe Lor is gone," says Mrs. Pfefferman, a tear sliding down her cheek. "I keep expecting him to walk in the door. Look, he was the fattest baby who ever lived."

I know I should leave, but the emotion in the room pulls me in like a whirlpool. I stand behind my mother and watch as Mrs. Pfefferman turns through the pages of her album—pictures of

238

baby Lor, becoming kid Lor, then becoming Pfeff, the boy I knew. Drinking milk from a bottle. Hugging a stuffed animal. Sitting proudly on a tricycle. Reading a book of fairy tales. Eating a doughnut.

My mother cries, low-key and continuously, while she bends over Mrs. Pfefferman's book and makes thoughtful remarks. "Oh, he looks so happy." "I can see how much he loved you." "My goodness, he was handsome." "He got so tall!" "He had a good sense of humor, didn't he?" She asks questions. "Where were you all in this one?" "This must be seventh or eighth grade, am I right?"

Mrs. Pfefferman cries less but seems hungry for every photograph to be witnessed and appreciated. "You're very kind," she says to my mother.

My father sits next to us with his face in his hands. Mr. Pfefferman remains on the porch.

The last picture is Pfeff grinning in his high school graduation gown, laughing at a party with one arm around George's neck. "He had run away," Mrs. Pfefferman says softly.

"Pardon?" asks Tipper.

"He left home and didn't tell us where he went," Mrs. Pfefferman explains. "We— My husband and I are divorcing."

"Oh. I didn't know."

"How could you? But it has been a hard year. At home. And Lor was—well, a boy gets angry when his world shatters, you see. My husband, he wouldn't let me have the house. And I refused to move out." She twists the napkin in her lap, still speaking low. "Lor didn't want to spend the summer at home, with us in so much conflict, but his father got him a job in the law office. Very official, answering phones and the like while different secretaries took their vacations. We felt it would be good for him to learn some responsibility before college. And then one night, we had—I shouldn't tell you this, but we had a big argument, my husband and I. And the next morning, Lor was gone. He didn't even leave a note."

"Oh no."

"He didn't call me for a whole week, and when he did, he said he was at George's girlfriend's summer house. And he wasn't coming home. He said he was staying forever and didn't give a phone number or anything. He was so unhappy with us, he just—he ran away," she says. "We hadn't heard from him since that one call."

"I'm sure he would have come home to you," says my mother. "He was just having a break, that's all. Finding himself. A good boy like that wouldn't really run away."

Mrs. Pfefferman wipes her eyes. She puts the book back in her satchel. "You girls are very lucky," she says to me. "You have a wonderful mom."

I smile. "I know I do."

"Don't make her sad, you hear me?" Mrs. Pfefferman says. "You be sweet to her, always. When she's old and her hair is gray, you be good to her then, as well as now. When you go to college, always call and write."

"Okay."

Harris stands up slowly, as if waking from a dream.

"Look at the time," says Mrs. Pfefferman. "I'm sorry I took up so much of your evening."

"Oh, it was lovely to see the pictures," says Tipper. "I am so sorry for your loss."

"Let me help you wash up."

Tipper laughs and puts her hand on her chest in mock horror. "I would never let you," she says. "After all you've been through." Her voice is suddenly bright and hostessy. "Go on, the two of you. Head up to Pevensie. The coffee maker is loaded and there are some breakfast things in the fridge, but you come see me around seven and I'll have the muffins out of the oven by then, juice and all that. Or come later, if you need to sleep in. The police promised to visit before noon."

The Pfeffermans depart. Tipper gives herself a shake and heads to the kitchen.

"I'll do it," I tell her, following. "Let me do it. You go to bed."

She pauses. "Is this because she told you to be sweet to me?"

"Maybe."

Tipper has never left any of us to clean the kitchen without her. But she hugs me and nods. "I am missing our Rosemary," she tells me, her voice choked. "God, I miss her."

"Me too." So much, so much.

"Every day," she says. "My little girl. Each morning I listen for the sound of her footsteps and I realize she's never coming down the stairs again. And I walk by her room when I'm heading up to bed, and I poke my head in to check—and remember she won't be there. You know, one night I thought I saw Rosemary. When we first got to the island this summer, she came into my bedroom. She looked like she had crawled up from the sea, just crawled out of it, as if to tell me I hadn't kept her safe. I couldn't bear looking at her tiny face, with that wet hair around it. I was looking at my worst mistake, my most tragic failing, and I felt so desperately sad and helpless that I ran away. It was just a dream, or my imagination, of course, but I told myself I couldn't let my mind play tricks on me like that. I mustn't think of Rosemary and how I failed her, or I'd fall apart. Sometimes I feel like I can't live without her," says my mother. "Like how on earth can I keep existing when my baby is dead? How can I?" Tears are coming down her face again. "But I have to, Carrie. I have to go on. People depend on me. There's always another pie to bake, or someone needs something. Right? It's better that way. Your dad needs me, you girls need me, the dryer's on the fritz or something else is broken. People need to eat supper, every day of the week, rain or shine. It's better to be busy. To be useful. That's how I get by."

I don't know what to say. I don't know if it is better to be busy and never talk of things.

"I'm sorry." Tipper wipes the corners of her eyes. "It just gets to me sometimes. I do think perhaps I should lie down. I'll be better in the morning, I promise. One hundred percent. Back to normal." She smiles at me.

Impulsively, I hug her again. I am taller than she is, and she seems frail in my arms. She is brave and in denial, limited and powerless, generous always, my mother.

"Come on, Tipper," says Harris, coming to stand in the kitchen doorway. "I'll take you up."

"It's fine. I'm fine," she says.

"Tipper."

"I don't need help, Harris. I'm just a little headachy, is all. It's been a real week."

"Neither of us is fine," says my father. "Let's go upstairs."

66.

I CLEAN THE kitchen, putting leftover food in stacking containers, loading the plates and cooking utensils into the dishwasher. The tablecloth and napkins go into the laundry. The wineglasses must be washed by hand, and so must the cast-iron pan.

Bess and Penny don't offer to help, and I don't ask them to. When I am halfway through, they turn off the TV, call good night, and head upstairs.

I want to see Rosemary.

I have never called for her, not once all summer. She says she doesn't know why she comes when she comes. "It's just when I wake up. I wake up and visit you, is all."

I whisper her name as I wipe the counters. "Rosemary."

I dry the wineglasses and put them away. "Rosemary, I am sorry."

I fill the coffee maker for tomorrow morning, just the way Tipper likes it. "Rosemary, I am sorry I left you. I am so sorry."

I take the trash out the door that leads to the staff building and put it in the bins over there. "Rosemary, buttercup," I say, walking to the center of the living room. "I am ashamed. What I did was selfish and mean. I don't know how to be a good person sometimes. If anyone else left you like that, left you when you were scared, I would be angry. I would hate anyone who treated you like that, and I hate myself for it, please believe that I do. I don't know if you can hear me, but I do love you a million loves. I miss you. And Penny misses you. And Bess misses you. And Mother and Daddy." I don't know if she can hear me. She probably can't. But the words pour out. I say everything I have been feeling. "We are trying to go on without you, but we can't do it. Not really. We're pretending to go on and everything's terrible. We are terrible. It's not your fault, darling Rosemary. Don't feel bad about it. We just have to—we have to learn how to live, over again, I guess. And it isn't easy."

After that, I sit in silence.

She does not come.

I wait, but still—nothing.

Then I walk to the kitchen. I rinse a stray teacup and wipe the fingerprints off the refrigerator. I turn out the lights.

When I return to the hall, ready to head upstairs, I notice a light on in the den, where the television is.

I go in to shut it off and Rosemary is there, in her cheetah suit. She is sitting on the couch, petting Wharton's red-gold head.

"That was a big speech," she says.

"I'm really sorry."

"Yah, yah."

"I am." I kneel in front of her.

"Okay, but I think I'm done talking about hard stuff for now," she says. "I didn't come for that."

"I didn't wake you up?"

"You *can't* wake me up. I told you that a million times, Carrie. I wake up 'cause I'm worried or I want something. I'm supposed to be asleep, but I can't be."

"Why are you up now?"

"Well, duh. It's eleven-thirty. Right?"

I glance at the clock. "A little after."

"And it's Saturday. Right? Well, ghosts can't sleep if they never saw *Saturday Night Live*," says Rosemary. "It's like unfinished business."

"You have not been haunting me because you never got to watch *Saturday Night Live*. That is not a reason."

"No, it's not," she admits. "But everyone is in bed now, right? And I totally want to watch it so bad. Come on. It'll cheer you up and get your mind off all your terribleness."

I turn the TV on, the volume low, and settle on the couch. Wharton thumps her tail. Rosemary curls up into me.

On the screen, the Pretenders sing "Don't Get Me Wrong." There is sketch comedy. A guy pretending to be Reagan.

"I don't understand it," says Rosemary. "But it's so good. I bet I'm like the only cheetah that ever saw *Saturday Night Live*."

67.

BEFORE THE POLICE arrive on Sunday, Tipper, Luda, Bess, and I spend the morning cleaning Goose. Penny sleeps in and Harris works in his study.

Tipper did go to the cottage to show the police Pfeff's room, but the work that needed doing in Pevensie has preoccupied her until now. She puts her hands on her hips as she looks at the chaos of the kitchen. "This is appalling. How did they live like this?"

"I came every other day, like you said," says Luda.

"I know you did," says Tipper. "It's not your fault in the least. They were just piglets."

We run the washing machine and the dishwasher, wipe counters, pour half-empty beers and cans of soda into the sink. Tipper takes the curtains down for cleaning. Luda vacuums under all the cushions of the couches. "You'll have to get them reupholstered. God, there's like, dried—oh, I don't even want to know," she says. "I can cover them with quilts for now."

Upstairs, I stand in the doorway of Pfeff's room. His clothes are still on the floor. The bed is unmade.

He is gone.

I haven't let myself feel sad or sorry. I can't afford to.

I can't think about how his parents loved him and how broken and lost they are. I can't think about how he was my first kiss, my first everything. I can't think about his beloved sci-fi novels and his ridiculous socks, the way he kneeled before my mother at the Lemon Hunt, the way he swam to my boat in his hoodie, the way he kissed me at the tire swing. I mustn't think of how he worked to make me laugh, and how he made up silly song lyrics, and how he didn't want to waste the moonlight. One day, he might have left Amherst and traveled far away, to Italy or Mexico, in search of beautiful food and adventure. Maybe he'd have found a job at a restaurant, worked his way up to manning the kitchen, made friends everywhere he went. Cooked the hell out of the dinner shift every night. Made small things exciting and beautiful, the way he knew how.

No. I have to stop these thoughts.

He was hurting Penny. He wouldn't have stopped. He was a terrible person. And then he was dead.

246

There was nothing else to do once he died but drown the body like we did. It was the only way. And now we have to live with it.

My job is to make myself believe the story we told, to let that story erase what really happened, like ocean waves erasing marks in the sand. He wasn't a ridiculous, beautiful moonlight boy, and he wasn't a terrible person, either. He was a cute guy I fooled around with a bit. A fling. A summer acquaintance. He drank too much, went swimming, and got eaten by a shark. What a sad tale. I feel shocked that he died, and shaken, but I didn't know him that well. That's my story.

It strikes me, suddenly, that Pfeff might come back. He might crawl out of the sea, shirtless and dripping. His ghost might return to this haunted island to—what?

Apologize?

Take revenge on me and my sisters?

Hurt Penny again?

A shudder runs through me.

I slam the door to Pfeff's room and run downstairs to the safety and bustle of the cleaning project. Without Tipper asking, I get on my knees and scrub the sticky spots off the kitchen floor.

LATER, WHEN GOOSE is fit for company again, my mother and Luda take themselves over to Pevensie to look for quilts. I head toward Clairmont alone. I am passing the stairway to the Tiny Beach, when I hear a sound, carried on the wind. Almost like a voice, whispering.

A tune from *Mary Poppins*.

Take no prisoners, do some crimes
Know your math facts! Step in time.

68.

SHAKING, I WALK slowly down the steps.

The phrase repeats, so quiet I can barely hear it. Maybe I am imagining it.

Take no prisoners, do some crimes
Know your math facts! Step in time.

When I reach the beach, I see Pfeff at the far end of the cove. He's standing in the shallow water, looking out to sea. He wears his blue striped board shorts and his Live-Aid T-shirt. His hands are clasped behind him.

He turns when I am near. "I was hoping it was you."

"Don't come back here, Pfeff," I say loudly. "We do not want you."

"I'm sorry, Carrie," he says. "Can we talk?"

"You have to go. You can't haunt this island." Rosemary never visited our mother after Tipper sent her away. Not once. If I banish Pfeff, I think he will go.

"I came to say sorry," he says.

"It's too late for that."

"I saw my mom last night, up in Pevensie." Pfeff walks

forward, through the water. He looks alive and solid, squinting in the sunshine. "I had to say goodbye to her," he continues. "Make sure she's all right."

"Okay."

"And—she made me see I have a lot to apologize for. She cooked me some eggs and toast in the kitchen up there."

"Did you tell her how you died?"

"No." He scratches the back of his neck. "I was trying to— you know. Make her feel better. Tell her I'm okay."

"What do you remember?" I ask. "I mean, about—about how you died?" I don't want him to tell his mother the truth.

"Not much, actually," he says. "I was drunk. Everything's kind of fuzzy because of that."

"And?"

"I was on the dock with Penny. And I felt a sharp pain in my head. I might have screamed. There was blood in my eyes. Then everything went dark and very quiet. Like a long sleep. It was comfortable after that, actually. Like a rest."

That's what Rosemary says, too. That it's comfortable. The actual dying didn't hurt.

"Then I woke up again last night," Pfeff continues. "And I found myself on the beach. With like, my feet in the sand. I was hungry and everything. Just like being alive. It was so strange. I thought, *I'm here for some reason, I guess.* And I walked up to Pevensie because that seemed like where I wanted to go. And I knew I was right when I saw my mom sitting on the porch. She was staring out at the night. So I talked to her. I wanted her to know I loved her and stuff. I was worried she didn't know, because we'd kind of been in a fight all summer. So I told her.

After that, we just hung out. We kept talking, and I filled her in about the summer, about George and Major and living in Goose. The stuff we did. And also about you and me."

"What did you tell her?"

"How it ended badly when I scammed around with Penny."

I stare at him. Shaking.

"She asked a lot of questions," Pfeff continues, "and . . . she made me think how it might have felt to you. For all that to happen. And I really am sorry. That I hurt your feelings."

I should banish him. I need to, so Penny and Bess and I can stick to our lies. So Penny and Bess can be safe. But I have wanted Pfeff to be sorry since I first saw him with Penny. I need to hear him out.

"I see that you must have been very upset," says Pfeff. "And that I probably led you on. And that Penny wasn't the best person to— I was wrong." He holds his hand out in my direction. "Can we say sorry to each other and set it to rest?"

Wait. "You want me to say sorry?"

"I'm saying sorry," he says. "So yeah. You owe me an apology, too. Don't you?"

"No."

"I think you do. You got so mad, and you turned Yardley against me and all that. Even George and Major. George and I had a whole argument about it. And Penny. Penny is confusing, you know? One minute she's all *Come hither* and *Let's be alone* and *I know how to make a guy feel good*, and the next minute she's changing her mind. She doesn't account for a guy being drunk and revved up or whatever, and she's saying no, but not like she means it, and now you've both decided I'm this terrible person. That's the problem, right? That Penny told you I'm terrible."

I stare at him.

"Did it ever occur to you that Penny says shit behind your back?" he goes on. "Did it ever occur to you that I wouldn't have been with her if she didn't like, explicitly go after me in the first place? That she put me in that situation?"

"Leave us!" I shout, the words exploding out of me. "I don't want you here!"

"Aren't you sorry?" he cries. "Aren't you sorry at all?"

Saying no

but not like she means it, he said.

She doesn't account for a guy being drunk

and revved up

or whatever.

She put me in that situation.

"No, Pfeff," I tell him. "I'm not sorry. For anything. At all."

In this moment, I don't care if his mom loves him. I don't care if there were good things about him. He was hurting Penny, and my loyalty is with my sister, no matter what else she has done.

"Carrie," he persists. "I'm like, back from the dead to talk to you. You don't want to apologize?"

"I'm through with you, Lawrence Pfefferman," I say.

"But—"

"No. You don't get to say sorry. Not to me, not to Penny. We won't forgive you."

"You wanted to talk to me," he says. "We were standing right here. Remember? You were begging me."

"And you didn't care."

"Come on." He takes a step toward me.

I put up a hand to stop him. "Nothing you do matters

anymore. You are not welcome here. Stay away from my family."

He stands there, looking at me.

"I mean it," I say.

Pfeff shrugs. "You're going to feel terrible about this later," he says. "You're going to wish you'd said sorry. You're going to wish we'd made up."

"No I won't. Just leave us and never come back."

Pfeff walks forward into the ocean. The water hits his middle and he begins to swim. He swims out past the sharp rocks, beyond the cove to the open water.

I watch until I cannot see him anymore.

WHEN THE POLICE boat arrives, it contains the same two officers we met with earlier. They have really come to speak with the Pfeffermans, but we all gather in the Clairmont living room, almost like a tea party. Tipper serves hot drinks and stacks of white toast with butter.

The weathered, pythony officer takes the lead. He explains that divers and rescue teams on boats have searched the area since Pfeff was reported missing. Sometimes bodies are found quickly, if they drown in shallow water, he says. Or if they are in a discrete area, like a pond. But in deep water, or in very cold water, it is common for a body not to surface. Depending on various factors, the body could float, or not.

In a situation like this one, a shark attack is certainly a possibility. "White sharks are widely known in Cape Cod waters. They have a migration pattern."

252

"Will you continue to search?" asks Harris.

The officer shakes his head. "I'm sad to say the search is closed," he says. "If you want my evaluation, I'd say the shark."

Mrs. Pfefferman breaks down crying. Mr. Pfefferman puts an arm around her.

Penny, Bess, and I busy ourselves clearing teacups and tossing uneaten toast into the trash.

69.

LATER THAT DAY, after Harris has taken the Pfeffermans back to the mainland with Lor's possessions, Tipper knocks on my door.

She sits on my unmade bed. Self-consciously, I begin picking up dirty clothes and putting them in the hamper. I straighten the objects on top of my dresser.

"I know you must be devastated," says Tipper after a silence. "You are holding up so well. I wanted to tell you how beautifully I think you are doing."

"Thank you." I am not sure what she means.

"He was a great boy. Dashing and smart and funny— everything a girl could want, really. Your dad liked him. And Amherst, that's a very good school," she says. "I could tell you were happy together."

Some part of me wants desperately to confide in her. I could tell her how I found Pfeff with Penny. I could share how cold he was, and cruel, could let her see how wrecked I've been. She would comfort me. I could snuggle into her arms and be her baby again, the one who needs the most care. I could become the priority, like I was when my jaw was infected.

But would the whole story spill out? If I tell her the one thing, will I tell her what happened after that? Will floodgates open? I cannot burden my mother with the story of a murder and a cover-up. Her world would shatter completely. She might never forgive us.

Even if I could stop telling the story at the breakup, even if I could tell her only that Pfeff didn't love me, and explain how he treated me, telling her would be foolish. The story of his death depends on everyone believing that Pfeff made an excellent apology and we agreed to go boating together with my sisters. Once people question that, our story will begin to seem suspicious.

And anyway, Tipper is not asking if I'm all right. She is telling me how well I've done pretending everything's all right. She thinks I have lost my first love to the sea, and she knows nothing more, but she wants me to keep on saving face.

"I'm sad, but it wasn't really serious between us," I say. "Just a summer fling before he went to college." It is the same lie I told the police. "I would never call him a boyfriend, really."

"Oh," she says. "I see."

"You know I really like Andrew at North Forest." Another lie. There is no Andrew.

"Oh yes, I hadn't realized Andrew was still in the picture," she says with a slight frown.

"I hope so," I tell her. "He's the soccer player, remember?"

She nods and fingers my green patchwork quilt. "This needs repair. Shall I take it down and fix it?"

"Sure," I say. "Thank you."

"I made the chocolate mud pie you like," she tells me as she folds up the quilt. "The one I always say is too much trouble."

I know she is trying to take care of me the only way she knows how.

70.

PENNY PEELS HER fingernails until her hands look like raw stumps. Bess brings bottles of wine to her bedroom at night. I up my dosage and spend hours asleep in the afternoons.

We no longer eat supper at the big picnic table. It feels too empty.

We are not well, but we do settle in to a quiet life.

A week goes by. Then two.

Rosemary visits now and then, for no particular reason that I can see except she's bored. Or lonely.

Harris spends a few days back in Boston, handling things at his office. When he returns, we have a visit from his lawyer, who gets taken out on the sailboat and stays a night in Goose.

One day, we all visit Edgartown to hear a famous cellist play an evening concert at the Old Whaling Church. It is dull and beautiful at once. We buy fat rectangles of chocolate fudge and eat them on the long, cold boat ride home.

Yardley calls me the next day.

"George came crawling back after Pfeff died, but I wouldn't have him," Yardley says. "It took like three days of arguing and tears to basically be still broken up."

"My god."

"Now he's off being a camp counselor for August." She sighs. "I love that stupid butthole, but if he's not going to back me up and believe in me, I honestly don't want him. Plus, what are we going to do, go out long-distance at college? I'm just done. I want the whole thing to go away." A pause. "Anyway," says Yardley. "Lor Pfefferman. Rest in peace. Did you really not see him go down?"

"I really didn't."

"No shark fin or anything?"

"Nuh-uh."

"And why were you out early with him?" asks Yardley. "I can't help thinking about that, honestly, Carrie. After he and Penny . . ."

I knew this question might come. It is why I haven't called Yardley. She was with me when I saw Pfeff with my sister.

I tell her the same lie I've told the police. And Tipper. "I wouldn't call him my *boyfriend*. It was a summer fling, and I mean, I like this guy at North Forest anyway. So after he apologized, I had to just get over it. It wasn't worth the drama."

"No," says Yardley sharply.

"What?"

"You were together. You and Pfeff. You were holding hands

256

while we watched TV and lying in the hammock together and sneaking off to be alone all the time. It went on for weeks, Carrie, and I know you never had anybody before that. At least, you told me you didn't, right?"

"Right."

"And after being totally into you for weeks, that dirtbag, I'm sorry he's dead and all, but that dirtbag weenie made out with your slimeball sister without even bothering to go somewhere private. It was one of the worst things I've ever seen anyone do to *anyone*. And I don't think you should have to pretend—not to me, at least—that Lor Pfefferman was a saint or even a decent guy, just because he died, Carrie. He was a messed-up whoring dirtbag of a person, and I will never forgive him, never, for what he did to you, when your heart is so open. You would never, ever hurt anybody like that."

"I know," I say.

I love Yardley.

I ask again about George, and the memorial service, and shopping for college, and manage to end our conversation without ever explaining why I chose to go boating with Pfeff and Penny.

Your heart is so open (she said).

You would never, ever hurt anybody (she said).

That dirtbag made out with your slimeball sister

one of the worst things I've ever seen anyone do to anyone

a messed-up, whoring dirtbag of a person

I will never forgive him

you were together

you never had anybody before that

I don't think you should have to pretend

you would never, ever hurt anybody
I don't think you should have to pretend
you would never, ever hurt anybody.

All those words of Yardley's, they ring in my ears now. They jumble and tangle as I tell this story to my son Johnny.

Johnny sits in my Beechwood kitchen, asking me to help him understand our family, asking me to help him understand what it's like between me and my sisters, asking me to help him understand his own life and his death. *Did you ever get in trouble? . . . Tell me. What's the worst thing you did? Come on, spill it. The absolute worst thing you ever did, back then.*

I owe him the truth. I owe him everything.

If I do not stop lying, I worry that he and his friends will never be able to rest.

Yardley's words spill out of me as I tell Johnny about the call I had with her. Then I am saying them over and over, jumbling them without stopping, talking nonsense to myself, mixing them up, giving them new shapes. I cannot stop until I find the meaning I need.

And when I do, they become
words I need to live by.

71.

I DON'T THINK you should
pretend

don't pretend
don't pretend
don't pretend
Don't pretend you would never hurt anybody.

DON'T PRETEND YOU would never hurt anybody.

PART SEVEN

The Bonfire

72.

I HAVE NOT been truthful here.

I have, until now, done what I always do—which is to tell a story about our family in which I, the eldest, am the savior of two needy younger sisters.

But really, it was they who saved me.

I did say at the start of this story that I am a liar.

And I did explain that it is hard, nearly impossible, for me to tell this story honestly.

It does not want to come out, after being buried for so very many years, but recounting Yardley's words to Johnny has changed me.

Yardley spoke with so much love and indignation.

She was the only one who saw how hurt I was by Pfeff and Penny. The only person who said to me how much it mattered, that I didn't deserve it, that he had *been with me*. She was a witness to my feelings.

Don't pretend you would never hurt anybody.

I believe I am finally being punished.

My punishment is that Johnny is dead. Others are dead, too.

Those deaths can never be undone. The loss is a canyon, yawning wide, rippled with stones and striated with layers of clay and silt. I have been thrown into the canyon and will never be able to climb out. I must live out my days in this loss.

I deserve that.

I TOLD THE story of virtuous Cinderella and her
    unworthy,
    unlovable
    nonbiological sisters,
    stepsisters who commit violent acts out of jealousy, cutting
off their heels and toes.
    I also told the story of the stolen pennies, in which a
    guilty daughter
    is unable to rest and lives on after death, in agony
    because her crime has stained her conscience.
    And I told the story of Mr. Fox, in which a
    person who seems lovable
    has a very grand house and
    turns out to be a murderer.

HERE IS THE truth about what happened the night Lor Pfefferman died.

73.

I WOKE FROM Halcion sleep at one a.m., like I said before.
But not because Bess was opening my door.
    No one needed me.
    I woke chilled, and got up to drink some water and turn off
the fan that sat in my window. My head was foggy because I
had taken extra pills.

I heard a voice. A soft sound, outside my open window.

It said, "Please, Penny. Please."

Pfeff.

I understood immediately. Penny had chosen Pfeff over me, for the second time. The "please" he'd once said to me, he was now saying to her.

I thought then, as I told you before, that Penny

knew how her betrayal had wounded me the first time, she

knew how cracked and broken it made me feel, she

knew because I told her, and still,

none of that mattered in the face of her need to be wanted, to be the prettiest girl in the room, to make Erin jealous, to be the straight girl my parents wanted, to kiss a boy she thought was hot—

all of that mattered more than I did.

I was not her full sister. She could feel it. I was convinced of it. I know now that this idea is false, that families are made and earned and need not be built on biology, but in the moment, it seemed undeniable. I was not enough. I was not worth even a small amount of self-restraint.

I went downstairs and stepped outside via the mudroom door.

I ran along the walkways to the dock. There, I could see the outlines of the sailboat and Guzzler, black against the moonlit sea. And I could hear Pfeff again. "Please, Penny."

I was so angry at him for wanting her, and so angry at her for going near him again. How could she? After Erin was gone. After she'd said sorry, however unconvincingly. After she saw the hurt she'd caused.

74.

WHEN I TOOK up the board,
    and when I brought it down,
    over and over,
    with all the strength of my batter's swing,
    when I brought it down,
    my head spinning with jealousy and rage,
    I wasn't sure if I was hitting
    Pfeff, the boy
    who dumped me for my sister,
    who wouldn't apologize and wouldn't even talk, or
    if I was hitting
    my sister, my beloved sister,
    who'd had so many boyfriends,
    who was really our father's
    firstborn,
    who's always been the
    beauty of the family, and
    who has never, ever hesitated to take what was supposed to be
    mine.
    It was Pfeff I killed. But I could just as easily have killed Penny.
    I am Cinderella's terrible, jealous stepsister.
    I am the ghost whose crime went unpunished.
    I am Mr. Fox.

75.

I LOOKED DOWN at what I had done and Pfeff lay on the dock. His shirt was off. It was a plain gray T-shirt and it lay crumpled on the ground. His belt buckle was undone, and his jeans were unbuttoned, pulled partway down on his hips along with his boxers.

He was wearing sneakers. His socks had small red lobsters on them.

I touched his wrist, not knowing what else to do.

There was no beat.

Penny had run away, down the dock to the sand. She was knee-deep in the water, rubbing her hands together and cleaning her face, as if trying to wake herself from a nightmare.

As I turned to go to Penny, Bess appeared at the end of the dock.

"I came to see," she said softly, when I got near her. "They said they were going for a walk."

I realized I was still holding the board. I dropped it with a clatter.

Penny came out of the water toward us. "Carrie saved me," she said. "I don't know what you saw, Bess, but Pfeff—all of a sudden his shirt was off and he was like, tugging my pants down and his pants down."

She told us everything, about the *Please, Penny* and how scared she felt, and then she explained that I came to her rescue.

And all the while I thought, *I tried to kill my sister.*

Did I try to kill my sister? Did I know what I was doing? Or did I want to kill Pfeff?

I did not have an answer. And I do not have one now. But I can say this:

I was not rescuing Penny.

As she spoke, telling the story to Bess, it dawned on me that she saw me as the hero. The protector.

She threw her arms around me. "I'm so sorry, Carrie. I'm so sorry. I don't deserve you. I'm so glad you came."

For my sins, I was delivered my sister, loving, penitent, and grateful.

76.

THINGS HAPPENED AFTERWARD as I have told you.

We got supplies from Clairmont. We loaded the boat and scrubbed the dock.

I went back for whiskey and found Rosemary in the basement. I abandoned her in her time of need to finish the drowning of Lor Pfefferman.

We had to wait at Goose Cottage for Major and George to go to bed.

Penny held my hand.

Bess handled Pfeff's room. I made coffee.

I was startled to witness my sisters' unquestioning loyalty. I knew I was only half theirs, only half a Sinclair, and yet they stood next to me in this crisis as if the three of us were one. As if they believed me heroic and good.

We drove the boat out far, far.

We weighted his body with the anchor and gave it to the sea.

We burned the paper towels and talked about camping with Buddy Kopelnick. We slept, briefly, under the stars.

We came home and we lied.

77.

TWO WEEKS AFTER Pfeff's death, when there are only the five of us and the staff on the island, my parents plan Bonfire Night.

It's a thing we do every year in August. No real reason. After supper, we go down to the Big Beach and burn stuff. Old newspapers and copies of the New Yorker, recipes cut from magazines that Tipper no longer wants, the name cards from the Who Am I game, things like that.

We make s'mores and sing camp songs from when Tipper and Harris were young. "Show Me the Way to Go Home." "Hot Time in the Old Town Tonight." "Be Kind to Your Fine Feathered Friends."

In my bedroom the day of the bonfire, I find an old

notebook, one that I wrote and sketched in back when I was the girl I used to be. In it, I now write:

I, Caroline Lennox Taft Sinclair, killed Lawrence Pfefferman.

I killed Lawrence Pfefferman.

I killed Lawrence Pfefferman.

I write it over and over until the words cover several pages. Then I take the notebook with me to Bonfire Night.

As we burn Harris's magazines and Tipper's fabric scraps, as we sing the silly songs we have sung together since childhood, I throw the book into the flames.

This is the only time I will ever tell, I say to myself.

I have burned the confession.

It is over.

And I never do tell anyone, until now.

MANY PEOPLE COMMIT crimes when they are young. Violent acts, felonies. In lots of states, once you come of age, you can seal your juvenile records. In other states, your records might be expunged.

The idea is that we can be forgiven for terrible things we do as children. That we can be redeemed, given the chance to start again.

I cannot say whether Pfeff would have been redeemed. Sometimes I think of him as incorrigible—I believe that he would have taken what he wanted from Penny and from countless girls after her, had he not been stopped. Saying no but not like she means it, he said. She doesn't account for a guy being drunk or revved up or whatever.

I think, then, that nothing would ever have taught him right from wrong. Guys like him go to prison or run the country, and in neither case do they become anything more than rapists who fancy themselves rogues.

Other times, I think of his deep love for life, of his enthusiasms and his generosities, his shame and his small kindnesses. And I think he could have become a good man.

Either way, I do not think he deserved to die.

I know he was capable of terrible things.

But so was I.

THE POLICE STOP by one more time before the end of the summer. They shake hands with my father like old friends when he and I meet them on the dock. Everyone walks up to Clairmont, where Tipper offers cold drinks and fresh-baked shortbread. Bess and Penny come down to listen and be decorative.

The officers tell us that Pfeff's status is now Missing, Presumed Dead. Given that he was last seen swimming in open water, they explain that they can "presume death" without waiting any longer.

Tipper says the family has already had a memorial.

The police say that often happens. Families need closure. Communities need to grieve.

"We should have gone," says Penny, sounding upset. "You didn't tell us about it."

"We couldn't go," says Harris sharply.

"Yardley went," I say. "She told me about it, after."

"We could have gotten to Philadelphia." Penny is a wonderful actress.

"Not without a tremendous hassle," Harris says. "And the Pfeffermans wouldn't have wanted us. They wouldn't like the reminder."

"I sent flowers," says Tipper. "Don't worry."

When the officers are gone, Harris asks to see me in his study.

78.

THE STUDY IS a large room at the back of the ground floor, decorated with manly objects I suppose could be described as trophies: those original New Yorker cartoons in frames, a taxidermied swordfish, shelves and shelves of books. Harris sits behind the desk and I take a seat opposite him.

"Now that the boy has been declared dead," my father says, "I want to tell you that I ran out of sleeping pills a few weeks back."

I stare at him and try not to move my face.

Can he possibly know I took them? Did he count how many he had in the bottle?

He continues. "I ran out of sleeping pills, and before your mother got me some more, I had a few sleepless nights. Do you see where I am going?"

I shake my head.

"Well. One night, I found myself awake around two a.m. I couldn't get back to sleep. I tossed and turned for a good long while, read my book and so on, but then I gave up. I thought I'd heat some warm milk, maybe make some cocoa to help me sleep."

He stops talking and lights a cigarette, leaning back in his chair. "I looked in on you girls," he continues. "I do that when I can't sleep. I have, ever since you were babies. I like knowing you're all safe and sound in your beds. Now, sometimes this summer you all have been out late, over at Goose with the boys. I get it. I don't worry about you. But at this point, it's about two-thirty in the morning and I'm expecting you're asleep. But you are not. Not you, not Bess, not Penny. Hm. I begin to be a little concerned. So I go downstairs, pour myself a glass of bourbon, and step onto the porch."

My hands feel cold. My throat is closed.

He takes a drag on his cigarette and ashes it carefully into an ivory dish. "I gave up on the hot cocoa, you see, because I was curious. I walked out of the yard, and when I passed the turnoff to the dock, there was movement on the water. What do you think I saw?"

"I don't know."

"Guzzler, rowing out to sea. You and Penny at the oars. Bess hanging over the edge with her fingers in the water. I watched until the boat was out of sight. And I thought, *Why are they rowing?* I didn't put it past you silly things to take the boat out in the middle of the night. I was a boy, once. But just the three of you? Without Major, George, or Lor? And why not use the motor? What could be such a secret that you'd row *that* far out? It's not easy work."

He taps his fingers on the wood of his desk, looks out the window and then at me. "So I went back to the house," he continues. "I got one of the heavy flashlights we keep in the mudroom and I went down to the dock to see what you had been doing. The dogs came with me." Another drag on the cigarette. "And a funny thing, Carrie. Right away, we all four noticed a strong smell at the end of the dock. Dogs were sniffing around. And do you know what the smell was?"

"No."

"Bleach. *How is that?* I wondered. *What are my girls doing with bleach in the middle of the night?*"

My hands will not stop shaking. I twist my fingers together and breathe slowly.

"The dock looked wet, I noticed," Harris goes on. "And when I looked around a little further, I noticed that board. You know, the warped one I pulled up?"

I do not answer.

He speaks very, very slowly. "Do you know the board I'm talking about, Carrie?"

"Yes, I do."

"All right, then. That board smelled of bleach even more than the rest of the dock did. I picked it up and it was soaking wet. I shone my flashlight on the length of it. And then I shone my flashlight on the nails. And do you know what?"

"What?"

"The nails were sticky."

79.

I FEEL LIKE all the blood has left my head. I might faint. "You took the board," I say. "That's why it went missing."

"I took the board," he says. "I brought it up to the house and

274

I scrubbed it over the sink. Then I went to the attic and stashed it behind a pile of boxes. I didn't know *why* I was doing it. I didn't know *why* my daughters had gone rowing in the motor-boat in the dark of night, leaving the dock stinking of bleach, and a heavy board they had tried—and failed—to properly clean lying there with some hellish sticky substance on it—but I sure as sure was going to protect them, no matter what was going on."

He loves me, I realize.

He treats me like I am his flesh and blood. He cares what happens to me, no matter what I've done.

For the first time since I learned about my parentage, I feel myself completely part of my father's family. I belong.

Harris goes on. "In the morning, I learn that the boy seems to have been the victim of a shark attack. The three of you are screaming and carrying on like hysterics, but I put two and two together. I'm damned glad I had the sense to move that board before the police arrived, I tell you."

He stops. Leans forward in his chair. Stares at me.

I stare back.

I will not tell him what happened.

I cannot tell him. About not being loved enough, about Pfeff, about Penny, about what I did and why. Even though he knows someone did something and we covered it up, he cannot know the full ugly truth of the matter.

"Do you have anything to add?" he asks finally.

"No."

"All right, then." He leans back. I know he is curious, but silence on difficult topics will always earn his respect. "So we got through it, and we got through it," he continues, "and when things were settled down, I told your mother it was time for Bonfire Night." He gestures toward the beach. "Now that board is nothing but ash and smoke."

"You had the dock rebuilt."

"Well, we can't have anyone wondering where that one board went. Or noticing that lingering smell of bleach." He smiles with tight lips. "Tipper wanted a new dock anyway, so she's happy."

"Why are you telling me this?"

He tilts his head to look at me. "Your mother says she told you about Buddy Kopelnick."

I nod.

"So."

I wait.

He explains: "The way I figure it, you—unlike your sisters—might need a reminder that this family is very important to me."

"I know it is."

"I will do a lot to protect it. And that includes you, as well as Penny and Bess. Do you understand?"

"Yes."

He puts out his cigarette and arranges some papers on his desk. "I told your mother I only went down to the kitchen that night. That I drank a nightcap, and read for a while, and came back to bed. I am letting you know what I really did so that you can stop mooning about Buddy Kopelnick, stop messing around with my sleeping pills, and be the Sinclair I have always considered you to be."

We stare at one another in silence for a moment.

" 'No way out but through,' " I say.

Harris smiles. "Robert Frost. Yes." He clasps his hands. "We will carry on as usual. Chin up, all right?"

"All right."

I realize then, and understand even more in retrospect, that we have gotten away with murder not only because we were clever, and not only because we were lucky, but because my father helped us. Because he has resources—an attic, a bonfire, the money for a new deck. Because the police believe a man like him is an upstanding citizen. Therefore, they assume that girls like us—educated girls from a "good family"—they assume we are telling the truth. We get the benefit of the doubt, the presumption of innocence, conferred by our family name.

Harris stands, as if to dismiss me, so I stand, as well. "I believe your mother is planning Midsummer Ice Cream for tonight," he says, smiling again. "The Hadleys and the Bakers arrive at four o'clock."

"I'll help her," I say.

"That's my girl."

80.

A COUPLE HOURS later, the Hadleys and the Bakers tumble off the big boat and into Goose Cottage.

There are little kids and parents. Everyone wants to go swimming, then go on the sailboat. The adults want to drink cocktails and eat cold lobster salad on warm potato buns, cucumber salad with dill, and thick slices of cantaloupe. The children need someone to teach them croquet.

After supper, Tipper and Luda set out Midsummer Ice Cream on the porch—five kinds of homemade ice cream, custards made ahead all week and churned in the big machine. They've made peanut-brittle, pale green fresh-mint, vanilla, chocolate, and strawberry. Tipper serves hot fudge, butterscotch sauce, whipped cream, and walnuts in ceramic dishes. The music is old barbershop quartets, and the tablecloths are striped red and white like peppermint sticks.

We each make our own, layering whipped cream and nuts with ice cream and sauce, holding our curved glass parfait dishes and dipping into them with long silver spoons.

When the guests are all served and my parents are gently drunk, I walk to the far end of the porch and sit in the hammock with a dish of fresh-mint and hot fudge.

My mother laughs at someone's joke. Bess shouts as she helps the youngest Hadley with his croquet mallet. The children have all spilled off the porch onto the lawn. Some of them are spinning in the tire swing. The women sit on the steps, watching the kids; the men have gone down to the bottom of the yard, where they can look out at the sea and smoke cigars.

I spoon ice cream into my mouth and close my eyes.

I want

to escape the tyranny of this family's expectations and make instead some new life, some city life.

I want

to stop carrying obsessive thoughts of stories I hear on the news and instead to reach out, understand, see with my own eyes.

But even more,

I want

to be in this family, messed up as it is.

I want

to be my father's daughter,

to solve my sisters' problems,

to be the one who receives my mother's black pearls,

to be Rosemary's favorite.

To be a Sinclair, and to have the security and good standing that all our

hard work and

dirty money and

unearned privilege and

intelligence has bought us.

I see that now.

It may be my greatest weakness, this family. But I will not leave.

Penny comes and sits next to me. She has filled her parfait dish with only hot fudge. It is just the two of us, here on the hammock side of the porch. We are practically alone.

"Having fun?" I ask her.

She spoons fudge into her mouth. I wait for her to swallow.

"Did you ever find out about that picture?" she says, instead of answering me.

"What picture?" I ask—though I know what picture.

"The one you thought was Uncle Chris or whatever," she says. "With the face scratched out. That I said was Daddy."

I turn to look directly at her. I cannot read her expression. "Why?"

"I'm asking," says Penny. "I kinda couldn't stop thinking

about it. That secret photo of Tipper's. And I thought—it could be Buddy Kopelnick. The guy who wanted to take you camping and gave you all the jelly beans. Don't you think?"

I look at her again.

She leans over and kisses my cheek, her lips warm from the fudge. "I didn't tell Bess," she says.

PART EIGHT
After

81.

SUMMER AFTER SUMMER, though I get older, Rosemary is always ten years old.

I ask her if she is lonely during the winters, when the island is empty.

"I'm just asleep or something, Carrie," she tells me. "It's fine. I'm cozy. Then I wake up."

She visits me the summer I am eighteen, when I have graduated from North Forest and am headed to Vassar College. I chose Vassar because it's only ninety minutes from New York City, the closest I could get. That year I am taking both codeine and sleeping pills during the day. I spend much of my summer asleep or stupidly numb.

She visits the summer I am nineteen, too, after my first year of college, when Penny and I both have boyfriends visiting. Penny is forcing herself into the shape my parents wish for her. A straight girl, a Sinclair, the stiff upper lip, a daughter to be proud of. She is headed to Bryn Mawr, though. An all-women's college.

That summer Penny and I drink and forget, reveling in sex and loud music and excursions to the bars in Oak Bluffs on Martha's Vineyard, where no one ever asks for ID. We ignore Bess, who responds by insinuating herself with our parents, being the hard worker with the bright smile, the noncomplainer, the athlete, the well-read dinner-table conversationalist. Rosemary sees me only now and then, that year, bribing me to read to her with potato chips she's stolen from the Clairmont pantry.

She visits the summer after my second year of college, when at twenty years old I have left Vassar for a rehab center. My time at the center involves weeks of withdrawal and therapy and hope and support—but when I get to the island, I slip back into old habits and take any pills I can lay my hands on.

I am no credit to the family.

Rosemary visits the following summer, as well, but that year, when I am twenty-one and have stumbled through a third year of college hardly attending any classes, I spend June and July back in rehabilitation. I don't arrive on Beechwood until August.

I get to the island a little heavier, very fragile, but sober and optimistic. I began making jewelry in the rehab center: rings and bracelets of thin bands of silver twisted around one another. I would like to learn to work with stones. Or maybe with fine metals. There are studios in New York where I can take classes.

I have a sober friend from rehab, Deja. I am quitting college and will share an apartment with her in September.

I hope dearly that I have kicked the pills for good this time.

It turns out to be true.

I see Rosemary only once that August. I wake one morning and she is sitting at the foot of my bed, eating a blackberry muffin. She has broken it into several pieces inside a yellow china bowl from downstairs.

"Hi, buttercup," I say. "You're up early."

"You sleep late," she says. "I like to get a muffin when they're still warm."

284

"You can heat it in the microwave," I tell her. "Twenty seconds."

"It's not the same."

Rosemary looks tired. Her skin is pale underneath her tan. She's wearing a Muppets T-shirt and worn jean shorts.

"Are you okay?" I ask. "I've missed you. It's good to see your freckle face." I sit up and lean my head on her small, bony shoulder.

"I'm not really that okay," she says. "I like coming to see you, but I'm so, so tired."

"How come?"

"I can't come here forever," says Rosemary. "I mean, I want to, but it's like—it takes a whole lot of energy." She pokes her muffin crumbs with a finger. "My bones hurt and it's hard to keep my eyes open."

"I thought maybe I imagined you," I tell her. "I thought maybe it was the pills, making me see you. But I don't take them anymore. And you're still here."

She laughs. "I'm totally here."

"Good."

"You take way too many pills, Carrie. You used to, I mean."

"So they tell me."

"You have to get better," says Rosemary. She is so small and earnest. "I can't make you better, but I keep coming because I'm worried."

"Is that why you come? Because you're worried about me?"

"Um-hm."

"I thought you came because you needed me."

She shakes her head. "I was worried you'd be an addict and do terrible things, and you did do them." Her face crumples and she begins to cry. "You did that one thing, first. It wasn't what I thought you'd do. It wasn't what I thought, at all. But then there was the cover-up and I couldn't stop you with the drugs and I've been so worried," she says, sniffling. "I can't stop anything. I'm just a kid. But I keep coming because I can't stop when you're not okay."

"You thought—you thought I would kill myself?" I say, understanding. "After you died?"

Rosemary nods. "But you didn't. You did him instead."

I didn't know she knew. About Pfeff. A true Sinclair, she never said a word.

I begin to cry, as well. Because Rosemary has loved me knowing the most hateful thing about me.

Because she is dead, and not really here to love me at all.

Because Bess and Penny have stood by me and will never tell, but our bond will always be stained with the blood on our hands. Our sisterhood will never recover. We will always be each other's secret-keepers, and it is my fault that we are this way.

My darling Rosemary, she has been pushing herself for four summers to come back, worried I would cut my wrists or drown my own unworthy self, then worried I would kill myself with pills, burdened by knowledge no little kid should ever have.

She should have been riding her bike up and down the wooden walkways. She should have been developing a figure and outgrowing her stuffed lions and learning to put on makeup and reading Judy Blume books and folding down the pages on the sexual bits. She should be having crushes, on pop stars and athletes and ordinary people. She would have been

286

starting boarding school, and I could have sent her letters and cards, tucking cash into the envelopes.

Dearie Rosemary (I'd write),

Rehab was hard, this second time. I won't lie. I was scared I wouldn't make it. But I am handling things okay here in New York City.

My roommate, Deja, waits tables, and I am working behind the counter at a boulangerie on Bleecker Street. The bakery smells so good, all the time. You would love it. But the bakers themselves are very bitchy in the back room.

The front of the shop is cute and painted blue. It is like working in the sky. When I come home at Christmas I will bring a bag of croissants.

I take jewelry class on Monday nights, and we can have studio time any night of the week, so I go in there a lot of evenings and do things with PLIERS. (I like pliers.) Other nights, I go out with friends, to coffee shops that are open twenty-four hours, or for Chinese food. There are a couple people I know from North Forest here, finishing college in the city, and a couple new friends from the jewelry class. Maybe I will try ceramics, too. I did a one-day workshop and it was really messy. I think you would like it.

I think about you every day, buttercup. Here
is some money so you can buy stuff without
having to ask Mother. I hope the beasts of North
Forest are being good to you and your tennis
game is vicious. (Daddy said it's vicious, that's
the word he used.) Anyhow, we will play next
summer on the island. And swim. And generally
loaf around. And you will be my favorite thing
about spending time on Beechwood, and I will
endeavor (most seriously) to be your favorite
thing, too.

> One love, two loves,
> a million loves
> from your big sister,

> Caroline Lennox
> Taft Sinclair

That is what I would have written her.

I can see my own letters so clearly, as if I were already living that life, as if Rosemary were really at North Forest, playing
tennis and making friends. I can see them even as I sit next to
Rosemary's exhausted little ghost body now, sobbing and strok-
ing her hair. I wrap my arms around her fragile frame and tell
her I love her.

Relief floods through me, even as I weep, because I can see
my own letters, and that means I can see a future beyond this
island, beyond this addiction. Although I will
never, ever escape what I have done, and although I might

never forgive myself, and although I will

never free myself of the Sinclair family, and will

always want my father's love and the place in my family it confers, and

although I will never love Bess and Penny free of resentments and obligations and shared secrets and guilt,

I will,

in a small way,

in a limited way,

move on.

"I want you to stop worrying," I tell Rosemary. I breathe slowly and my crying stops.

"You always say that." She sniffs. "You always tell me cheerful things, like Mother used to, and you want to play games and read stories, and that's nice. But you see, I'm still so worried. I'm so tired, Carrie. I don't know what to do."

"I want you to rest."

"I need to." She takes a tissue and wipes her nose. "I don't feel good here, even this one visit. It hurts to be here, but I'm scared to not come."

"I am not going to kill myself," I whisper. "I was not and I am not."

"For real?"

"Yes. Is that what you need to hear?"

"Kind of," she says. "But you—" She gestures around, as if there's a bottle of pills somewhere. "You can die doing that stuff. That's like a fact that people know."

What can I say to reassure her? What can I say that will be true? "I have been really sick and sad," I tell her after a minute.

"Sick in lots of ways. And guilty. And ashamed and angry. I have been all these things for a very long time, and trying to numb myself out of it and forget my way out of it, burying it all as deep as I can bury it. You know what I mean?"

Rosemary nods.

"But I am telling you, now, all these feelings. So they're not buried anymore."

"Okay. So what?"

"What are the feelings?"

"Yah."

"Okay. Um . . . I have been sad, because you died. And that still feels fresh, nearly as fresh as when it first happened. And I've been so angry at Pfeff and Penny, and so horrified and ashamed of what I did, I couldn't live with myself. I've been punishing myself for that, and at the same time, I've been escaping from it all. The pills let me do both at once, I think."

Rosemary sniffs. "That's strange," she says. "'Cause you took them before. Before he died."

"There's not just one reason I took them. It's a tangled-up mess of reasons," I say. "And I can't promise to be happy, and I can't promise to be well, even, but I am telling you how I feel because telling you is showing you that I'm not trying to be numb anymore. I'm going to live with the sadness and the shame, and actually feel them or whatever, and somehow not hate and punish myself so much. I'm going to just go on, one day and then another day."

"And then another day and another day," says Rosemary.

"Yeah, you got it."

I will go to New York in September.

I will find a job and live with Deja.

I will stay sober.

I will meet people. Learn to make jewelry.

This new life won't redeem me. It won't fix the world crises that still bubble and boil at the back of my mind, hot and sad. It won't change the fact that I killed a man, a rotten man in many ways, but still a human whose life should not have ended. It won't change that I covered it up, that *we* covered it up.

But still. I can see that I have a future. And maybe that is enough.

I do not love my father's way of thinking, but much of it has become mine anyhow. Perhaps he and Robert Frost are right on this one: "No way out but through."

"Okay," says Rosemary. She blows her nose loudly. "That was all super mushy."

"Yeah."

"But all right. I won't worry so much anymore."

"You can go rest?"

"I think so."

She climbs into my lap, smelling of suntan lotion and muffin. "Snuggle snuggle," she says.

We sit there for a bit, not saying anything.

"Is this goodbye, buttercup?" I finally ask.

"Um-hm."

We sit for a little longer, and then Rosemary climbs out of my lap. She takes my hand and I climb out of bed.

She leads me out of my room, down the hall, and up the stairs to my parents' floor. Their bedroom door is closed.

We climb the steps to the turret.

82.

THE ROUND ATTIC room is still stacked with boxes of Rosemary's books and toys. The rolled carpets are still there, and the trunks. "Do you know my stuffed lions live here?" she asks. "And my 8 Ball?"

"Totally."

She opens a cardboard box full of lions and rummages through it. "I love them all," she says, "but Shampoo is the best for sleeping with." She holds up her favorite lion, washed so many times it is very floppy. "Okay, now I'm going to be able to sleep super well."

"You can take Shampoo with you?"

"I don't know for sure, but I think so."

"And where do you go now?"

Rosemary walks to the turret window and pushes up the sash. It opens about a foot. She pushes up the screen.

"Oh no, buttercup," I say.

"I could swim out to sea, but I don't like swimming anymore," she says. "This is the best way. And I have Shampoo with me."

She pushes a box beneath the window and climbs onto the sill.

"Don't go," I say nonsensically.

Rosemary shakes her head and tears begin to fall. "I have to."

I start toward her, wanting to hug her one last time, but

she is through the opening and out the window in a flash. She stands on the ledge, Shampoo in one hand. "I love you, Carrie," she calls. "Goodbye and good luck and be good."

She jumps.

I rush to the window and thrust my head out, looking for her thin little body on the rocks below—but it isn't there. I look into the sky and she isn't there, either.

The island is peaceful in the morning sunshine.

Rosemary is gone and all I can do is keep my promises to her.

83.

NOW.

My son Johnny and I sit in the Red Gate kitchen. Between us are cups of cold cocoa and the remains of a blackberry pie Bess made.

One of Penny's dogs, Grendel, has taken a shine to me this summer and lies at my feet. My sisters are here on the island with us, but they are nestled into bed in other houses, sleeping their agonized sleeps. They do not see ghosts.

Johnny cannot help me, except by listening. And I cannot help him, except by telling this story. But we have had some good last times together.

He is very tired, I can tell. He can't keep visiting Beechwood Island much longer. His hands shake and his eyes are bloodshot. He moves slowly, as if in pain. It is nearly time for him to leave, and maybe my story has given him what he needs to say goodbye and rest.

I lay my head on the table. A wave of exhaustion runs through me. The clock reads 1:45 a.m.

Johnny stands and runs his fingers through his hair. "Thanks for telling me all that," he says gently.

"Sure thing," I say.

"It was kind of a lot."

"I know." I sit up to look at him.

"Can't have been easy." He picks up a spoon and eats a large bite of pie, straight from the plate. "I'm gonna have to think about it, I guess."

"Okay," I say. He drops his spoon back into the pie plate. "You done with that?" I ask.

"Yeah. Just eating for fun. I'm not hungry." I stand and cover the pie with foil.

Johnny shakes his head. "God, I don't know what to even think. All of that's true?"

I look him in the eye. "All of it."

"I can't all the way deal." He comes over and gives me a kiss on the cheek. "I'll bounce for now," he says. "But I'll come see you tomorrow. Sound good?"

"Mm-hm."

"You all right?"

"I think so."

"I'm gonna go meet the others at Cuddledown, then."

"It's so late," I say.

"We're up all hours."

"Okay."

"You go to sleep. I'm living the nightlife while I can," he says.

I nod and watch him as he heads to the door. Then I follow and watch some more as he heads through the yard and closes its red gate behind him.

I AM CINDERELLA'S stepsister.

I am the ghost whose crime went unpunished.

I am Mr. Fox.

I am white cotton and sandy feet, old money and lilacs, yes—and yet my insides are made of seawater, warped wood, and rusty nails.

My name is Caroline Lennox Taft Sinclair, and I am the bastard daughter of Tipper Sinclair and Buddy Kopelnick, who loved each other deeply and foolishly.

I am a former athlete. I used to have a different face.

Yes, it's true I killed a man and threw his body in the ocean, and that may be the primary thing you choose to remember about me. But now that I have told that story, I think I may be able to tell a new story about myself.

Once upon a time, there was a girl whose sisters were loyal to her.

Once upon a time, there was a girl whose father claimed her and protected her, even though she was not his own.

This girl recovered from a narcotics addiction and was stronger for it.

Once upon a time, there was a woman who had children— and though she wronged them in some ways, she was good to them in many others. And they loved her.

Once upon a time, after her divorce, this woman fell in love with a man who would make sacrifices for her. He made her laugh, and life with him was always interesting. And in turn, she fought for him. Though he didn't know everything about her, he loved her with a joyful heart. He said what he needed from her. And though it was hard for her to give him what he needed, and though she had to anger her father and quarrel with her sisters, she eventually found a way.

Once upon a time, this woman lost her eldest son and thought she might descend into darkness forever. But then her son returned to her as a ghost. He met her with open arms and forgave her worst trespasses, before he had to leave.

And so she began to heal.

Once upon a time, this woman chose to stay loyal to her family. She could have left them. They weren't easy. But she chose them and accepted the consequences.

Going forward, she did her best to live a

joyful

but conscious

life.

That wasn't easy, either. But she tried.

PERHAPS I AM Lady Mary after all. After all, she pulls the severed hand from the pocket of her wedding dress, where she has hidden it. Do you remember? She pulls the severed hand and holds it up for everyone to see. She exposes the horrors she has uncovered, the corpse she has hidden beneath white linen. She forces her brothers to bear witness. This, says Lady Mary to her brothers, *this is the worst I have seen. I expose it because I do not want such horrors to be my future.*

This, I said to my son, this is the worst I have seen and the worst I have done.

Please bear witness.

I do not want such horrors to determine my future.

What does Lady Mary do after that? Well, what would any of us do after pulling a chunk of bloody corpse out of our pocket?

I'm sure she washes her hands. And burns her wedding dress.

I imagine she says some words of sorrow over that poor dead woman's bloody hand and consigns it to a grave.

And to Mr. Fox, killed by her brothers, she says, "Good riddance."

Later in the day, perhaps, Lady Mary goes down to her kitchen, where the uneaten wedding breakfast has been shoved into the fridge. She finds some lovely carrot muffins and some special sausages. She brews a large pot of strong tea and heats the sausages in a pan until they fill the kitchen with their meaty smell.

She calls her brothers.

The sun rises and I call my sisters. My remaining son. My nieces and nephew. My father. My love.

They come to my house, or come downstairs with bedhead. Someone makes eggs and someone else puts ketchup and silverware on the table. The dogs get underfoot and Grendel steals a sausage. My younger son asks if he can eat the blackberry pie from yesterday. I say, "Fine, there's not much left, but do it."

The breakfast is quiet. Some people read. The little boys eat quickly and run out to the yard. The teenagers make coffee and dose it with sugar and cream.

My sisters and I step onto the Red Gate porch and finish our second cups of tea there. We are very small, next to the ocean, beneath the open sky.

I do not think it will always be this way.

ACKNOWLEDGMENTS

Many people helped with this book, in its creation and as it found its way out into the world. Colleen Fellingham, Dominique Cimina, Rebecca Gudelis, Mary McCue, John Adamo, Christine Labov, Barbara Marcus, Adrienne Waintraub, and everyone on my team at Penguin Random House, I am very grateful for your support and hard work. My editor, Beverly Horowitz, that goes for you x 100. Elizabeth Kaplan, Jonathan Ehrlich, and Kassie Evashevski, thank you for your creative and stalwart advocacy. Gratitude to the folks at Allen & Unwin and at Hotkey for their early enthusiasm and support.

Len Jenkin did mystery novel exercises with me in the early stages of the book. Ivy Aukin, Gayle Forman, and Sarah Mlynowski gave insightful early reads, and Gayle gave me the push I needed to begin this project in the first place. Bob was terrific. Hazel Aukin let me borrow and rewrite some of our best conversations. The Minkinnen/Bourne family made raucous sausage jokes and allowed me to write them down. Daniel was excellent and had my back at all times. The cats were useless, but I'm grateful to them anyway.

ABOUT THE AUTHOR

E. Lockhart is the author of the #1 *New York Times* bestseller *We Were Liars*. She also invented a super-hero for DC Comics. Her books include *Whistle: A New Gotham City Hero*; *Again Again*; *The Disreputable History of Frankie Landau-Banks*, a National Book Award Finalist and a Printz Honor Book; and *Genuine Fraud*, a *New York Times* bestseller and a finalist for the *LA Times* Book Prize.

EmilyLockhart.com
@elockhartbooks

@elockhart

Bonus Material

AUTHOR Q&A

QUESTIONS AND ANSWERS

BY E. LOCKHART

I hate you for breaking my heart.
Thank you.

Seriously. Why do you do this? It's very upsetting.
I am trying to get the inside of my brain out onto the page.
That's the kind of stuff that's in there.

Did you grow up like the Sinclair family?
I did not. My family growing up was just me and my mom.
For some of that time we lived in communal living situations.
She is a psychotherapist and was raised Christian but now
practices a new age religion. My dad is a playwright and a
secular Jewish person.

So how did you end up writing about this kind of exclusive
world?
I spent many summers on Martha's Vineyard with my maternal

grandparents, and some of the texture of Sinclair family life comes from their (more modest) summer ways. Also, I was a scholarship student at some fancy educational institutions, where I had friends who lived pretty large. In other words, I had one foot in and one foot out of a couple different highly privileged environments, and I often write from that position.

Do you believe in ghosts?
If we're talking about actual spectral beings who require exorcists or ghostbusters or whatever, then no. But inside my head there are many.

Why publish a prequel to We Were Liars eight years after the first book came out?
I didn't have an idea for a story before that. Occasionally someone would ask about a sequel or a prequel, and I just didn't have an idea I thought worthwhile. Then one day, I did. I decided to think of the two novels as related to one another like an anthology TV show in which thematic material repeats in a new season, with different meaning or a fresh approach. Here is another drug-addicted heiress, another difficult romance, intense summer friendships, and unspeakable truths told through fairy tales. But (I hope) a very different journey.

Where did you get the idea for what happens?
I started by thinking about the three Sinclair sisters on this island, separated from the rest of the world. What was their shared wound? And what would upend their story world? The answers: the loss of Rosemary and a boatload of cute boys.

Why are the dogs named McCartney, Albert, Wharton, and Reepicheep?

In *We Were Liars*, Tipper and Harris named their dogs after royalty—Prince Philip and Fatima. That gesture is a form of self-aggrandizement, I suppose, and a sign of their sense of entitlement to cultural artifacts not their own. Here, the dogs are named for Paul McCartney (rock royalty), Prince Albert of Monaco, and Edith Wharton (literary royalty).

Uncle Dean is a fan of C. S. Lewis's Narnia books. Pevensie is the last name of the family in the first of those novels. Reepicheep is the name of a heroic talking mouse in Narnia.

How do you come up with plot twists?

I am not really sure. A lot of my writing comes from somewhere unconscious. But I do write out the basics of a story in a pitch document that I show my publisher before I begin to truly write a novel. And I revise that pitch over and over until I feel I have a story that will turn out surprising (if it's that kind of book). Then I worry a lot about whether I will be able to carry the whole thing off. It takes significant rewriting to set up a twist effectively.

What is Rosemary's song?

"Don't You (Forget About Me)" by Simple Minds. You can find it on the mix tape below.

Why did you write about Carrie instead of Penny? Penny is much more important in *We Were Liars*.

In *We Were Liars*, Carrie is the one who sees ghosts. Penny does not, so I felt she could not be my protagonist for this tale. Also, Carrie is the sister who eventually (after many awful missteps) challenges the family and wins (in *We Were Liars*). She will marry Ed and still retain her connection with Harris.

What else should I read that's kinda like *Family of Liars*?
Two faves: *Boy, Snow, Bird* by Helen Oyeyemi: a morally complicated fairy tale reinvention, clever as clever can be. And *A Deadly Education* by Naomi Novik: teenagers trapped in a magic school, navigating a toxic and authoritative culture and the evil that lies inside them.

I know "Cinderella." But are "Mr. Fox" and "The Stolen Pennies" real fairy tales?
Yes. "Mr. Fox" was originally collected by folklorist Joseph Jacobs. "The Stolen Pennies" was collected by the Brothers Grimm. I retold all three fairy tales in my own words, bringing out themes I thought were important to Carrie's story.

Why did you pick those two tales?
I went looking for stories of ghosts and terrible boyfriends.

Do you have other books with fairy tale elements?
Besides this and *We Were Liars*, I wrote a collection of tales for children called *Brave Red, Smart Frog: A New Book of Old Tales*. It is published under my legal name, Emily Jenkins.

Will there be a movie?
I really don't know.

Okay, some lightweight questions. What's your favorite coffee drink?

An almond-milk latte, hot.

Favorite candy?

Tony's Chocolonely milk chocolate bar.

Do you have a green thumb, like Tipper?

I kill all plants. But I am a good baker, so I'm like her that way.

What's the last thing you baked?

Blackberry crumble.

Do you collect anything, like Harris?

No. I am something of a minimalist. But I do adore looking at other people's collections.

Is anything about you like Carrie?

I have been neither an addict nor a criminal. But I have a lot of issues with my teeth and jaw. I have done things I am ashamed of. I have wrestled with forgiveness. I have dreamed of a different life and not known how to get it. I have loved unfaithful people. I have had friends betray me as Penny betrays Carrie. I have felt unlovable. I have loved a number of ten-year-olds who were magically unique and delightful.

SOME THINGS TO EAT AND DRINK

HERE IS WHAT to eat while you argue about *Family of Liars.*

Things You Might Buy: Nibbles and Drinks

premade lemonade, plus fresh lemons and limes to
    squeeze into it
sugar-free soda (Bess drinks this)
roasted, salted cashew nuts
black olives—kalamata if possible
yellow cherry tomatoes
blackberries
cucumbers (peeled, sliced, and sprinkled
    with salt and pepper)
thin, buttery cookies such as Pepperidge Farm Bordeaux

A Snack Mix to Make: George's Special

This is the snack mix George makes for the last viewing of *Mary Poppins*. I will confess, it does not sound good to me. But teenagers I know strongly disagree, so have at it.

12 ounces semisweet chocolate chips (usually a whole bag)

8 ounces small roundish pretzels, like Snyder's of Hanover Mini Pretzels or Snaps (half a family-size bag)

9 ounces Frosted Mini-Wheats cereal (usually half a box)

5 ounces mini marshmallows (usually half a bag)

salt

Mix the items together in a bowl.

Taste it. Does it need salt? If it does, add some.

Tipper's Lemon Pound Cake

This is the lemon pound cake Tipper makes in the book. It's adapted by me from a cake by Deb Perelman of Smitten Kitchen. It's easy to find Perelman's original recipe online by searching "Smitten Kitchen lemon pound cake." But I did make some adjustments.

A nice thing about this recipe is it makes two loaf cakes, so you can bring one to your book conversation and save one for yourself. It makes a good gift, too. I wrap mine in foil and tie a bow on.

INGREDIENTS FOR CAKE:

1 cup (2 sticks) unsalted butter, at room temperature

3 cups all-purpose flour (plus more for dusting the pans)

1/3 cup grated lemon zest (you'll need a bag of lemons for this)

1/4 cup fresh lemon juice (supplement with bottled if you don't have enough)

2 cups granulated sugar

4 large eggs, at room temperature

1/2 teaspoon baking powder

1/2 teaspoon baking soda

1 teaspoon kosher salt

3/4 cup buttermilk, at room temperature

1 teaspoon vanilla extract

INGREDIENTS FOR SOAKING SYRUP:

1/2 cup granulated sugar

1/2 cup lemon juice

Directions:

Preheat your oven to 350° F.

Grease two loaf pans with butter, then flour them.

Zest your lemons—in other words, grate the rind off them. If you want to make things easy, you can cut the yellow part of the peel off with a knife and then zap it in the blender, if you have one. That way makes more dishes, but it's quicker. Otherwise you'll get the peel off the lemons with a grater.

Squeeze your lemons. Chase any seeds around and throw them out. Make sure you have enough juice for the cake *and* the soaking syrup. If you don't, supplement with bottled lemon juice, or get some more lemons.

Make the soaking syrup by heating the ingredients together on the stove until they look syrupy. It's only *some* of your lemon juice in there. Save the rest for the cake. Let that cool.

Cream the butter and sugar together. Beat these a really long time (5 minutes) at a high speed, so that the mixture gets super fluffy.

Add eggs, one at a time, mixing on medium speed.

Add the lemon zest to that mixture.

Scrape down the sides of the bowl and mix a bit more.

In a new bowl, mix flour, baking powder, baking soda, and salt. You can sift them all together if you want to get fancy, but frankly I don't bother.

In another bowl, put your 1/4 cup lemon juice, your buttermilk, and your vanilla.

Add the dry and wet ingredients alternately to the butter mixture, mixing between additions. Begin and end with flour.

Scrape down the sides of the bowl and mix a bit more.

Divide the batter evenly between your two greased, floured loaf pans. Smooth the top.

Bake for 45 to 60 minutes, until a knife you poke in the center comes up clean.

When cakes are out of the oven, let them cool for ten minutes. Then carefully flip them onto a rack set over a tray. If you don't have a rack, just use a plate. It's a little messier but it'll still taste amazing.

Gently poke the top of your warm cakes with a chopstick or a knife to make some holes for syrup.

Using a pastry brush if you have one, or a spoon if you don't, slime the soaking syrup all over your warm cakes. Get the sides wet with the syrup if you can. Make sure the syrup goes down in the tiny holes you've made.

Then let the cakes cool.

You can eat it plain or get fancy by serving it with whipped cream and/or strawberries. Or put it alongside some cookies topped with chocolate, like Lu's Little Schoolboy/Petit Ecolier cookies. Or try it for breakfast with strong coffee. Tipper eats it that way quite often, I think.

A *FAMILY OF LIARS* MIX TAPE

BACK IN 1987, when *Family of Liars* takes place, we used to make each other mix tapes. You'd get a cassette-to-cassette re-corder and carefully plan out a mix tape for your friend, or for the person you were romantically involved with. You'd pick a theme, or a music genre, or just your absolute favorites from that week, and figure out the playlist so the songs would flow from one to the other. It took forever, and you had to write the names of all the songs in tiny handwriting on a little-bitty paper insert. It was precisely *because* it took forever that a mix tape made a really good gift.

So—I made one for you. Okay, you do have to actually go on

314

Apple Music or Spotify (where you'll find playlists named *Family of Liars*). Or you can source the songs into a playlist yourself. But I really did try to make the songs flow from one to the other—from a late-night dance party in Goose to a beachy afternoon to a romantic epiphany. Also, I put down all the songs in tiny handwriting on a little-bitty paper insert!

The mix tape is meant to bring you to Beechwood Island. It's all eighties songs that stand the test of time—to my ears, anyhow. But it's no definitive soundtrack to 1987. Music experts on the internet do a much better job of that than I ever could. It's the music the Sinclair girls loved, and I hope you love it, too.

Sit down on a wide cotton blanket on the sand on one of Beechwood's two beaches.

It's a sunny day. The tunes come out of a beat-up portable cassette player.

You've got a cooler full of lemonade, some

icy sliced peaches in a square plastic box, and some

roast beef sandwiches with horseradish and watercress on sourdough bread.

The waves lap the sand.

Your skin smells of coconut sunblock.

Later on, you might swim, but for now, you're just

lying still and

listening to the music.

Maybe you'll dance on your back with your feet up in the air.

The mix tape includes most of the pop songs mentioned in book, as well as songs by the artists Carrie talks about. Not everything in the book is here, though—just the songs I like best. Everything dates 1985 to summer 1987. If you're looking for Rosemary's favorite, it's Simple Minds' "Don't You (Forget About Me)." That's where "Hey hey hey hey" comes from, and "La la la la la."

Listening should bring you to the best parts of (the sometimes terrible) Beechwood Island. It's a soundtrack to Carrie's long days on the beach, to Bess curling her hair in front of the mirror, to Penny and Erin alone in their bedroom, and to the nights spent in Goose Cottage, when no one was up to any good.

xo E

A FAMILY OF LIARS MIX-TAPE

A-side: Dance party to Beach Day

- Notorious – Duran Duran
- Kiss — Prince
- Faith — George Michael
- Higher Love ♥ – Steve Winwood
- Wishing Well – Terence Trent D'Arby
- West End Girls – Pet Shop Boys
- Don't You (Forget About Me) – Simple Minds
- Wild Wild Life — Talking Heads
- Fall on Me — R.E.M.
- I Still Haven't Found What I'm Looking for — U2

B-side: Beach Day to Romance ♥

- Don't Get Me Wrong – Pretenders
- If She Knew What She Wants – The Bangles
- Thorn in My Side – Eurythmics
- If You Leave – Orchestral Manoeuvres in the Dark
- If You Let Me Stay – Terence T-D
- No One Is to Blame – Howard Jones
- Life in a Northern Town – Dream Academy
- Don't Dream It's Over – Crowded House
- In Your Eyes ♥ – Peter Gabriel
- Sometimes it Snows in April – Prince

xoxo E. Lockhart

A Side

"Notorious" Duran Duran

"Kiss" Prince

"Faith" George Michael

"Higher Love" Steve Winwood

"Wishing Well" Terence Trent D'Arby

"West End Girls" Pet Shop Boys

"Don't You (Forget About Me)" Simple Minds

"Wild Wild Life" Talking Heads

"Fall on Me" R.E.M.

"I Still Haven't Found What I'm Looking For" U2

B Side

"Don't Get Me Wrong" The Pretenders

"If She Knew What She Wants" The Bangles

"Thorn in My Side" Eurythmics

"If You Leave" Orchestral Manoeuvers in the Dark

"If You Let Me Stay" Terence Trent D'Arby

"No One Is to Blame" Howard Jones

"Life in a Northern Town" The Dream Academy

"Don't Dream It's Over" Crowded House

"In Your Eyes" Peter Gabriel

"Sometimes It Snows in April" Prince

A MAP OF BEECHWOOD ISLAND

HAND-DRAWN BY E. LOCKHART

MY EDITOR ASKED me to sketch Beechwood Island in 1987 so that the map designer would know what to draw for the finished book. Here's my drawing. Find the romantic spot to take advantage of the moonlight. And watch out for sharks.

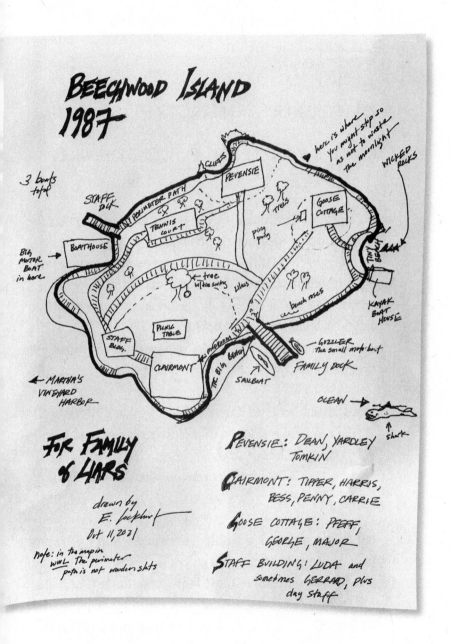

BEECHWOOD ISLAND 1987

FOR FAMILY of LIARS

3 boats total

here is where you might stop so as not to waste the moonlight

WICKED ROCKS

CLIFFS

PEVENSIE

TREES

GOOSE COTTAGE

STAFF DCK

PERIMETER PATH

TENNIS COURT

Ping pong

TINY BEACH

BOATHOUSE

BIG MOTOR BOAT in here

tree w/ tire swing

LILACS

beach roses

KAYAK BOAT HOUSE

PICNIC TABLE

THE HYDRANGEAS

THE BIG BEACH

STAFF BLDG.

CLAIRMONT

SAILBOAT

GUZZLER the small motorboat

FAMILY DOCK

MARTHA'S VINEYARD HARBOR

OCEAN

shark

drawn by E. Lockhart
Oct 11, 2021

note: in the map WWL the perimeter path is not wooden slats

PEVENSIE: DEAN, YARDLEY TOMKIN

CLAIRMONT: TIPPER, HARRIS, BESS, PENNY, CARRIE

GOOSE COTTAGE: PFEFF, GEORGE, MAJOR

STAFF BUILDING: LUDA and sometimes GERRARD, plus day staff

A SINCLAIR FAMILY TREE

HAND-DRAWN BY E. LOCKHART

I DREW THIS family tree so my editor could pass it on for
more professional treatment in the book.

In the mid-twentieth century, it was common in certain
kinds of novels to have a list of characters at the beginning—
Agatha Christie did it in a lot of her books, for example. And
in middle school and high school, I read a lot of plays. Those
always have a list of characters, very often with descriptions. For
Family of Liars, I kind of wanted to have one of those opening lists.

> *Harris Sinclair*: father to Carrie, Penny, Bess, and Rosemary.
>   He can hold his liquor, quotes Robert Frost, and used
>   to row in the Harvard heavy eight.
> *Rosemary Leigh Taft Sinclair*: a cheetah in the shape of a ten-
>   year-old girl.

But in the end, I felt a family tree would set-up the themes
in the novel better (parentage is such a part of the story). It also
felt like a nice companion to the family tree in *We Were Liars*.

I find family trees fascinating (and useful for keeping track
of the Sinclairs!), but I do acknowledge their many limitations.

When I was about four years old, my step-grandfather made a family tree of my mom's side of the family. He branched out his children and my granny's children and their spouses and ex-spouses—and below them, the grandchildren. I loved looking at that document. My mother and all her sisters had copies. So I suppose that's where my interest in family trees comes from—although I have also written about how the tree model can exclude people who live in less typical or alternative family structures. It wouldn't have represented my home life at all well when I was a kid. Because my mom and I lived communally, and later with a boyfriend of hers, a tree had no way to represent the people in our household. Educators are beginning to use alternate activities to teach about family connections and heritage. I tried fitting the dogs into the tree, but in the end it seemed too weird that way, so I put them off to the side. They are still members of the family, I think.

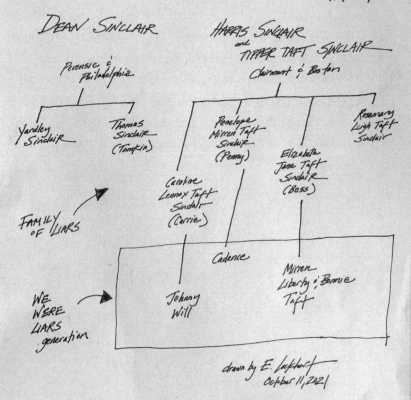

SINCLAIR FAMILY TREE

Dogs in 1987:
Wharton
Albert
McCartney
Reepicheep

DEAN SINCLAIR

Pevensie &
Philadelphia

Yardley
Sinclair

Thomas
Sinclair
(Tomkin)

FAMILY
OF LIARS →

WE
WERE
LIARS
generation →

Johnny
Will

HARRIS SINCLAIR
and
TIPPER TAFT SINCLAIR

Clairmont & Boston

Penelope
Mirren Taft
Sinclair
(Penny)

Caroline
Lennox Taft
Sinclair
(Carrie)

Cadence

Elizabeth
Jane Taft
Sinclair
(Bess)

Mirren
Liberty & Bonnie
Taft

Rosemary
Leigh Taft
Sinclair

drawn by E. Lockhart
October 11, 2021

322